I0567841

Athen 'Blackeye' Mavromatis, roving lieutenant with the Beverly Hills Police Department, is trying to enjoy a rare day off. It doesn't look like it's going to happen when the mayor hands him a twisty missing person's case. A Saudi Princess has vanished. Because of royal protocols, Athen must conduct his investigation under the wire. He doesn't mind doing that, but it soon becomes apparent that the princess, who's also a wannabe actress, might have been murdered. Her apartment appears to be one big giant crime scene.

But just who is Natasha Al-Khan, AKA Natasha King, and who wants her dead? Though Beverly Hills has the reputation of being crime-free, this is the second murder case he's tackled in the short time Athen's been with the department. Not only does he have to solve this one fast, but he and his lover, Grady, are dealing with Athen's delinquent niece who's just come out to them. Oh, and somebody very near and dear to them may turn out to be a deranged psychopath . . .

The unauthorized reproduction or distribution of this copyrighted work is illegal. Criminal copyright infringement, including infringement without monetary gain, is investigated by the FBI and is punishable by up to 5 years in federal prison and a fine of $250,000.

This book is a work of fiction. Names, characters, places, and incidents either are products of the author's imagination or are used fictitiously. Any resemblance to actual events or locales or persons, living or dead, is entirely coincidental.

Fancy Man Blues
Copyright © 2020 A.J. Llewellyn
ISBN: 978-1-4874-2984-3
Cover art by Martine Jardin

All rights reserved. Except for use in any review, the reproduction or utilization of this work in whole or in part in any form by any electronic, mechanical or other means, now known or hereafter invented, is forbidden without the written permission of the publisher.

Published by eXtasy Books Inc or
Devine Destinies, an imprint of eXtasy Books Inc

Look for us online at:
www.eXtasybooks.com or www.devinedestinies.com

Fancy Man Blues Blackeye

By

A.J. Llewellyn

"I love to see my baby smile
You say you love me now but
You've got a fancy man on the side"

Fancy Man Blues, The Rolling Stones.
Music and lyrics; Keith Richards

DEDICATION

For Lisa Marie

CHAPTER ONE

Unknown Number. Normally, Athen ignored calls like that because they were telemarketers or scams. But he was a cop. He couldn't ignore calls, especially when they kept calling back. Two-forty a.m. Who the hell could it be? His cellphone crackled.

"Hullo? Athen?"

Athen squinted as the voice from his distant past interrupted his, er, uptown funk. He finally had his lover, Grady, right where he wanted him, naked and in bed, the house dark and silent.

"Jay-zus. Cricket?"

Charlie *Cricket* Pritchard chuckled. "You still got that thing for me, eh?"

Athen rolled his eyes but couldn't resist laughing, too. "Oh, yeah. I got sleepless nights over you."

Grady sat up in bed. "Who the hell are you talking to?"

Athen held up a finger. Grady's eyes hardened in a way that Athen knew would mean he had a lot of 'splaining to do. The truth was, he'd missed Cricket, his old partner. Athen thought he'd retired. Why was he calling now?

Cricket coughed. He was still smoking, by the sounds of it. "Listen. We need to talk."

"Sure. When?"

Athen reached out a languid hand and stroked Grady's belly. Grady stiffened, shoving his hand aside and rolled away from him. *Ouch.*

"I'd say now, except it's not a good idea. I'm on surveillance. Can we talk tomorrow? Can you meet me?"

"Sure," Athen repeated. "When?"

"I'll let you know. Sleep tight. Nighty-night. Keep this on the QT." Cricket ended their call.

"Whatever," Athen said, even though Cricket was gone, and Grady had his back to him.

"Who the hell's Cricket?" Grady asked, not turning to look at him.

"My former partner."

"Wait." Grady half turned. "You mean Charlie?"

"Yeah." Athen grinned in the darkened bedroom.

"Half rodent, quarter insect, quarter human Charlie?"

Huh. Grady hasn't forgiven Cricket. Grady had come into his life just as Charlie was being ordered to bedrest after a quadruple bypass.

"Isn't he dead yet?"

Athen stared at Grady's barely visible back. "Apparently not."

"Hmph." Grady leaned farther away. "You can thank that old coot for my iffy stiffy."

Athen lay back against the pillows. The chill between them frustrated him. He was as loyal as they came. He hadn't had a decent, active case for a month, and at the first sign of something brewing . . .

Grady's soft snoring told him everything he needed to know. Athen might not have much on *his* plate, but Grady had to be exhausted. He was working on a huge TV show and handling Athen's thirteen-year-old niece, Despina. She was closer to being shipped off to boarding school than she probably realized.

Athen loved sex. So did Grady. And Athen *loved* sex with Grady. Despina did her best to come between them, and now, it seemed, so did Cricket. Athen felt like the guy on the State

Farm TV ad whose wife catches him in a late-night phone conversation with Jake, a security specialist and doesn't believe him.

Huh. Cricket, like Jake from State Farm, wears khakis. At least he did. Wonder what the hell he wants from me? Thoughts paddled around his brain. Memories of the last case he and Cricket had worked on still rankled. He tried to push the upsetting thoughts from his mind. And then, sleep claimed him . . .

Stumpy Lake, Virginia Beach, Virginia, February. Midnight. Five Years ago.

Athen felt ridiculous, in the dead of night, to be waiting to meet a man who'd claimed he could help him with his case. A man who was blind, no less. Athen shifted his feet a little farther apart on the edge of the damp, rock-strewn lakefront. His boots were wet, but the water hadn't soaked through to his socked feet. Yet.

He let his flashlight blaze a trail around him. The lake was considered perfect for watercraft, especially kayaks and canoes, but not for swimming. Athen had already been warned it was filled with deadly snakes.

Something terrible had happened here to someone beautiful, and he wouldn't rest until he solved the mystery of Allie Madden's disappearance. He focused his gaze on a ripple of movement in the water. He didn't want to get bitten and die before he could find her.

Her disappearance and apparently brutal murder ached in his gut like an ulcer.

He took some deep breaths and it only hurt his throat more. *How cold is it? Last time I checked it was thirty-two degrees. Much colder now.* Athen switched off the flashlight, tucked it into the pocket of his pea coat, and rubbed his gloved hands together. It didn't help him get any warmer.

I should have worn something else. This old coat won't cut it. A fleeting sense of passion scissored through him for his lover, who'd lent it to him. Another worry invaded his thoughts.

What if the tracker doesn't show?

Was it this cold the night Allie Madden was dragged out here?

He slid his left foot across the sand to his right. Then he drew it back, bringing the right foot toward the left. He shuffled this way repeatedly until the heat from his feet traveled up his calves and moved up toward the rest of his body.

He let out a breath, condensation evaporating from his frigid lips.

Keep moving, man.

He continued sliding his feet back and forth, a trick he'd learned from his days working for the US Marshals. An actress he'd protected from a stalker had taught him this routine from her long days standing on movie sets. *Where is she now?* She'd been stalked by an ex-lover and he'd guarded her for two months in Savannah, Georgia. It had been hot and sticky and . . . *Yeah. That's the ticket. Pretend it's hot right now.* Her wonderful smile came to mind, and her wicked sense of humor. She was the closest thing he'd come to falling for a woman.

And the nearest thing he knew of perfection.

Athen kept his gaze swiveling across the deserted beach.

Where is this guy? Was this a hoax? The skin prickled at the back of his neck. *The gift of fear. No. Not a hoax.* He detected movement. The old man was close.

Or somebody was.

Athen stopped shuffling and listened intently, his gaze flickering to his left. He almost shouted a greeting as an old man made his way toward him. Athen noticed a younger man helping him carry a canoe over the bumpy terrain.

The young man lifted a hand in greeting and Athen nodded back to him, stepping closer to them. The old man didn't glance in Athen's direction. He stopped walking and stared out at the rippling water.

"Hi," the younger man said. "My name is Andrew Laurie. This is my grandpa, Kaikane." He pronounced it *Ky-kah-nay*. "Everyone calls him Kai."

Only Andrew shook Athen's hand.

"Kai is the Hawaiian word for water, isn't it?" Athen asked.

"Yes." Andrew gave him a fleeting smile. "Kaikane means strong."

"Strong water. Somehow that seems apt." Athen flicked a gaze at the solid-looking man who exuded a quiet confidence. "How do we do this?" For the first time in his career as a cop, Athen felt a cold stab of fear. *Am I crazy to meet two strangers like this?*

"I'll be paddling with you. Kai will navigate. He — we both want to help."

"He's a blind navigator?" Athen blurted.

"Yes." This was the first time the old man spoke. He turned his head toward Athen, his eyes seeming bright and alert in the moonlight.

Before Athen could respond, Andrew continued. "Kai is Hawaiian. He comes from a long line of *kahuna*. High priests. His gift is tracking the missing. Especially in water."

Kai held up a hand. "I'm blind, not mute." He stared at Athen. Hard.

Athen had met some intriguing people in his time, but Kai was one of the most unusual. He had an odd scent to him. A mixture of kerosene, it seemed, hair pomade, and a woodsy smell. Athen had a mental image of the old man living on a boat using kerosene for fuel.

Kai's long, grey hair had been pulled back from his face and he wore it in two braids. *He reminds me of Willie Nelson.* His attire was an odd mix of western and tropical clothing. His skinny legs were adorned in jeans that seemed three sizes two big, and he was barefoot. *Barefoot. In this weather.* Over

5

what looked like an ugly Christmas sweater, he wore a large swath of cloth Athen recognized as *tapa*. Tree bark beaten and fashioned into distinctive tan and black fabric.

"Please tell me everything you know about Allie's disappearance," Kai said.

Athen took a breath that was so cold he could feel it in his lungs. "Allie Madden is missing, presumed dead after she and her husband were seen arguing in a bar, an exclusive private club on Atlantic Avenue—"

"I know the official story." The old man's tone was sharp. "I want to know *your* impressions." He jabbed a finger at Athen. For a guy who couldn't see, he seemed to know exactly where Athen stood.

"Are you really blind?"

"I see shadows. You're right to be afraid. This beach has known evil."

Damn. Athen swallowed.

The old man seemed to be waiting.

"I came into this case late," Athen admitted. "As a favor to the US Marshals. I've worked dozens of missing people cases around the country."

"I know *your* story. I want to know about *hers*." Another jab to Athen's chest.

"She is—was—married—"

"Ah. So, you believe she's no longer alive."

Athen hesitated. The local authorities had been quick to release way too much information on the case, hoping somebody who knew Allie Madden, or felt badly enough about the disappearance of the young married mother of a baby boy, would come forward with information. Despite nationwide publicity, not a single, credible clue had emerged.

"We know the husband, Phil Madden, has a mistress, Leta Gordon, but she is in fear of her safety. The story she tells is . . . chilling." Athen paused and closed his eyes. He felt badly for Allie Madden, and for Leta, who had believed Phil's lies. She was young and naïve, by her own admission, and became caught up in something she would never be able to get over.

"I am telling you this in the strictest confidence and because my commanding officer says I can trust you." Athen sucked in another frigid breath. "I tracked Leta down to a hunting shack on Pine Mountain. I guaranteed her protection in exchange for her cooperation."

"What did she tell you?" The old man seemed alive with excitement.

"That she helped her lover, Allie's husband, Phil, kill his wife on the edge of this lake. She was crying hysterically when she described how Allie begged for her life as he stabbed her multiple times. She said it took a long time for her to die." Athen paused. "Then they took his old rowboat out here and dumped her body in the middle of the lake."

A look of anguish crossed the old man's face. "And she has regrets?"

"Plenty. She found out she was just one of three mistresses. And Phil has been threatening her ever since they killed Allie."

Kai looked surprised. "*Dakine*. Let's go."

"We've searched the lake and there's been no sign of her. Nothing. And we can't even find the alleged rowboat," Athen pointed out.

"Let's get on with it. I'm due back on Maui in two days. I miss my wife." Kai frowned at him. Athen could see it by the faint light of the moon. Another jab to Athens chest. "No more yackety-yackety."

They dragged the canoe to the waterline, pushed it in and all three climbed aboard. The old man sat in front, his hands trailing in the water as Athen and Andrew paddled.

Kai muttered something under his breath as he leaned

close to the water.

"It's a chant for protection," Andrew whispered to Athen between strokes.

Athen nodded, curious, as Kai waved a hand in one direction, then another. He held up a hand in a 'stop' gesture at one point and turned to face Athen. "What was down there?" He pointed right beneath them.

Interesting. Navy divers had found an old tire iron and a chain at the bottom of the lake. The investigators had told nobody about the objects, and they'd been deemed too rusted and crusty to be of any value.

"Did they contain metal?" Kai asked as though reading Athen's thoughts.

Shocked, Athen mumbled. "Yeah. An old tire iron and a chain."

"Hmm. This way." Kai pointed to the left and once again, his search pattern seemed whimsical. Not the methodical grid the military had used.

"Stop." Kai's hand churned in the water. "I know why you never found her here."

"Why's that?" Athen asked, so cold now, it hurt his whole face to talk.

"She was never out here in the first place." Kai made smaller, calmer circles with his hand then suddenly withdrew it, as though stung. "She's not here at all."

Chapter Two

"Wakey, wakey."

Athen resisted the pull of Grady's growling early-morning voice and the smell of fresh coffee. He burrowed deeper under the covers. *Warm. I'm warm. Thank God. Man. Why am I dreaming about that case?* Anguish gnawed at him. *Why can't I have wet dreams about Grady instead of missing people?*

He knew it was the late-night call from Cricket.

"Get up." Grady seemed tense.

"Leave the coffee on the table," Athen mumbled.

"Nothing doing. I know you. You'll go right back to sleep."

"But it's my day off." Athen raised his head and opened one eye, then the other. Grady had put two cups of coffee on the nightstand and was opening the plantation shutters on their bedroom's bay windows.

"Why does it always rain on my day off?" Athen stared as fat drops spattered the beveled glass panes Grady had polished until they gleamed the day before.

Grady handed him one of the cups. "Because you have bad luck."

"No, I don't."

"Yes, you do. Worst luck of anyone I know." Grady sipped his own coffee. "Charlie, sorry, Cricket called you for a reason. I'm thinking we may need to bring in an exorcist." He pulled a face. "No sugar. This one's yours." He reached over and switched cups, a grumpy look on his face as he parked his butt on the edge of the bed.

"Does this make it my bad luck, or yours?" Athen asked, taking a sip.

"Yours. It just traveled to me. It's like catching somebody else's cold." Grady's eyes widened. "I'm inheriting your bad luck."

Athen had a feeling that the long, lavish breakfast and fast and dirty lovemaking he'd envisioned were off the calendar this morning. He swung his feet to the floor and steadied the sloshing contents of his cup. "Don't say that. I don't have bad luck." He took another sip. *Mm, mm. Good.*

"You have very bad luck." Grady rose, moving around the room with the gait of an angry tiger. "Every time you have a day off, the city of Beverly Hills makes alternative arrangements for you."

True. Athen took another sip. Perfect. He waited a beat, but Grady was now in full flight.

"You watch. They'll call you with a homicide or missing person's case. And God knows what Cricket wants."

"Right." Athen stared at him but Grady shifted his gaze. "Babe. Is there something you're not telling me?"

"Other than the fact the mayor's on hold wanting to discuss a missing person's case?" Grady stared at him. "Absolutely nothing."

Athen gasped. "He's been on hold all this time? What's the matter with you?" He fumbled for his cellphone. *Nothing there.* He glanced at the landline phone on the nightstand. It had two lines on it. One was blinking. "How come I didn't hear that?"

"Because I muted it. You needed sleep." Before Athen could respond, Grady stomped out of the room.

Athen took the call. He, Grady, and Despina, had come to call the landline the bat phone. No good calls came from it. The instrument was a gateway between them and catastrophe. Many times involving Despina.

"Sir?" Athen wondered if he'd have time to finish his coffee and take a quick shower before tackling hazardous duty. Sometimes he felt like one of *Charlie's Angels*. Four weeks ago, he'd handled the first homicide the city of Beverly Hills had had in several years. Now there was a missing person. Athen always got his orders from the mayor, Scott Aubrey, via phone. A bit like Charlie's private eyes.

Scott breathed heavily. Athen narrowed his gaze. "Sir?" he repeated.

"Sorry, Athen. I'm at the equestrian center and I'm in the middle of a ride."

It was hard to imagine Scott Aubrey atop a horse. He was an elegant man who preferred suits and ties to just about anything. A bit of a bubblehead, he was happiest with a microphone in his face.

"How can I help you?" Athen wondered about the mayor's attire. What had possessed him to take up any form of exercise?

"We have a missing person. A girl. Woman." *Huff, huff.* "I just got a call from the Saudi Arabian consulate. This *cannot* escalate, Blackeye. *It. Can. Not.*"

When Athen didn't respond, Scott barked, "Okay?"

Athen knew that Beverly Hills had a large Saudi population. Their *riyal* had feathered a lot of the city's coffers. It was an uneasy alliance because Saudi customs were so foreign to America. The Saudis lived by their own rules as though they were part of a secret society where nobody else mattered. They had, however, forged a strong foothold in the most prosperous city in the US. They had escaped the current government's travel restrictions even though they were Muslim. But they were rich Muslims, and money changed things. A lot of things.

"Who is she?" Athen asked, getting ready to jot down details.

"This must be done in secrecy. She's a Saudi prince's daughter. Her name is Natasha King, only she keeps her identity secret. Her real name is Natasha Al-Khan. The consulate contacted me in strictest confidence. She's been missing for a day. Didn't show up for her Got Set yesterday. Her friends say this isn't like her. She—"

"Her what?" Athen asked, not sure he'd heard right.

"Got Set. She booked a studio to shoot some scenes for her show reel."

"Oh. So, she's an actress?"

"Wannabe," Scott said. "She also set up a photo shoot she never showed up for yesterday and Maggie Harman, her friend who reported her missing—"

"I thought you said the consulate reported it."

"She reported it to the consulate." Scott's tone became testy.

"I see. Then they contacted you." Athen took a swig of coffee. "You got a contact name and number there?"

"No, I don't. I already told you the call came to me in the strictest confidence."

Athen said nothing.

"Hold on," Scott barked.

Athen's thoughts raced. The murder of New York Times reporter, Jamal Khashoggi, in the Turkish Embassy in Istanbul, had caused shockwaves among Beverly Hills' Arab community the previous year. Its impact was still being felt. Young, progressive Saudis continued to flutter in and out of the US, a lot more careful now about their tweets, Snapchat, and Instagram posts. They feared what was often perceived as radicalism by the heavy hand of the ruling Saudi kingdom.

Particularly vulnerable were female activists. A few prominent young women had been imprisoned over their support for a new law allowing women to drive in Saudi Arabia. Was Natasha King a party girl or a humanitarian? *I have to Google her.*

He moved out of the bedroom and into his home office. His desktop computer had numerous passwords and encryptions to stop Despina from accessing the Internet and buying stuff she didn't need on Athen's dime. All the security however made it arduous for Athen to get online himself.

Scott was screaming at somebody in the background. Athen cradled the receiver against his ear as he typed one incorrect password after another.

I give up. He returned to the bedroom and pulled out clothes for the day. He wondered if Scott had forgotten about him as he swigged his coffee. In the bathroom, he checked Google for information on Natasha King. There was one photo of her from some big fundraiser. She was a beautiful, exotic-looking woman, posing with some Hollywood actor. The photo was tiny however, and for some reason he couldn't enhance it.

She had a million-dollar smile and a sparkly silver dress that was hard to forget. There wasn't much else about her online. Nothing under her real name and only two references for Natasha King. *So, she's one of the careful ones.*

The affluent Arab community in Beverly Hills had its own banks, restaurants, clubs . . . everything. They were well looked after in the city, so they didn't stray far from its confines, because they liked to splash the flash. But there was a truth most people ignored. Many of these visitors behaved badly in Beverly Hills. Some women came to LA and still wore their *abayas* and other traditional garb. Many did not. Away from parental rule, the younger set got up to a lot of mischief that rarely made the headlines.

"Sorry." Scott came back on the line. "Maggie Harman's worried Natasha won't turn up for acting class today. She says if Natasha doesn't show, then something is very wrong because this particular class is important to her. Natasha's been preparing for it for months. I — " He stopped huffing and puffing and a wild scream almost shattered Athen's ear drum.

"Sir? Are you okay?" Athen yelled into the phone. A commotion on the other end of the call was punctuated by a horse's neigh.

"Please tell me you didn't photograph that," Scott bawled at somebody on the other end of the phone.

Athen bit his lip. "Sir?" he asked again.

Scott came back on the line. "Sorry about that, Blackeye. I'm out here doing a photo spread."

"I see," Athen said, trying not to laugh.

"My wife's idea. She set this whole thing up. I think I just got a wedgie."

Athen closed his eyes. The last thing he wanted to envision was the mayor's underpants bunched uncomfortably up his butt. "Sir, where do I start?"

"This photo shoot is important," the mayor continued.

"Hers or yours?"

"Mine. I've decided to run for governor."

God help us all. Athen rolled his eyes. When he didn't respond, the mayor continued.

"My wife's conception. She's my campaign manager."

I bet she is. Athen fought another wild urge to laugh. *Wait till I tell Grady about this. He'll laugh for days.*

The mayor muttered, "Take the horse," to somebody on the other end of the line then came back to Athen. "Natasha lives in the Bermuda Triangle on Linden. I'll text you her address. I'll also send you her friend Maggie's number. You can contact her, but leave the consulate out of this, and *do not* file any official paperwork, and *do not* discuss this with anyone at headquarters. Keep me posted."

Fuck you. "I have a question, sir. If nobody knows our missing woman is royalty, why did this Maggie Harman call the consulate and not the police?"

A long pause ensued during which time Athen heard crickets.

"I don't know. You're the cop. Go check it out." Scott ended the call and Athen ignored his orders, calling Lucy Lane, the acting chief of the Beverly Hills Police department. Rumor had it she would probably be offered the permanent position within a matter of days. He hoped so. Athen liked and respected Lucy very much. They went way back to the Allie Madden murder case that spanned three states and was still waiting to be settled in the courts. Without a body, the prosecutor's office had been reluctant to press charges. They were in no real hurry because there was no statute of limitations on murder, and so far, Phil Matthews still denied he had anything to do with her disappearance. There was no proof.

It rankled Athen that the guy had broken up with Leta Gordon and had started a family with yet another woman. His wife was still officially missing, and he couldn't apply to the courts for permission to declare her legally dead for another five years. It would take another ten years after that for it to become final.

Why was I dreaming about her? Tears pricked the back of his eyes. Every cop had a case like Allie Madden. A case that clung like barnacles and never left them.

Lucy took his call, saying, "Don't tell me you're working on your day off."

"I am, sir," he said. Chiefs were always called sir, regardless of their gender. He gave her a brief rundown.

"I've never heard of Natasha King, but I appreciate you letting me know about this. Once again, the mayor is trying to ignore my presence. Hopefully Natasha just overslept or something. If she's living in the Bermuda Triangle, then she has money." A beat. "If you find something more serious going on, I can assign you a detective. Who would you like to work with?"

"If it can't be you, then Paulie Hansen." Athen liked and trusted the guy. He'd been a godsend in their recent homicide investigation.

"Gotcha. And thanks for the compliment. And, Athen, you did the right thing letting me know. You work for *me*. And the city's lucky to have you. *I'm* lucky to have you. Please keep me posted, and the lone ranger, too."

Athen burst into laughter. "You know about that?"

"Yeah. He's using my horse for his damned photos. I hear she threw him off. Twice."

They both laughed at that. They ended the call on a warm note and Athen took his coffee into the bathroom. He took a two-minute shower, though he longed for a lengthy, scorching one. He dried off, and just as he was feeling good about himself, he used the wrong bottle to spray his pits. He studied the label. It was Despina's latest fragrance. Lush Go Green. *Great. I always wanted to smell like a Christmas tree.* He banged the bottle back on the vanity and stomped off to the kitchen.

"You have time for another quick coffee? Or I can give it to you to go," Grady offered, leaning into him for a kiss.

At least he's giving me that. Athen tried not to fret about Grady's moodiness. "To go would be great. And I'll have the bacon I see there. And that piece of toast." Athen nuzzled Grady's gorgeous neck. "You used the wrong bottle, too."

"I swear. I tried to find her something more pleasant, but she loves Lush's bath bombs and she begged me for the perfume." Grady handed Athen and their dog Bella slices of bacon. Athen threw his rasher onto a piece of toast then slathered cashew butter all over it. Grady winced at the spectacle. Bella drooled as she watched.

Athen gave her half of his toast and eyed Grady. "Babe, what do you know about Got Sets?"

Grady threw him a dirty look. "Why do you ask?"

"You're in the biz. You must know something about them."

Grady chomped on a piece of toast. "I do." He swallowed. "They're bad news. Big, *big* open secret in Hollywood. Actors pay a fortune to record a scene or two for their reels."

Athen knew that actors took snippets of work they'd done then put them on DVDs — known as reels — that they sent to casting directors, producers, and agents, in the endless hunt for acting work.

"Most of them look fake," Grady said. "When they first showed up on reels, casting people took them for lousy, cheap productions until they could find no record of them on the International Movie Data Base. Then the same sets, and the same damned scenes kept turning up over and over again. In the early days, about three years ago, professional crews did the Got Sets and the results were great." He jabbed a finger at Athen. "And if you ever tell anyone I said that, I'll deny it emphatically."

"I'll keep that in mind." Athen loved it when Grady got all worked up over something. "So, what changed?"

"People who think they're Martin Scorsese jumped into the pool and wrecked if for everybody. No finesse. No talent. They charge these actors hundreds, sometimes a couple grand to shoot a scene somebody else just did in the same studio. It's become so bad, casting directors have instructed talent agents to make sure there are no Got Sets on their clients' reels, or they won't even look at 'em."

Before Athen could respond, Grady went on. "Some of those scenes are painful to watch. A girl in a prison jumpsuit, for example, sits opposite somebody, usually a man in a suit and she raves on about the false accusations surrounding her arrest. This scene crops up all the time, but a lot of actors have no idea. Got Set people will shoot the scene with different dialogue but the same premise.

"I don't know if you're aware that the day of actors going

on auditions is fading. Most casting directors want virtual auditions now. They'll do it via Skype or the actor gets a friend to tape their audition then email the video to the casting director. Still a losing game. Big names are having trouble getting work and they're desperate to jump into the TV mud pile. They'll get the jobs over little-known talent any day."

"And Got Sets are that easy to spot?"

Grady rolled his eyes. "They're designed to bilk actors out of a lot of money. Just like the endless demands for new head shots. The quality's usually horrendous and the lighting is poor. No stuff going on behind them in the scene. The focus is purely on the actor in question. They rarely show you the other actor's face. Just not authentic to TV shows and movies."

"So the actor in question's wasted a whole lot of money for naught." The mention of money made Athen think of his niece. "Despina's awfully quiet."

"That's what happens when she's off school. Stays up all night playing video games and texting her friends."

"But she hasn't nicked your credit card lately?"

"Not yet. But the day is still young. And I keep hiding my wallet."

Despina had all the time in the world to get up to mischief. Her school, like millions of others had been cancelled for the rest of the schoolyear thanks to the outbreak of the coronavirus. She was at a loose end until the new year started in September.

And like a lot of Hollywood workers, Grady's TV show had yet to return to production, so her care frequently fell on his shoulders.

Athen knew that it was a daily ordeal dealing with her. Despina longed to hang out with her friends at the Beverly Center, but she'd been caught shoplifting there and had been banned from going there by the security personnel for three months. He and Grady didn't know if they could trust her unsupervised alone in the house. She was a handful at the best of times. They'd talked about more drastic measures in dealing with her, but so far hadn't made any decisions.

Grady handed Athen a travel mug that had a pair of eyes painted on it and the words, *I See Guilty People.*

I sure do. "What game is she playing these days?" Athen leaned over and kissed his lover then twisted off the cap from his mug. He inhaled the deep, rich fragrance, taking deep sips.

"Horizon Zero Dawn," came Grady's prompt reply.

"That the one with the female warrior and the robot dinosaurs?"

"Yep." Grady stopped fussing around the kitchen island. "She's moving around now. She's had about three hours' sleep so she might be grumpy. Get out now while you can, unless you want an argument."

"Good idea." Athen recapped his coffee, kissed Grady and Bella, who flopped to the floor, licking the spot where her toast had been.

"Will you be gone all day?" Grady asked.

"No idea, babe. I'll call you."

Grady blew out a breath. He glanced at Athen, then fixed his gaze away from him at the collection of family photos on the living room shelves. "I don't know why I forgot Cricket's nickname. And I'm sorry I was an ass last night."

Athen had plenty that he wanted to say but the truth never hurt. "Maybe because he wasn't very nice to you."

Grady focused on him again. "Yeah, there's that."

Athen wished things were hot, and not heavy between them. "I love you, G. I'm headed for the Bermuda Triangle."

Grady's eyes widened. "Don't say that too loud. Despina will want to go with you. She's fascinated by it."

"Really?"

"She's in her early, *early* goth phase."

"Geez." Athen made a run for the door.

CHAPTER THREE

The Bermuda Triangle was a patch of prime real estate in the flats of Beverly Hills. Most people never even noticed the small, triangular piece of land with a swathe of emerald green grass, crowded with swaying palm trees south of Sunset Boulevard. It made Athen think of a miniature *Gilligan's Island*. It was the gateway to one of the most sinister intersections of the city, and certainly the neighborhood. Freaky stuff happened between Whittier Boulevard on one side of the triangle, and Linden Drive on the other.

Despina had ferreted out some strange tidbits such as actor Boris Karloff the original movie *Frankenstein,* and his friends' obsessions with his rose garden. Legend had it that his friends loved that garden so much, they asked for their ashes to be buried there. He must have been a popular guy because the garden contained hundreds of people's cremated remains. Though the Bowmont Drive house had been through multiple renovations, the garden remained unspoiled and well-tended.

It was right near there in 1946, when Howard Hughes crashed his private, experimental XF-11 plane into a row of upscale houses on North Whittier. Hughes had been piloting the aircraft for the first time. He took off from Culver City Airport several miles away but somehow wound up in the Bermuda Triangle. Critically injured, doctors said he was lucky to survive.

A year later, the gangster Bugsy Siegel, enjoying a quiet evening with friends after dinner, was gunned down in his living room via a drive-by shooting a few blocks away on North Linden.

In 1966, singer Jan Berry of the popular surf music group Jan & Dean crashed his sporty Stingray into a gardener's truck driving south of Sunset on Whittier Boulevard. Like Hughes, he suffered severe injuries, but Berry never fully recovered from massive head trauma.

More recently, in November 2010, Hollywood publicist Ronni Chasen was shot to death in her Mercedes-Benz E350 at the corner of Sunset and Whittier in a botched robbery attempt. Oddly, the spot where Chasen's vehicle came to a violent stop, was mere yards away from the living room where Bugsy Siegel died from 30-caliber military M1 carbine fire.

Chasen's death had been the last murder in Beverly Hills until Athen's woman-in-the-carpet case a month ago.

The rain had slowed to a drizzle but it shook him to remember that the day he started his investigation into the brutal murder of Paulina Martinez, the rain had been unbelievable. It had hampered his investigation. He hoped it wouldn't be the same today.

As he headed north from his home on Arnaz Drive toward Sunset, he pondered calling Maggie Harman, Natasha's friend who'd reported her apparent disappearance. Why was Natasha's missing a Got Set and a photo shoot such cause for alarm?

He checked her address. She lived on North Linden. He hoped the mysterious triangle hadn't claimed another victim. He asked his virtual assistant, Alexa, via Bluetooth, to Google Natasha King.

"One listing. IMDB," the mechanical voice told him over the radio's speaker. "No further information."

"What is the listing?"

"She has an agent, but you don't have a business account and you need to pay to view the agent's name."

He shook his head. "Anything else?"

"She has a Facebook page, but you need to be a friend to view the contents."

Boy, do I feel rejected.

"Her Instagram page is private. A request for access must be sent." Alexa paused. "There is a photo of her on Google with the actor Jean-Claude Van Damme."

I saw that photo! Man, Van Damme must have had massive plastic surgery. I didn't recognize him in the image I found online. "Thanks, Alexa," he said.

"Thank you, Athen."

He wasn't sure which of them ended the call, but he arrived at Natasha King's residence a few minutes later, relieved that the rain had stopped. If there was a crime scene, and if it involved outdoor activity, he didn't want to lose precious evidence to a deluge. He thought once again of the woman in the carpet and shoved the memory aside. He parked and stepped out of the vehicle, glancing around. No crashed aircraft. No beds of roses.

The only people on the street were two gardeners opposite, working on already immaculate landscaping of a white mansion. They were covered from head to foot in long sleeves and pants. Each wore straw cone-shaped hats. He approached the massive white building Natasha called home. There were six apartments listed at the intercom. No names except for unit four, which boasted a slip of paper with the word *manager* typed on it.

Athen pressed the buzzer and waited. Through the iron bars he viewed the exterior of Natasha's home. Golden pillars, koi ponds, and elaborate tile work shrieked money. He buzzed three times, beginning to feel like a beggar as he called out, "Hello?"

He saw no evidence of security cameras. No ring camera on the front gate. Nothing. He turned to check the house directly opposite the apartment building. No cameras that he

could detect. He'd encountered the same issue when he'd begun investigating the body-in-the-carpet case. Beverly Hills
residents had come to take the luxury of their own, vigilant
police department, for granted.

A man poked his head around the front door of the apartment facing the street.

"Who you?" he yelled.

Posh. Real posh. Athen held up his wallet with his badge and
ID card. "Lieutenant Athen Mavromatis, Beverly Hills police."

The dark-haired, swarthy-looking man uttered a curse of
some kind and came out to the gate. *He's wearing pajamas. Oh,
man. Cowboys and lassos. How old is he? Nine?*

"How can I help you?" the man asked, though his facial
expression indicated he had no desire to do any such thing.

"Are you the manager?"

The man nodded.

"What is your name, sir?"

"Cameron Deck."

Athen was surprised. It seemed like an American name.
He'd assumed the man was Arabic. "I'm looking for Natasha
King. Do you happen to know if she's home?"

Cameron Deck looked surprised. "No. And it's weird.
You're the fifth person to come around here looking for her."

"You mean today?"

"Two men very late last night and a woman this morning.
Then another one. You just missed her."

"Do you know any of them?"

"Yeah. Woman who came earlier was her friend Maggie.
She took Natasha's cat home with her."

"Was the cat inside?"

Deck unlocked the gate and let Athen onto the property.
"Normally yes, but it's been outside for two days. We don't
allow cats in the common area and it was walking around crying all day. Ever heard a cat cry? It's like a baby crying." He

gave a shudder. "I suppose you want to look inside her apartment."

"Yes, please."

Deck sighed. "She wanted to come in. Maggie, I mean. She got real upset because she had a key to the unit. She said the lock's been changed in the last week." He gave Athen a smile that was so feral it almost scared him. "She's right. *I'm* the one who changed it."

"And why was that?" Athen donned latex gloves as they walked down the side of the property.

Deck stopped moving. His gaze stayed on Athen's hands. "She had a break-in last week and I said I'd change the locks. No idea how she got broken into. This place is usually so safe."

Athen had no idea if this was true, but this was the most spectacular apartment building he'd ever seen. Ivy covered portions of the exterior walls and long, lavish infinity pools laden with lotus bulbs gave the place a luxurious feel. Athen wasn't sure if he'd stepped inside an Arabian oasis or a majestic villa on the Greek Isles.

"Was anything taken?" he asked. *Why do I smell roses? Are dead people buried here, too?* They passed an open bathroom window where a naked woman stood in front of a mirror applying makeup as she bounced along to Gotye singing *Somebody that I used to Know.* For some reason, the song made Athen shiver. He averted his gaze and caught the smile on Deck's face. Deck was trying not to laugh.

Athen adopted his most terse tone when he repeated his question. "Was anything stolen?"

"Oh. Just her camera and laptop. She bought new ones." He tripped on something along the walkway and went flying. Athen caught him, steadying him. Deck was shaking.

Why is he so rattled? Is it the near-fall or something else?

"You okay?" Athen asked.

"Yeah."

"Did Natasha report the theft to Beverly Hills police?"

"She says she did."

"But you don't believe her." It was a statement, not a question.

"You do realize she's a Saudi princess, right?" Deck asked, moving forward again. Athen's head swiveled from one direction to the next. He took in the stained-glass windows on each unit and what he was sure were hand-painted tiles on the exterior walls.

"Yes, I realize that," Athen said.

"She wouldn't report it to the police. Her father's some kind of sultan or sheikh or something, and she's always worried he'll make her go home." Deck stopped outside unit number five. "This is it. I live right next to her."

"When did you last see her?"

"Two days ago."

"You have security cameras, Mr. Deck?"

Deck's face turned an interesting shade of magenta. "No. I'm always home. I've become a bit of a yenta. I notice everything. The older I get, the more like my grandma I become. She—er, Natasha, not my grandma—was taking some clothes to the cleaners."

"How do you know she was going to the cleaners?"

"She had her favorite red dress hanging over her arm. Ask her friends about that. Isla Sanchez claims it's hers and that Natasha stole it. Big upsetness there." He flapped a hand. "Natasha probably wanted it cleaned fast. She's got a big audition today."

"What time did you see her go out?"

Deck gave a nasty half-smile. "About two o'clock. That's when she usually gets out of bed." He dropped his voice. "She has a lot of boyfriends. Bet she's with one of them and she would have gone straight there." He knocked on Natasha's door several times. Not home, he and Deck decided.

"Are you very friendly with her?" Athen wondered how this guy knew her sleep schedule and everything else about her but tabled the questions for later.

Cameron gave him a hooded look. "I have a crush on her like everybody else. She can be a bit of a bitch, but she's damned beautiful. I can let you inside. Do you want me to stay or go?"

Athen appreciated Deck's directness. "I take it you're giving me permission to enter the premises."

Deck scowled. "Yeah."

"I need to record this, sorry." Athen had been scrutinized by his own department for his investigation of the woman-in-the carpet case. He'd passed with flying colors, but Lucy had warned him the media and other law enforcement officials were still leery of Beverly Hills Police Department's handling of Ronni Chasen's murder. Some people felt the case had been bungled and not thoroughly investigated. Lucy had been clear that Athen was a showy hire for BHPD and he had to conduct thorough inquiries.

He always did, but neither of them expected a new case to crop up so soon. Athen shot several seconds of footage with Deck giving him permission to enter Natasha King's apartment.

"I'm not just the property manager, I own the premises," Deck said with a haughty air.

Even better. Nothing like a property owner giving you permission to enter an apartment. It would make Athen's life a lot easier when he needed a search warrant. Nobody could say he'd violated the Mincey Warrant by barging into the missing woman's abode.

"Please stay," Athen said, ending the recording, "but don't touch anything. You haven't let anyone in here?"

"Nope. Not even Maggie. She was here the night Natasha said she was robbed. I'm not discounting her being involved."

That was a surprise. "Why?" Maggie had reported her friend missing and was now babysitting her cat. "Why would you think that?" Athen paused at the threshold and turned to stare at him.

"They're both actresses and extremely competitive. It's a cutthroat business, Hollywood, even when you're a wannabe."

"Right." Athen knew this was true. He walked around the apartment, aware of the mingled scent of wet cat fur and some unidentifiable perfume. Nothing seemed out of place that he could tell, but he caught his first real look at Natasha via a stack of eight by ten glossies on what looked like an antique writing desk. She was stunning. Slim with gleaming dark hair and a dazzling smile, Athen wondered how long it would be before she got an acting gig.

In spite of being asked to remain by the front door, Deck was following him. Athen glanced at him. "Can I ask you what the rent is here?"

"Five grand a month."

That's steep. But then again, she's royalty. "And when did she move in?"

"Six months ago. She paid twelve months' rent upfront. The property owner was thrilled."

"You just said you're the property owner."

Deck reddened like a cranberry in boiling water. "I forgot." He shrugged. "I don't tell too many people. Anyway. I didn't run a background check on her. She paid in cash."

"How did she find you?"

Deck frowned. "She never said. She arrived toward the end of November. A vision in a red mini dress. I saw her climbing out of a silver limousine. She walked around, smelled really good, then offered me the money." He blushed then spread his hands. "I make the residents feel as though there's a family of us running things. I want to convey the feeling that I'm not alone. Just a henchman. I don't like trouble."

"Do you get much trouble?"

He pointed to the photos of Natasha. "Looks like she's bringing plenty my way."

"Do you have a copy of her lease?" Athen asked.

Cameron Deck's face flushed. "She never signed it. Hey, nobody pays a year in advance. I figured when we renew the lease, I'll make sure she signs it."

The arrangement sounded bizarre to say the least. "Can you recall the exact date she moved in?"

"Between Thanksgiving and December first." Deck scratched his head. "I really don't know when she traveled here. I got the feeling she hadn't been in LA very long." He followed Athen from one room to another. After a cursory inspection of the apartment, which was huge by most standards, he was surprised how few personal items were in evidence.

"No laptop," Athen said. "Do you know where she usually keeps it?"

"Wherever she goes, it travels, too. She keeps it in a Hello Kitty laptop bag she blinged the heck out of."

"So, it's not strange that it's missing."

"No." Deck's voice grew faint. "Not strange."

The massive flat screen TV in the open-plan living and dining rooms seemed to be the focus of the residence. A stack of DVDs on the coffee table were screeners, the kinds of DVDs folks in the industry got for free during awards season. He and Grady had a ton of them at home. Still, the place felt cold, remote. He couldn't get a feel for Natasha at all. He swept his gaze over the minimal wall art and the white-on-white furniture that looked like it came from a catalogue. Beautiful, but no character.

"Did she rent this place furnished?" Athen asked.

Deck looked surprised. "Yes. The only things she brought

in herself were blackout curtains for the bedroom. I helped her put them up."

In the kitchen, Athen found what he was looking for. Signs of Natasha's life. Her appointment calendar was stuck to the side of the fridge with round magnets, filled with so many activities he wondered when she slept. Over the last two days, she'd booked sessions for something called a V-steam, a yoni massage, dental bleaching, manicure, an AB, whatever that was, and a haircut.

He wondered if she'd kept any of those commitments. It was only eight-thirty, too early to call and check. He jotted down the names of the businesses listed on the wall calendar and took a photo of it with his phone. "Do you know anything about the Got Set appointment she has for today?"

"Yeah. This is her third time doing it."

Athen gave him some side eye. "What's a Got Set?" He'd already heard Grady's take on the subject but wanted Deck's opinion too.

Deck gave another shrug. "They're fake sets where you go and shoot a scene but not all sets are created equal. She found a high-class one though and shot some impressive footage." He gave Athen another terrifying grin. "Who says money doesn't buy happiness?" When Athen didn't respond, he added, "She's shooting a third scene for her reel. She keeps DVDs of her work over there." He pointed to a cabinet next to the fridge. It was filled with an array of jewel-colored DVD cases. Athen pulled one out, examining it.

Natasha King Reel, 2020 a label on the case read.

Below these words was a real surprise. *Contact: Maggie Harman Management 310-243 2282.*

Athen tilted his head as he skewered Deck with a stare. "Maggie Harman's her manager?"

Deck seemed to be attempting to stifle laughter. "She had trouble managing the cat. There's cat litter all over the bathroom. Couldn't even get the tray out of here without making a mess."

"Ah." *Wow he really hates Maggie Harman.* Athen paused. "I thought you said you didn't let her in here?"

Deck swallowed and looked around. Athen though the guy might have a heart attack.

"Breathe," Athen said, putting out a hand to steady him.

Grady couldn't stand it when Despina got into one of her moods. She was banging around the house and he predicted a snit-fit with a chance of a full-on meltdown over nothing. He was ready to send the kid back to her parents. Sometimes, he felt as though his relationship with Athen hung on a slender thread. If they had Despina for much longer, Grady didn't think he could handle it. He took a deep breath. Athen's sister, Sia, was undergoing chemo and not doing well. She needed a lot of rest. She'd lost both breasts and was still recovering from a double reconstruction surgery. She'd lost her sense of smell, taste, and her vision had become blurry, thanks to a hellish round of chemo the hospital staff called the Red Devil.

To help him, Sia and her husband Jordan had urged Grady to download an app called MyFlo Tracker. It had been a godsend for him and Athen. Neither of them had coping mechanisms for a teenage girl with enormous emotional issues, let alone monthly changes. The app had been her idea in fact. Whatever her friends tried, she had to try as well. Grady wasn't sure if she monitored her own cycle, but the app helped Grady track it, and also offered excellent advice on how to handle her see-sawing moods.

He tapped the app, which sent him lengthy emails each week. He always intended to read them, but often forgot.

The app loaded up and let him know she had entered her *Luteal phase. Menstruation begins next week.* Moodiness was a seventy-five percent guarantee.

No wonder she was so unpleasant at the moment.

Gulp.

The app suggested taking her hot air-ballooning. *Ha!* He wouldn't do that when she was in a great mood, let alone dealing with her stomping gloominess. And it was raining. He braced himself for her arrival in the kitchen. She approached in a cloud of her cologne, wearing a tank top and shorts.

That's weird. She had on a different outfit when she went to bed last night. And do I smell cigarettes? Grady brushed the thought aside and smiled at her. "Good morning, beautiful. How are you today?"

She stared at him grumpily and with a frightening look on her face, barreled into his arms. He held her, kissing the top of her head. It shocked him and he considered deleting the app.

"I want breakfast," she announced, pulling herself away from him. *She's been smoking. I can smell it on her hair. When? How? It didn't happen in the house. Is she sneaking out at night?*

She gave Bella a brief head pat and threw herself onto a stool at the kitchen island. "Where's Athen?"

He wanted to correct her with "*Uncle* Athen," but wanted to enjoy her rare bouncy side.

"Working on a case."

"Oh? What kind?" She twirled her long legs around the stool and wound a hair curl around her finger.

"Not sure." He didn't trust her not to post the tiniest detail on her Instagram. Grady opened the oven. She was the most finicky eater he knew, and he withdrew a pan of blueberry and peach muffins. "Gluten free, organic flour, cashew milk, and flax seeds instead of eggs."

Veganism was her passion du jour, but he'd been told by her best friend's mom that she ate a Burgerama meat burger with them the previous day. Grady hadn't tackled Despina about this and wouldn't. Unless she became a pain about the muffins, which she'd asked for yesterday.

She glanced at the six, golden goodies. "Organic fruit?" she asked.

Oh, brother. "Yes. Of course."

"Because, you know, my favorite food influencer says that if you eat regular fruit you may as well pour gasoline down your throat."

He stiffened. "The fruit's organic."

She tilted her head. "Are you sure?"

"Sure I'm sure. We get the produce box delivered each week and it's all organic." *And expensive. I'm not up to this. Maybe I should pay for her to go hot-air ballooning. Away from me.*

"Well, I'll try it."

Don't do me any favors. "Do you want tea or coffee?"

"Milk."

He stared at her and her cheeks flamed. "Um, almond milk," she said. "The one from Trader Joe's."

Grady poured her a glass and pushed a napkin and plate toward her. She took a muffin and nibbled at it. He wanted to scream.

"Not bad," she said, putting the muffin down as though it might bite. He resisted the urge to mention the burger. Instead, he said, "What do you feel like doing today?"

She plucked at a blueberry from her muffin. Away from prying eyes he knew she'd eat at least two if he left her alone. She shrugged. "I'm tired. I'm going back to bed." She left the milk untouched, pushed away her plate and trudged back to her room.

Grady sagged against the kitchen counter. *What the hell am I gonna do with her?*

Deck's eyes did funny things as though he was on the verge of choking to death. He gulped in air and burbled, "I only let Maggie in to get the litter box and the cat carrier." His cheeks reddened as Athen kept staring at him. "I . . . panicked when you showed up." He ran a shaky index finger cross his upper lip. "It was the first moment I realized something might actually be wrong. I mean, all those people showing up. Then you . . ."

The phone number for Maggie Harman on the DVD was different from the one Scott had given Athen. "I'm taking this DVD with me." This wasn't officially a crime scene. *Yet.* He paused. "So is she the one listed as Natasha's agent on IMDB Pro?"

Deck nodded. "Boy, you're quick. You looked her up already?"

"Yeah. And if Maggie's so inept, why would Natasha work with her?"

Deck gazed at something fascinating on the floor. "There's a group of girls who kind of formed a team. The players change as they squabble and fall out. But they act as each other's managers, submitting reels for different auditions. Been going on for years in this town, but Maggie actually comes across very well. She was a good choice. She sounds authoritative. I mean, hell, she talked me into letting her in here and taking the cat's things." He stopped. "She also wanted Natasha's Filofax, but we couldn't find it."

"So, she has another appointment book apart from the wall calendar?" Athen pointed to the wall.

"Yeah. Natasha is easily distracted. Gets caught up in things. She does day trading online."

This didn't really surprise Athen. It sounded as though Natasha was a girl with money to burn. She could afford frivolous beauty treatments and paid for pricey classes. Day trading though, was a real skill. Athen wondered how accomplished she was in the securities business.

"Natasha's invested a lot in her career. Takes expensive workshops and such," Deck said, as though reading Athen's train of thought. "I know, because a few of the girls in the building were going but they all dropped out of this one particular hot class because the price was too high."

"Who does she take them with?"

"Grant LoBell. He was on a TV series with that actor . . ." He snapped his fingers. Athen didn't supply the name though he knew it well. Tyler James. The eighteen-year old actor Grady was working with on a TV series.

"Tyler James," Deck said.

Athen nodded. He knew that Tyler hadn't worked with Grant LoBell. He'd replaced the actor in the hit series *Shout* now in its second season for Netflix. The show had already been picked up for a third season and Grady loved working on it.

"How do I get in touch with this guy, Grant LoBell?" Athen asked.

"I have his business card. I'll give it to you."

Athen was surprised how involved Deck seemed with all of this.

"My father was a big producer in this town," Deck said, once again seeming to read Athen's mind. "He died in a plane crash in New York and left me everything. The movie business is my passion, but I haven't made a movie myself." His eyes gleamed when he added, "Yet."

Athen didn't respond to that. He waited a beat. "I'll make some calls. Check if she's kept her appointments the past couple of days. And I'll need to talk to the neighbors sooner rather than later. I'll need names, apartment numbers, and contact details, please." Athen pointed to a notation for two o'clock. "Any idea why this acting class with Grant LoBell is so important today?"

"It's not Grant LoBell. This a different teacher. Grant is her cold reading coach. They say he's the best, but damned expensive so most students hire him for specific auditions. And believe me they pay the price for giving him short notice."

Athen made mental notes. *Cold reading coach. Grady must know what the heck that is.*

"Maxine Michaels is her main acting coach," Deck continued. "She pairs the students up with scene partners. This is a hard class to get into. She's a soap opera star. Does this class for rich people who think they have talent. Anyway, Natasha's been anxious and excited about today's class. She's hired coaches—Grant being one of them—and rehearsed her scene over and over. The girls have all been fighting over pairing up with this one actor."

"And who is that?"

"Bryce Felton. Handsome as shit. He's gonna go far. On looks. No ability to speak of, but that's never stopped anyone in Hollywood."

Shit is handsome? Athen studied Deck and realized the guy was jealous of Bryce Felton. *Man, he's got a serious crush on Natasha. Bet it's unrequited.*

"You'll see him on the DVD. He has a scene with Natasha. That alone caused her problems with the other girls," Deck said.

Athen mentally listed all the people he needed to contact. First things first. Neighbors, then the people she'd made appointments with, and Maggie Harman. The first thing he'd learned as a cop was to find out everything about the way a victim lived to understand how and why they died.

What am I thinking? Why do I think she's dead? He suddenly remembered his dream. Weird things had happened in his life since meeting Kai. He'd never told a soul, except Grady, that the old kahuna showed up in his dreams when murder was afoot. He took a deep breath. *I'm missing something.*

He turned to Deck and held up a finger. He retraced his steps and scouted the rows of bizarre health supplements lining the kitchen bench top. Pro and prebiotics. Gummy vitamins and supplements of every description. There didn't appear to be a single Hollywood fad Natasha King hadn't tried since moving here. He moved over to the fridge and studied the photos stuck on it. There was a photo of Natasha smoking at a restaurant, by the looks of things. He knew that women were forbidden to smoke in Saudi Arabia and public smoking had been banned there. It was illegal to smoke in Los Angeles bars and restaurants.

"Is this Maggie?" He pointed at the girl beside Natasha.

"No. Another friend. They had a falling out."

"You know a lot about her." Athen glanced at him.

Deck didn't skip a beat. "They had an argument a few weeks ago. Thick as thieves until then."

"What's her name?"

"Isla Sanchez." Deck paused and said, "She's the other woman who came here today. I was surprised to see her."

"And do you know what went wrong between her and Natasha?"

"That I don't know. Natasha usually tells me things. Especially if she invites me over for coffee or asks me to fix things." He looked a little stunned. "I think she's used to having household staff and won't lift a finger herself."

Athen didn't respond. He kept checking things. He spotted a phone bill, though it was months old. He hadn't noticed a landline, so it had to be for a cellphone.

For somebody with family in Saudi Arabia, there wasn't a single call registered to that country. All the calls were local. He flipped the page over. She had unlimited local calls but there was one registered overseas. Country code 61. Next to it, the word Australia. Since the call logged in at only thirty-five seconds, he wondered at its importance. He'd check it out. He ran over the local call list. Mostly to the same number he recognized as Maggie Harman's. *These two are as thick as thieves.*

"Is her number three-one-zero, five-five-five, one-two-one-two?" he asked Deck.

"Yeah. She wanted a five-five-five number because that's what they use in the movies."

Athen called the number, listening in case the phone rang in the house. It didn't, and the call went straight to voice mail.

"Hi, this is Natasha. You know what to do."

Her voice was husky, seductive, no trace of an accent.

"Hi Natasha. My name is Lieutenant Athen Mavromatis of the Beverly Hills Police Department. A lot of people are worried about you. If you pick up this message, please call me back at your earliest convenience." He left his number and ended the call. He had a sudden flash that he wouldn't hear back from her. Athen snapped a photo of both sides of the bill and left it tucked where he found it behind a container of coffee pods.

"There's no food in her cupboards. Nothing in the fridge. All she has is her fancy coffeemaker and that jar full of pods." Deck flicked a hand across the kitchen toward a Nespresso machine on the counter.

Athen and Grady had one, but Natasha's machine seemed more complicated.

"She's a coffee fiend." Deck sighed. "All I know is, something happened between Natasha and Isla, and Natasha asked me to change the lock to the front gate."

"This was after the robbery?"

"Yeah. She offered to pay for it." He shrugged. "But I do it periodically anyway. She'd been letting Isla come and use the pool. Isla tried to get in a couple of times. One time we had a maintenance guy working out front and he'd propped the gate open with a brick, against the rules here, and Isla slipped in. I asked her to leave. She was livid." He chuckled at the memory.

"What did she say when she came here today?"

"She said she got a weird phone call from Natasha and

couldn't reach her. Natasha's voice mail was full."

"That's weird. It wasn't when I called it just now."

"Um. Yeah." Deck's color crept up his face again.

Huh. Somebody had cleared Natasha's messages. "Are you worried about her?" Athen asked.

Deck scoffed. "No. I think all of this is ridiculous. She's a princess. She acts like one."

Athen turned on his heel and headed to her bedroom next. Lavishly decorated all the way to red and gold brocade window treatments and bedspread, it was neat. The faint fragrance of some heavy perfume, a different one he'd detected upon entering the apartment, hung on the air. He spotted a walk-in closet and stepped inside, surprised when he didn't find the one thing he expected.

Not a single *abaya* or *hijab. How weird.*

He started to wonder about the red mini dress Deck said she wore the first day she'd arrived. It wasn't in the closet either. Where had she come from when she arrived in her limo? From the airport or someplace else?

Everything about her closet troubled him. Wouldn't a Saudi princess keep at least one traditional outfit in her wardrobe? He moved over to her shoe racks on the left side and sniffed. A sweet smell he recognized. Cleaning fluid. Something squished underfoot. He looked down.

Cameron Deck, who was right behind him gasped.

"Get back!" Athen yelled. When Deck swayed, Athen shoved at him. "Stay where you are. Don't move." Athen took out his phone, ignoring the pale look of horror on Deck's face. Focusing on the carpeted floor, Athen stood where he was and activated the ultra-violet light app on his phone. It wasn't apparent to the naked eye, but he recorded what he saw around him. He could hardly breathe as he realized his missing persons case had taken a horrible turn.

Somebody had cleaned up, and not done a very good job

of getting rid of what was seeping underneath Athen's feet.
Blood.

Lots and lots of blood.

CHAPTER FOUR

Deck let out a blood-curdling scream, so strident Athen wondered if he needed to smack some sense into the guy. He made Deck remove his shoes then took off his own. He gripped them by the shoelaces as he led Deck outside. While Deck leaned against a stone column and hyperventilated, Athen called Paulie Hansen. It wasn't easy juggling the shoes and the phone.

"You need an ambulance?" Paulie asked. "What's all that noise?"

"Landlord of a missing woman freaked out when he saw blood. How fast can you get here?"

"On my way."

"And bring a crime scene crew." Athen's thoughts raced.

"That might take a while. We just got a robbery in progress at the Morgan Price jewelry store on Rodeo Drive. It's all over the news. Security guard shot. Our crew's on scene dusting for prints. I can put in a request with the chief for immediate response. Gimme your address."

"Is the guard okay?" Athen couldn't believe the city had two major cases in one day. Beverly Hills was usually so sedate. They hadn't had a single jewelry store robbery since he'd been here. The last one was two years ago. Thieves had broken into Jason of Beverly Hills in the middle of the night and taken off with 1.4 million dollars in diamonds.

"He's okay. Man and a woman posing as customers," Paulie said. "They held everyone up at gunpoint. He confronted them. Damn he's got some balls on him. They shot him and took off, but Bonnie and Clyde were caught on tape. Crime scene analysts are there. Guard's in the hospital." Paulie took a breath. "I'm watching it all on TV. Our guys have the suspects in a highspeed chase on the 101. Why do they always run? They know they're gonna get caught."

"Just get here. And bring Sullivan with you." Athen knew that very soon he'd need a female officer to help him interview the other residents in the building and Sullivan Tang was the best, next to Lucy, of course. "And Paulie, I'll let the chief know you're on the way."

"Is this why she benched me? Kept me on hold for you? I was getting jealous that Lorne Brand caught this one." He gave a slight chuckle.

Lorne Brand. A capable detective but Athen couldn't stand the guy. He was thrilled to know Brand was out of the way at the jewelry store.

"I asked for you. Gotta go." Athen ended the call just as Deck started yelling again.

"Where'd all that blood come from, man?" He doubled over. *Oh, crap.* He was having an anxiety attack.

Athen told him to sit on the stoop. "Put your head between your legs and breathe. I'll be right back." He put a call through to Lucy Lane. His only thoughts were, *could somebody survive losing that much blood?*

"What's going on?" a woman asked, running over to him.

Athen held up a hand to ward off more questions and took note of Lucy's instructions.

"Do not talk to the media. Did you find a passport, or any other kind of ID?"

"No, sir."

"Damn. Get back inside and search. I'll leave you to it. I'll get you evidence analysts, but it'll be at least fifteen minutes." She paused. "Maybe it's time to call in SID."

"Yeah. That might be a good idea. Paulie told me about the jewelry heist."

"The offenders look like teenagers. I can't believe it." She took a deep breath. "Talk to this Maggie Harman woman. Do you want to involve the Saudi consulate at this time?"

"Yes, sir."

"You want to do it, or do you want me to handle it?"

"If you could call them, I'd really appreciate it." Athen hated dealing with royal muckety-mucks. He preferred to let Lucy be the politically correct one. "I have no contact number there, though Scott told me that Maggie reported Natasha missing to the consulate this morning. He specifically told me not to contact them."

"Screw him. I'll take a hit for the team, Blackeye. I'll get back to you. In the meantime, this *cannot* get out. It must be contained. I can't stress that strongly enough. Is Paulie gonna be enough help?"

"Yes, sir," he responded. "He's bringing Sullivan Tang with him. I trust them both. I want to keep this contained as well. Until I know what we're dealing with."

"Roger that." She ended their call.

Athen squinted at the woman bouncing on her toes beside him. He recognized her as the naked woman dancing in her bathroom. Now she was sporting tiny white dolphin shorts and a tight white T-shirt that read, *Blink If You Want Me*.

"Do you have any brandy at home?" Athen asked her, hoping like hell he didn't blink.

"I have cognac." She cast a surprised glance at Deck, whose head remained bent as he choked and cried.

Athen nodded. "Bring him some please. He's had a shock."

The woman's ruby-red-painted lips parted, but she took off with the grace of a gazelle. Athen popped his state-issue Chrysler 300 open remotely and managed to get both pairs of shoes into evidence bags. He removed paper booties and disposable gloves from his trunk then paused for a moment. *I need a blue felt-tip marker and transparent tape for my cellphone.* He had some in the evidence kit he kept in there and pocketed them.

As he returned to the apartment building, the ruby-painted gazelle walked over to him with a brandy balloon. Its amber contents sloshed the bottom of the glass, coating it with tiny, liquid waves.

"Thank you." Athen took the glass from her and nudged Deck who leaned his head against a creamy white and gold column, shaking. "Here. Drink this."

Paulie and Sullivan arrived a minute later. It had taken them two minutes, one more than the Beverly Hills Police Department allowed, but they'd hustled to get here judging by his harried appearance. Deck's freak-out forced Athen to tend to him before he could deal with Paulie. It was then Athen realized he was still wearing only his socks. He quickly donned booties and handed a pair to Paulie.

"Want me to call Grady and ask him to bring you another pair?" Paulie asked.

"Thanks, I'd appreciate it but first, I want you to look at something." Athen turned to Sullivan. She was a lovely, warm woman. A natural blonde, according to Grady.

She wore a black pant suit paired with black lace-up shoes. *She's ready for anything.* Sullivan was beautiful and calm and deceptively strong. Didn't take crap from anybody. She was Athen's kind of person.

"Can you keep an eye on things out here for me?" he asked, placing the bagged shoes beside her. "I'm leaving these with you. Please don't let them out of your sight."

"I won't, sir."

"Hit me up when the crime scene analysts show up." He paused. "Special Investigations Division might show up since we now have two active crime scenes."

She nodded and glanced down at Deck who was blinking up at her through tears. He smiled, but she looked appalled.

Is he really coming onto her? "Shoot him if he makes a pass at you," Athen whispered to her. She grinned at him.

Athen and Paulie had so much to do Athen had to decide where to start. He nudged Paulie, handing him a pair of paper booties. Paulie was already slipping on gloves. "Follow me." They headed over to Natasha's apartment.

"The whole place feels off to me," Athen muttered. "Staged. She's had a recent break-in and I couldn't find a purse with ID anywhere. Her cellphone and laptop are missing. Her friend and manager Maggie Harman came and took Natasha's cat this morning."

The faint scent of heavy perfume still lingered.

"Shalimar," Paulie said, taking a sniff.

Athen welcomed Paulie's attention to detail, and his keen sense of smell.

"Is that a common perfume?" Athen asked.

"No. Well, it was back in the day. I had an auntie who used to wear it. She always wore that, or Charlie perfume." His expression became pained. "Isn't Natasha King young?"

"Yes. But she's a Saudi princess. Maybe they wear things like Shalimar over there," Athen responded. "Okay, now here's where things get real."

He led Paulie to the patch of carpet in the walk-in closet that oozed blood. He knew that the crime scene techs would do their own blood analysis but Athen needed to know now how bad things were.

"Strong smell of cleaner," Paulie said.

"Yep." Athen pulled out the transparent tape and blue marker from his pocket. After covering his LED flash on his phone with the tape, he swiped the blue pen across it. He repeated this process.

"Man, I love this hack," Paulie said. "Want me to record?"

"Yup." Athen had just turned his phone into a black light. He pressed the video record function and the small room lit up like a bizarre Christmas tree.

"Holy crap!" Paulie recorded it all, neither man saying a word as they took in the wide arc of smears and evidence of crazy blood spatter.

"Oh, this is creepy," Paulie said when Athen stopped his phone.

"Yeah."

"I'll send you what I got," Paulie said.

"Thanks." Athen went to the bathroom. "I don't see anything in here we can use for trace." He opened cabinet doors and drawers.

"Didn't you say there was a cat in here until this morning?" Paulie asked.

"Yeah."

"No litter on the floor. I don't care how neat and tidy you are, there's always gonna be a few litter grains."

Athen thought for a moment. "True. But according to the landlord, the cat's been locked out the last two days."

His phone pinged and Athen quickly removed the doctored tape from his phone. "Can you send it on to Lucy as well, Paulie?"

"Sure thing, boss."

Athen's phone rang. Sullivan let him know the crime scene crew had arrived. As he and Paulie stepped outside, the building's residents came running out of their units to see what was going on.

Athen handed one of the techs the bagged shoes, letting him know which pair was which, and sighed. *God knows when I'll see mine again.*

He nodded to Mike, one of the newest crime scene techs hired by the department.

"Sorry it took us so long," Mike said. "Been a busy morning."

"You were quick." Athen smiled at him. "Glad you're here." He turned to Sullivan. "I'm gonna need your help."

"You got it," she said.

Athen turned to the four female residents huddled together. "I need to talk to all of you and I'm going to ask you respectfully not to discuss anything with each other until we've asked you a few questions. Do *not* take photos of anything. No posting *a single thing* to social media. Don't call your friends to gossip. Nothing."

They all exchanged looks.

"Do any of you have security cameras in your apartments?" Athen asked.

Another round of hooded, guarded looks. Then they all stared at him.

"No," one of them said, casting a vicious look at her landlord. "Cameron won't allow it."

"You don't need it. I'm always here," he bleated.

"Yeah. Right. Tell that to Natasha King," one of the women said.

Athen sucked in a breath. "I'll be right back." He gave Sullivan a meaningful look.

"I'll be right here," she said. The look she swept over the group before her would have frozen time.

"Thanks. Mike. Front door," Athen said.

Mike and his team followed Athen and Paulie. Outside Natasha's door, Athen nodded to Paulie.

"Show 'em what we've got."

Paulie played back the footage as the four-man team clustered around them.

"Christ," somebody muttered.

"Obviously, I need to know if this is one person's blood and if so, could the victim have survived this kind of blood loss?" Athen asked.

"If it's one person, I'm gonna say no," Mike said.

In the small dressing room, Mike held out an arm to block anyone from coming closer. "I smell a household cleaner." He sniffed. "I believe it's four-zero-nine. That's a weird choice for carpeting."

"Whoever did this cleanup job was desperate," Paulie said. "I think they got rid of a ton of stuff in the process."

"Probably grabbed whatever was handy," Athen said.

Mike sighed. "Let me get to it. We'll start here and examine for other possible blood spatter and fingerprints." He stared down at the stained carpeting. "Particularly in the bathroom. Somebody went to great lengths to clean up here. But they panicked." He gestured to Paulie's phone. "The smeared, frenzied way they wiped at the wall. Probably thought the blood would dry up under the carpet before anyone came in here."

"Or they thought they'd have more time to finish up." Athen's voice was quiet. He wanted to take a closer look at Cameron Deck.

"They must have washed their hands at some point." Mike turned to Athen. "We got any cleaning products in the kitchen?"

"Not that I checked. Yet."

"Any DNA on the possible victim?"

"Not yet. Her fingerprints must be all over the place. But for hair or trace evidence, we couldn't find a hairbrush or toothbrush in the bedroom or bathroom."

"There isn't even any dirty laundry," Paulie said. "Not even a hamper."

"Cameron Deck mentioned he last saw her taking out laundry two days ago," Athen said. "Maybe she takes everything out to be cleaned."

Mike held up a hand. "We'll take care of a more thorough search. If I find good, useable prints, I'll run 'em through AFIS immediately."

"Okay." Athen nodded. "She was supposed to have arrived here almost six months ago, but without an exact date, it's gonna take some time for Homeland Security to check her prints from her arrival at LAX. She would have had to give thumbprints."

"You're right." Mike sighed. "They're backed way up. Without an exact date it could take days. But we can try."

"Paulie and I will check for a passport or some other form of ID then we'll get out of your way."

"Do that." Mike gave him a slight smile.

In the bedroom, Athen and Paulie methodically opened drawers and found underwear and bras. No socks or panty hose. *Huh.* Weird. Then he thought about the dresses he'd seen in the closet. Maybe this girl didn't wear jeans or jog. Yet, she was a fitness fanatic judging by the multiple supplements in the kitchen. The whole thing felt off. He knew that in Saudi Arabia, Natasha would have to wear an abaya, and that even showing her ankle would be considered offensive. Yes, she was a royal, but at some point, she had to respect her family's customs. He itched to speak to at least one family member to see when they'd last heard from her, but so far, he had nothing to go on.

Paulie checked the bathroom despite the fact the crime scene crew would take care of it themselves.

"I don't see makeup or women's stuff," Paulie reported to Athen. "Only a bottle of generic anti-dandruff shampoo in the shower stall."

He and Athen checked the two handbags dangling from the handle of the bedroom door. They were pricey designer bags that would have made Despina drool but contained nothing more than a couple of crumpled tissues. One of them had a parking pass to the Beverly Hills post office. Athen studied it. Beverly Hills was the only post office he knew of that not only issued passes but had valet parking as well. The ticket would have her prints on it, but so did other objects in the apartment. According to the timestamp, Natasha had been to the post office at 3:45 p.m. two days before.

Maybe they have security cameras. We'll check if she was alone and what she was doing there. He put the ticket on her bed and took a photo of it then handed it to Mike in an evidence bag. He dropped to his knees and checked under the bed. Nothing. Not even a dust bunny. The place felt devoid of personality and any trace of real, human life.

"What's bothering you?" Paulie asked.

Athen shrugged. "All of it. What vibe do you get?"

"I feel like it's almost empty. Maybe she's taken off and she's missing of her own accord."

"Maybe. But she's been here nearly six months and got a cat. Would she just take off and leave it?"

"I wonder. And how did her friend Maggie know to come get the cat this morning?" Paulie asked.

"Yeah. Does she know something we don't?"

"I tell you what else is weird. There's no perfume any-where in the place. No Shalimar. Either Maggie wears it her-self or she sprayed some from a bottle that was here and took it with her." Paulie pointed a gloved finger at the bedside ta-bles. "I'm pretty certain there were bottles on them and some-one swept them up. I still see ring marks. You're right. Some-body staged all this."

They looked at each other. Athen drew in a breath. He sus-pected that he and Paulie had just stepped into what was about to become a massive, international catastrophe. A Saudi princess being murdered. They moved on to the kitchen where Paulie examined the same surfaces Athen had before heading outside again.

Athen asked Paulie and Sullivan to interview each resident away from one another asking if any of them had information on Natasha. "Find out if any of them saw her leaving with her laundry two days ago."

Cameron Deck sat on a stone step, tears flowing down his face. He sipped the cognac, but it just seemed to make him more hysterical. Sullivan stood over him, an odd look on her face.

"Do you have any idea where Natasha takes her laundry?" Athen asked him.

"Naw. Some place in West Hollywood. It's a Chinese name. Sort of fake Chinese name. Heck. It might even be called The Chinese Laundry. I just forget what it is. They usually pick up, but she had an argument with their delivery guy last week. They shrunk her favorite dress and she went off the deep end."

Athen jotted a note in his phone to check for Chinese laundries in West Hollywood. He then stepped away and called Lucy Lane. She listened with grave attention as he gave her a brief rundown on things.

"No ID at all?" She blew out a sigh. "I called the consulate. Waiting for a callback now. How much blood is there?"

"A lot. It doesn't seem to me that whoever suffered, could have survived that kind of loss. I'll defer to Mike on that. I took my shoes off and got out of there. I gave 'em to the crime scene guys. I'll let you know as soon as I have any further news." Athen's thoughts raced. "Listen, we're gonna need to check Natasha's phone records. We need to know who she called last, and when. Can you use your charm to track them down? I've jotted down her number and according to an old bill I spotted on her desk, she uses AT&T. I tried calling her and it went straight to voice mail."

"I'll do that. Just give me the number," Lucy said.

"Will do. And I'll text you a copy of the bill. I'm wondering if she has a second phone. Not a lot of calls and most of those are to her friends Maggie and Isla. They both came here this morning. No idea who the guys were that came here last night looking for her."

"You need more help?" Lucy asked.

"Just you, Paulie, and Sullivan, right now. Oh, and I want

to check Natasha's appointments she had for yesterday, and today."

"Let me do that. I can share the load with Sullivan. You got numbers?"

"Yeah. I took photos of her calendar. I'll text that to you as well. She was supposed to be getting a V-steam and a slew of other things over the last couple of days. And what the hell is a V-steam?"

Lucy chuckled. "Vaginal steam. It's the latest thing."

Ugh. "If you say so. Today, she's supposed to be at an important acting class and her Got Set shoot. If you can chase up the beauty treatments, I'll work the business angle and let you know as soon as I have anything."

"Likewise. By the way, Scott fell off a different horse. Broke his collarbone. He's in Cedars-Sinai so no need to contact him. He's under heavy sedation." She paused. "Somebody recorded it on a cellphone and it's all over the Internet. He was wearing chaps over his suit pants."

Athen grinned. "Yippee Ki yay," he whispered, making Lucy laugh.

Before he could do anything, he got another call. *Unknown Number.* He suspected it was Cricket. He had enough on his plate, starting with the need to track down Maggie Harman and Isla Sanchez.

"I gotta talk to you. Where you at?" Cricket asked. The line crackled just like it had last night. Athen realized now it was Cricket's creepy habit of chomping on fried pork rinds. Huge bags of it.

"You still on surveillance?" Athen asked.

"Yeah. How'd you know?"

"The pork." Athen scratched his head. He was itching to get back on the case.

"Oh, yeah. Well, look. It won't take long but it's urgent."

"What's so urgent?"

"I guess nobody's told you." Cricket coughed. It sounded like the guy was about to lose a lung. Nasty. "We found Allie Madden."

Athen's jaw literally dropped. "Where?"

"Buried in a field ten miles from her house. We need to talk. Now."

"I got a big case."

"This is big, too."

"Where do I find you?"

"I'm across the street from your big case."

"What?" Athen swiveled his gaze. He finally picked out a snazzy-looking black Camaro parked two blocks away facing him. The headlights blinked on and off.

"You're following me?" Athen's fury flared.

"Meet me at the corner of Linden and Lomitas. Don't come near the car."

"Okay." Athen's thoughts raced. Cricket was watching him. Why? He got his bearings and told Paulie he'd be right back.

"I don't have any leads," Paulie said. "Nobody saw anything. And the natives are getting restless."

"I'll be right back." Athen realized Cricket was sending him away from the Camaro and the crime scene. He arrived at the appointed corner outside a clutch of swanky homes that must have had starting prices of around three million bucks.

Cricket was there, pork rinds in hand. He offered Athen the bag, then his gaze swiveled downward. "Nice footwear, Athen."

Holy cow. I'm still wearing booties. He waved away the pork rinds. "Oh, no. Thanks." Athen shook his head. Cricket's fingers were stained orange from the snacks. He looked the same as Athen remembered him, with maybe a few more short grey hairs, checked shirt and jeans with a crease. He couldn't look more like a US Marshal if he tried.

"We found Allie Madden six weeks ago. I know it hasn't been big news out here but back east it's been a huge deal."

"I'd say so."

Cricket was a big guy who looked like he should be fat but wasn't. given the chance to loiter in front of his TV a week or two and he would be. Not that Cricket would allow that to happen. He was as committed to solving crimes as Athen was. The Allie Madden case had affected them both.

"We found her by accident," Cricket said then. "Some poor schmoes doing routine grading work out in a field slated for development found what they thought were finger bones poking out of the ground. Turns out they were right. Local cops issued an excavation order and the forensic pathologist for the state of Virginia took over three weeks ago once she was ID'd as Allie."

He let that sink in for a moment.

Athen closed his eyes. The old man, Kai, had been right. Athen and Cricket had argued over Kai's insistence that she had not been dumped in the lake.

Cricket's tone turned husky with a trace of emotion. "She'd been shot in the back of the head. There was some DNA on her clothing. Semen stains on her jeans and on her jacket. Her purse was underneath her body. We think she was raped. Evidence of stabbing as well as the gunshot. Amazing the DNA survived since her remains were skeletal."

Athen was riveted. He and Cricket had worked hard on the case. "You're going to tell me the DNA doesn't match Phil Madden's."

Cricket's face fell for a moment. "How do you do that? You're right. And the DNA didn't bring up a direct hit."

"Really? So why am I here?"

Cricket's expression turned sly. "My niece has gotten involved in some very sophisticated form of DNA testing."

"And?"

Cricket's eyes turned flinty with anger. "I'm gettin' to it. If you'd let me finish speaking."

Athen couldn't believe she'd been buried in a field and not dumped at sea. He and Cricket had argued often over Athen's late-night consultation with Kai. Actually, he and Cricket had argued *a lot* once Athen got involved with Grady. Cricket had always known Athen was gay, but as long as it was an abstract theory and there was no real boyfriend at hand, Cricket was okay with it. But Grady had been real. Athen had been so focused on his career and his budding romance it had taken a while for him to realize Cricket rarely invited him to family events. They'd grab dinner together, or breakfast, when they were working cases, but once Grady came into his life, Athen felt he'd been iced completely from Cricket's family life.

"So, Phil Madden's girlfriend lied about Allie being tossed in the lake."

"Oh, yeah." Cricket shoveled a few rinds in his jaw. "You always said so."

Athen, like many cops, worked from intuition. Now he was feeling positively psychic. "Oh, man. You've gone rogue."

Cricket's shoulders sagged. "How do you do that? Look, I'm not completely workin' off the radar, but I have no probable cause to arrest the guy I think is good for it."

Athen squinted at him. He said nothing hoping Cricket would explain.

Cricket waved a hand around. "The DNA doesn't match Phil Madden."

"Yeah, you said."

"Nothing on file anywhere." Cricket flinched. "Which means the suspect hasn't ever been put into the system." He waited a beat. "My niece came up with an idea. The FBI has quietly been working with a couple of those genealogy websites where people submit their DNA to try and find long lost relatives. One of them is working with law enforcement."

"Sounds like a good idea to me." Athen was surprised that a genealogy website would do this since the work was supposed to be confidential.

"This website lets its users know that they share information with law enforcement and people don't seem to mind. Guess they think they've got nothing to hide."

"Or they think it may help them track hard-to-find family."

Cricket nodded. "Right." He let his chubby fingers root around the snack bag for a moment. "Anyway, my niece got in touch with the site, submitted the suspect's DNA."

"You got a hit." Athen was riveted.

"Yes, and no. The type of testing these sites do is called Genetic Genealogy. It's broader than DNA because they can get a general idea of a family DNA."

"I see."

"So, we got a hit. A family in Pennsylvania. This woman has been looking for relatives. I've been checking her out."

"Pennsylvania's nowhere near Virginia Beach, Allie Madden's last known sighting." Athen pondered. "Wait. Maybe a five, five-and-a-half-hour drive at most. Not that farfetched. Damn. Is there a name that came up that we missed during our investigation?"

"Don't do this to yourself. I've beaten myself up plenty and it's pointless. This suspect came up out of nowhere. That's why I'm here. The woman I mentioned in Pennsylvania. She's a widow. An empty nester. Husband died eight years ago."

"So, he can't be our suspect," Athen blurted.

"No. But I found *her* on Facebook. Been spilling her guts all over it. She has two daughters, and one son. It can't be the daughters obviously who raped and stabbed our girl. Must be the son."

"Okay. I'll bite. Who's the son?"

"Tyler James."

Athen stared at him. "Tyler James?" As in the movie star

Tyler James, who also happened to be Athen's friend and current landlord?

"We've been watching your house. You *are* aware he bought the place two doors down from you and he's been staying there?"

"No. He's in New York working on a show as far as I know."

"Nope. He's back. He has no idea we're onto him. But this is where you come in. He's hanging out with your niece."

"What? When?"

"She knows he's here. She's been sneaking out of your house late at night to see him. I've peeked in the windows. Boy, can she talk. It isn't sexual, but he listens to every word she says." Cricket paused. "I think he's grooming her."

Athen wanted to blurt out the truth about Despina, that she'd just come out as gay to Athen and Grady, but it wasn't his place. Besides, whatever her own truth was, it didn't stop a guy with an un ulterior motive from trying to groom a young woman.

Cricket blathered on, unaware that he'd just detonated an emotional neutron bomb. "Can't figure out why else he's spending so much time listening to a teenager who's as boring as batshit. Oops, sorry. No offense meant."

"None taken."

"If he's the guy who killed Allie Madden, then he's a vicious, sick killer. I haven't told you the half of what he did to that girl. And your niece is underage. I wish I could come up with a reason to bring him in for that, and cut him in his tracks, but I got nothing on him there. All they do is talk."

Holy shit. Athen was speechless. *I'm gonna ground her for life. Then I'm gonna kill Tyler James.*

Cricket looked at him. "So far, this Genetic Genealogy has only been used for one criminal case. That was the arrest of the Golden State Killer. Who, as you know, is still awaiting trial."

"What do you need me to do?" Athen asked. He knew the Golden State Killer case had been a huge one for investigators spanning more than three decades and several different California cities. Joseph James DeAngelo had been arrested but he'd eluded discovery and capture for years. Authorities believed him to be the most prolific serial rapist in US history. They still didn't know how many victims there were, but he'd managed to kill eleven people and was escalating those violent crimes. Athen believed he would have continued his long-term spree had he not been caught.

"I need you to get Tyler James' DNA. I don't care how you do it, as long as he has no idea we're onto him," Cricket said. "I can't do it legally, like I said. I've been watching him for days. He hasn't dropped so much as a discarded paper cup in his trash. So damned frustrating. You in?"

"Hell, yeah." Athen knew if they could get Tyler's DNA off something he'd thrown away, they could legally obtain it and enter it into a case's evidence. His phone rang. Lucy Lane. *911.* "I gotta go."

Cricket raised a hand in farewell. "And, Athen?"

"Yeah?"

"Sorry about your niece. Teenagers are a pain in the ass. I'm gonna forward you everything I have on the Allie Madden case."

"Do that." Athen turned and headed back to the crime scene. The thought occurred to him. He hadn't talked to Cricket in months. How did he know about Despina? *Damn. He's really been watching us. Maybe that's a good thing. An extra set of eyes on Desi.* "I'll be in touch," he said over his shoulder. He took Lucy's call. "Sir?"

"I just spoke to a representative at the Saudi consulate. You're not gonna believe this, but Maggie Harman never called the consulate this morning, and the guy I talked to has no record of Natasha King, or Natasha Al-Khan. She is no Saudi princess. And they have no knowledge of her. He said she could be a regular citizen and they wouldn't necessarily know of her, but if she were really from a royal family, she'd be on their radar."

"Hot damn." Athen swallowed. Hard.

"No such number. No such zone, as the song says." Lucy lapsed into silence.

"Then who the hell is she?" Athen ground out.

"That's what I'm hoping you'll tell me. I don't wanna find out she's some kind of suicide bomber. I don't want her to be a terrorist, Athen. Whoever the hell she is, tell me. And make it soon, Blackeye. Please."

CHAPTER FIVE

A then checked in with Paulie who said the crime scene analysts were still processing the apartment.

"Sullivan's got a funny feeling about one of the residents, but I don't know. I thought they were all pretty clammed up. Sullivan thinks they're all intimidated by Cameron Deck."

"I'm not surprised." Athen thought about how intrusive the guy seemed. In his mind, Deck had just moved up to the top of the list of suspects. Not that he had any others right now. "Which resident was this?"

"Felice Farmer. The one who thinks if you blink that you want her."

Despite the circumstances, Athen grinned. "Oh, her. Maybe we can have Sullivan try her again away from the building."

"She works in a cigar bar doing bottle service."

"Those girls make great tips," Athen said.

"Yeah. Apparently, Natasha worked there first and got Felice and her friend Isla jobs there. Felice was very close-mouthed about all that. Oh, the girls are getting restless. Can we let them go?" Paulie asked.

"Yep. I need you to come with me to talk to Maggie Harman." Athen told him quickly about Lucy's call.

"Wow. A mystery on top of a mystery."

"I'm heading back to you. I'll call Lucy for extra help. I want to keep a uniformed officer on Natasha's front door."

"Want me to call her?" Paulie asked.

"Do that. Please. And let's get a squad car here. They can

start going door to door and asking neighbors if any of them have security cameras. Maybe somebody saw something." Having Paulie organize things gave Athen a few extra minutes to call Grady. He had to warn him about his conversation with Cricket.

"Love of my life," Grady said, his voice warm and sincere sounding as soon as he took the call.

Athen was about to ruin his day. "What I'm about to tell you remains between us."

"Of course. What is it?"

Athen weighed his options. He would tell Grady only essentials. He needed to know Despina was lying to them and sneaking out of the house, on top of all the other drama she'd brought into their lives.

"Please don't let on anything to Desi."

"Oh, God." Grady sounded instantly distressed. "What's she done now?"

"She's been sneaking out at night."

"Yeah. I just figured that out. She gave me a hug—"

"She *hugged* you?"

"I know, right? Anyway, she was in a great mood until it was time for breakfast. I could smell cigarette smoke on her hair and skin."

Athen blinked. Tyler James smoked. They could get his DNA off his butts. But if he wasn't discarding trash, what the heck was he doing with them?

"I can't check the security cameras with Desi hanging all over me," Grady said. "Whatever's going on, we'll get to the bottom of it."

"I'm coming home," Athen said. "I need shoes."

"What happened to the ones you left in?"

"Covered in blood."

An intake of breath on the other end of the line. "I'm sorry I asked. "You coming alone?"

"Paulie's gonna be with me." Athen would have Sullivan talk to Felice Farmer again. On her own she might extract some information from her.

"Oh, he called me, but I was on the other line talking to your sister and didn't click over."

"Is Sia okay?"

"Yeah. She just misses her big brother. You need to call her."

"I will."

"Since you're bringing Paulie with you, I guess there's no time for a quickie then."

Athen grinned. "Later, gator."

"I just made some rosemary bread. I'll have a couple of sandwiches and coffee waiting for you."

"We don't have time for sandwiches—"

"Athen, Paulie's diabetic. He has to eat."

"How do you know that?"

"His wife told me. Newly diagnosed. Don't you two talk about this stuff?"

"Er. No." Athen would never tell Grady they liked to gripe to each other about family life. Athen's overly full one, and Paulie's desperate efforts to create one with his wife.

"And you need to eat, too," Grady scolded. "Giving half your food to the dog doesn't count as any type of meal."

"Roger that."

"When you get here, keep Desi distracted so I can check the security tapes. I hate what she's doing to us. I don't trust her and that makes me somebody I don't like very much. I'm afraid to let her out of my sight. How'd you find out Tyler James is in town, anyway?"

"I'll explain later. See you in a few." Athen reached the apartment building and ended their call. Neighbors were streaming out of the building as though they'd been let out of jail. A squad car pulled up out front. Athen gave the guys a wave and nodded to Paulie. "We'll take my car. I gotta pick up some shoes. Any word from the crime scene analysts?"

"Nothing. We have her prints, well, we assume they're her prints. We're checking AFIS and Mike will forward them to Homeland Security once we have a positive ID."

"Right." Athen knew he'd have to enlist help from other officers. He approached Sullivan who caught his gaze. She inclined her head away from a still-crumpled Cameron Deck. In Athen's opinion, the guy was laying on the act a little thick.

Athen moved over to where she stood, in a far corner of the iron fence. "Sullivan, Paulie tells me you think Felice Farmer's holding out."

"I do." She cut a glance toward the entrance to Natasha's unit where Mike's team was still dusting for prints. "She works at a cigar bar. Fabulaire's."

"Oh. I know of that place. Up on Doheny," Athen said.

"That's the one. She will only talk to you. Said she'd be there at four to get ready for her five o'clock shift. You must have made an impression on her." A slight smile from Sullivan. "Did you blink at her?"

Athen and Paulie laughed.

"Yeah." Athen shrugged. "Guilty as charged."

"She's expecting you," Sullivan said. "I'll text you her number. And, sir?" She held his gaze for a moment. "That Cameron Deck . . . I've seen him somewhere before. Not in person. In a connection with a drug case. I'm certain of it, but I can't place him. With your permission I'd like to forward his photo to the DEA. My former boss there can be trusted, and we've got state of the art facial recognition programs we don't have access to here. Can I send it to him?"

Athen stared at her for a moment. "And you trust this guy?"

"Jesse Davis is the best. Give me the word and I'll text him right away. I'll have him contact you directly."

"I really just have to say thank you," Athen said. "I appreciate the suggestion and your eagle eye. I'd like to keep you in the loop, and Paulie too, of course. Anything he sends to me should go to both of you as well."

"Thank you, sir," she said.

"Don't call me sir. Athen's fine. I'd like you to stay and keep an eye on Deck. We'll put up yellow tape right now, but I still don't trust him not to go into Natasha's unit and poke his nose in things. We have a squad car out front. Any problems with him, arrest him. Once the guys are done here, I'd like you to help me and Paulie check out some leads." He caught a glimpse of Mike waving to him.

"Great, sir. Um. I mean Athen. We'll stay in touch." Sullivan moved back over toward Deck who sat with his head in his hands.

"Landlord's prints are all over the joint," Mike muttered to Athen. "Talk about hands-on. This guy must be in here all the time. By the way, I'd like to go over the bedroom some more."

"Whatever you need to do."

"There are prints on the wall heading up to the ceiling." Mike held his gaze.

"That's unusual."

"He might have installed a hidden camera. I'll holler at you once I know more."

"Great, thanks. You're running her prints through AFIS?"

"Yep. I want to run the landlord's prints too. They're in the bedroom but stop near the bathroom. His prints aren't the ones near the ceiling."

"Huh. Okay. Paulie mentioned Homeland Security. If you can contact them with her prints, I'll have Lucy check for video of her arrival at LAX. Landlord says she moved here in late November, but he wasn't firm on the date, and who knows if that's when she really landed here."

"Most people come on six month visas these days. Maybe

her time was running out," Paulie suggested as he and Athen made their way to his car.

On the drive back home, Athen weighed his options. So much to do, and without a clear identity of his apparent victim, it made his job harder. He called Maggie Harman who answered the phone in a breathless, seductive manner that suggested phone sex as an alternate source of income.

"Maggie?"

"Oh, yes, this is Maggie," she said, her tone turning business like.

"My name is Lieutenant Mavromatis. I'm with Beverly Hills Police. I was wondering if my partner and I could come by and talk to you. I know you're busy, but it's about Natasha King."

A beat. "Okay. But I have a class at two. I just got an extension for me and Tash, in case she can still make it. I'm assuming you're calling about her. Have you heard from her?"

"Not as such. Can I have your address, please?"

"You want to come here?" Her voice turned into a squeak.

"Yes. We won't keep you long."

"Okay." She sounded reluctant but gave it to him and he recognized Spalding Drive as one of the most elegant streets in the heart of Beverly Hills. He longed to ask her who she'd contacted at the Saudi consulate but preferred to do this in person.

"We'll see you in twenty minutes."

"Okay," she said. "Gives me a chance to tidy up a little."

"Zillow the addy for me, will you?" he asked Paulie as they waited for the lights on the corner of Pico.

"Building's worth nearly four million. Nineteen-twenties. Four apartments. Wow. This is some classy joint. One of the units just rented out for four grand a month. What'd you say she does for a day job?"

"No idea. But pretending to be a manager for non-working

65

actors can't be paying the bills." Athen parked outside his house on Arnaz Drive and slapped his official neighborhood parking permit on the rearview mirror. The grey ghosts as locals called the parking enforcement had no respect for Athen, even though they knew his vehicle. They liked to fine him as though he had time to waste in the courthouse.

He led Paulie inside the house, sniffing appreciatively at the lingering scent of warm rosemary bread.

Grady came to greet them, Bella rushing toward them like a furry bullet. Despina stood behind Grady, a scowl on her face and her arms folded across her chest.

"I want to go to the mall," she announced by way of a greeting.

"We'll discuss that later." Grady sounded exasperated. He turned to Paulie. "Hey, Paulie."

"Hey," Paulie responded.

Athen leaned into Grady for a kiss and got one. He had no qualms about kissing his man in front of Paulie.

Paulie, meanwhile, tried to hug Desi, who took a couple of steps farther away from him. *Oh, boy.*

Grady scowled at her then glanced back at Paulie and Athen. "I have blueberry muffins in the kitchen. No sugar. You can have one of those without raising your blood sugar," he told Paulie. "There's also homemade rosemary bread sandwiches. Bottled water in the fridge. Twyla said you should take an apple and a piece of string cheese with you for a snack. You gotta have at least half a sandwich here. You can take the rest with you."

"My wife called you?" Paulie looked shocked.

"She's my new best friend." Grady gave him a smug smile. He glanced at Athen. "I gotta call the office. Mind holding the fort a moment?"

Athen knew this was code for checking the cameras. It astounded him that for her relentless criminal activity in their home, Despina seemed unaware that they'd installed cameras every place they could think of. She'd stolen a few pieces of makeup she didn't need from a beauty supply store at the Beverly Center—twice. Athen and Grady had been mortified the first time and grounded her after the second incident. At least three times a week she still stole their credit cards and would try to buy stuff online. They got camera alerts when she went into Athen's office, otherwise known as the perpetual scene of her crimes.

They'd viewed the footage and she seemed unaware she was being watched. Or, as Athen had begun to suspect, she just didn't care.

Maybe she didn't know he and Grady had wired up the house. Their security specialist had hidden them in light fixtures and inside the eyes of a couple of antique cat statues that belonged to Tyler James. He needed to consider the question of what to with her next. He wasn't sure he should let her stay here with Tyler James' new involvement in her life. On the other hand, he knew if he and Grady tried to extricate her from him, she would rebel.

There was also the issue of Tyler James possibly bolting and wrecking Cricket's case against him. Tyler had always been a low-key guy in Grady's opinion. *A wolf in sheep's clothing.* At the mere thought of that made Athen turned on his heel as Grady slipped away. Athen walked into the kitchen. He and Paulie sat at the kitchen island and threw down a couple of sandwiches. Athen made coffee with the Keurig and passed a cup to Paulie who sipped at the hot liquid the second he received it.

"That feels better. I was feeling a little dizzy." Paulie shot him a guilty look.

"You should have said something." Athen pointed at the coffee cup. "Are you allowed to have that?"

"According to me, yes." Paulie grinned and sipped.

Despina stood beside him frantically typing a text message. Athen didn't bother asking who she was talking to. He had access to her texts since he paid for her phone. He and Grady were forced to spy on her because she kept lifting their credit cards to make online purchases. They'd caught text messages requesting her to verify purchases they would never have otherwise known about.

Suddenly, Athen's phone pinged.

A text from Cricket. *File emailed to you. I'm watching Tyler James' house. He's driving a yellow Porsche. Hard to miss. He just got food delivered. Maybe he'll chuck out empty bags.*

Athen texted back *K.* For okay. He and Grady had been mulling over what to do about Desi. Her school was out until September and she refused to adhere to the structure of home schooling, even though they'd hired a tutor for her.

His phone pinged again. Paulie drained his coffee and glanced at him. Athen blew out a sigh. Grady had texted him. *She's out of this house today. We'll talk later. I'm driving her back to Santa Cruz. I'm taking Bella with me. You can tell your sister.*

"Despina!" Grady bawled from somewhere in the house.

Can you handle her? Athen quickly texted.

Watch me, came back the reply.

Athen hated leaving his life partner to deal with Desi but it was the best solution. He called Grady from the kitchen. "You okay? You sure you want to do this?"

"She had people in our house last night," Grady said with a hiss. "People. In our house," Grady repeated. "At two a.m. While we slept."

"How did we miss that?" Athen asked.

"She must have disabled the alarm. I'm gonna text you. Hold on." He ended the call and Athen received a string of texts. *I'm taking her home. Taking the dog for company. I don't want to talk to you right now, Athen. I am so damned mad at you. I'm gonna stay somewhere for the night and head back tomorrow.*

Oh. And while I'm away, change the damned locks. Tyler James was in our house last night. Touching things. At two a.m. he was outside our bedroom door! He tried to open it!" Grady stopped texting him.

These words chilled Athen to the core.

He tried calling Grady who wouldn't answer. *Damn.* He left a message. "I love you. And I'm sorry." He blew out a sigh. *Maybe Tyler drank from a glass or something. Nah. Even if he had, Grady is so fastidious he would have washed it by now.* Still, it more than rankled to know that Tyler had been in their home, uninvited. Athen and Grady slept with their door locked, Bella tucked away with them. Their bedroom was huge, and she tended to be restless if she wasn't with Athen and Grady.

Man, I'm gonna sleep alone tonight. He put on fresh running shoes then drove away with Paulie beside him. "I hate to ask you to do a personal errand for me, but can you check my security cameras for me on my phone?"

"Sure." Paulie took hold of it. "Problems?"

"Teenagers. She's been sneaking out at night. And our landlord just moved in two doors down. Grady says he was in our house at two o'clock this morning."

Athen took Olympic Boulevard all the way to Spalding. It was faster than Wilshire, which had lengthy traffic lights at each corner. He gave Paulie his security code. He'd change the locks when he got home tonight. The burden of Grady's anger toward him sat heavily in his gut. Grady was all the missing parts and pieces in Athen's heart and soul. Athen worshipped him. He'd never wanted to compromise his relationship with the most amazing man he'd ever met.

"You've got excellent security footage," Paulie muttered. "It's in color. I wasn't eavesdropping, but it was hard not to hear it. Grady was screaming. He said people were in your house. *Tyler James was in the house. I see him here. He let himself in. He has keys."* He paused. "He took his time going through your house. Jesus. He's one hella sneaky landlord."

"Yeah."

"You just got a text."

"Is it Grady?" Athen turned right on Spalding.

"Uh, yeah. He said he confiscated Desi's phone so she couldn't warn Tyler that she's leaving."

As Athen made his way to Maggie Harman's apartment, Paulie made a weird sound in his throat. Athen glanced at him.

"My niece was so jealous when she found out Tyler James was your landlord. I mean, you know. Hot movie star and all." Paulie shook his head. "There's something real creepy about this guy, boss. The way he's roaming around your house. Despina following him and giggling. He's got a predator vibe. Is he messing around with her?"

"I don't think so." Athen's gut felt like he'd eaten pebbles for lunch. *My life sucks at this moment.*

"He doesn't seem interested in her. It's like, I dunno . . ."

"What?"

"He's looking for something. Maybe he has secrets." Paulie tried to add a chuckle to his words, which only made Athen's heart sink farther. *Yeah. Tyler has secrets. Damn. What if there's something hidden in our house? And oh, crap. How did he get hold of our keys?* The thought hit Athen like a tidal wave. *Despina gave them to him. She'd told Grady she'd lost her set a few days ago, but I bet she passed them onto this idiot.* Athen needed to get those locks changed. Now. With Grady and Despina gone and Athen clearly not home, Tyler would have free access to their family home.

"I just realized something else," Paulie said.

"What?"

"He's wearing disposable gloves. This is really shady behavior."

"Tell me about it." Athen digested this nugget of information. "We're here," he said, hating the fury surging through his body.

CHAPTER SIX

A then called Cricket who picked up within seconds.
"Hey," he said.

"Please, do me a favor," Athen said. "I'm interviewing someone, and I have reason to believe Tyler James has free access to our house. Can you keep an eye on him and make sure he doesn't let himself inside again?"

"He's been in there? Recently?" Cricket sounded surprised.

"Last night. Weren't you watching him?"

"Damn. I got desperate and went to the gas station to take a leak. I switch off with a buddy so we can catch some shut eye. Musta drank too much coffee 'cos last night, I couldn't wait for the end of shift. Tyler James musta been in and outta your place real fast because I thought I was keeping a close eye on him. I couldn't have been gone more than seven, eight minutes. This was around two o'clock in the morning."

"Exactly the time Grady says he came in the house."

"Well, when I got back to surveillance, your niece was running over to his place from yours. That was at two-ten."

"And you didn't see Tyler come out of my house?"

"Naw. He was in his house. I watched him let her in. Jeez, I'm sorry Athen. Hey, wait up. I see Grady backing out of your driveway. Wait. He stopped. He's got your niece with him. She's crying her ass off and getting in the backseat. Oh. Now's he's taking the dog from the back seat and putting it in the cargo hold." A pause. "That's a handsome dog ya got there, Blackeye."

"Yeah. Thanks. Grady's driving Despina home to Santa

Cruz."

"Does Tyler James know that?"

"Apparently not. Grady confiscated her phone. Listen, we discovered Tyler's got keys. We think she gave 'em to him."

"Damn."

"She was running around our house with Tyler while we were sleeping. He's been in there, snooping." Athen caught a glimpse of Paulie's wide-eyed expression. He knew he'd have to explain himself. And soon. "What if he's done more than ah, the case you know about? What if this creepozoid's left souvenirs of his crimes somewhere in my house?"

"Holy crapola." Cricket went silent for several seconds. "I'm here for another hour then Murph takes over from me. I'll fill him in. We switch off every six hours in different vehicles. If Tyler James makes a move toward your house before you get home, we'll figure out a distraction."

"Great. Thanks. When I do get home, I need to change the locks and ah, maybe you could help me hunt for a possible hiding place for his souvenirs. Grady just told me he noticed Tyler wearing disposable gloves when he was in my house."

Cricket let out a snort. "Oh, that sorta gives the game away."

"Think he's onto you?" Athen asked.

"Nah. I change cars too often. I think he befriended your niece as a ruse to get in there."

"I think so, too." That thought relieved Athen more than the prospect of Tyler James grooming her for sexual manipulation. "I'll let you know when I pick up new locks and I'm heading home."

"Roger that." Cricket ended their call. Two seconds later, Athen's phone rang. It was Mike from the crime scene unit.

"I just heard from the office. Nothing from AFIS, so Natasha King's got no criminal record. I put a call in for an expedited search with Homeland Security. She didn't come here anytime in November, as far as they can tell. And I called in a bunch of favors on this one, Athen. If you send them a photo now, they'll work backwards but an arrival date would really help."

"I know. Cameron Deck isn't even sure of the date she moved in, let alone when she arrived in LA."

"Yeah, I know." Mike sighed. "I asked him myself. Well, we got a lot of prints. A lot on the walls in the bedroom but I don't see any reason for 'em. I did figure out the source of that perfume you and Paulie talked about."

"Oh, yeah?"

"Natasha King keeps these metallic rings on some of her light bulbs around the apartment. I think she was putting drops of perfume inside the them and the heat warmed the perfume, permeating the place."

"Okay. That explains the lingering scent. I'll let Paulie know." Athen ended their call and he and Paulie walked up the garden path. Maggie Harman opened the door before they could even knock. She was a beautiful young woman whose hair was dyed a shade of pink most people couldn't carry off. If Athen had to describe her, it would be as a young Marilyn Monroe, even down to the 1940s style floral dress and matching pink, open-toed high heels that she wore.

"I have an audition," she said, her tone breathless. Yeah. Marilyn Monroe. "I like to stand out."

Athen nodded. "I just have a few questions."

She didn't seem to want to let them in, but had no choice when Athen said, "It's better if we talk inside."

As soon as they entered, he wondered if the place had been messy when he'd called because it was in pristine shape, now. It was like something out of Architectural Digest. Clean lines. A single, massive pillar candle decorated the fireplace. A three-foot-tall replica of the Eiffel Tower, and a huge hardback edition of a Taschen book on Paris were the only decorations on the coffee table. The sofas grouped together in two sections were all white, with charcoal-colored faux-fur covered cushions placed on them. Athen did a doubletake. Not cushions. Two beautiful, charcoal-colored cats.

"Are they yours?" Athen asked.

"Lilac is. The other one, Violet, with the violet, heart-shaped tag belongs to Tash."

"They're beautiful."

Maggie smiled then, but the worried look never left her eyes. "Yes, they are." She kept glancing down at the cellphone in her hands.

"They must be siblings."

"Yes. We rescued them together last year from an alley in East LA. The mother cat had been hit by a car. I took one kitten, she took the other."

"Can I ask how you met Natasha?"

She hesitated. "Online."

"How long ago?" As Athen asked questions, Paulie moved around the room, studying the carefully placed books on the sprawling, built-in shelves. She had a long, but narrow worktable that jutted out slightly from the shelving units. He moved toward them. Maggie seemed to grow more uncomfortable. Paulie froze.

Athen knew he'd spotted something. *I gotta keep her focused on me.* "Who got in touch with whom?"

Paulie turned and pointed upward to a corner shelf and mouthed, "Camera."

Maggie's glance darted from Paulie back to Athen. She leaned against the back of one of the sofas, a finger on her chin. She shifted her gaze upward as though pretending to ponder the question.

"Look at me," Athen said. He rarely got testy with people, but Maggie Harman was playing games with him. "Come sit over here." He indicated a sofa which would mean her back would be facing away from Paulie. Athen moved to the sofa opposite her, leaning close to her.

"I have an audition," she said, rubbing her hands across her knees as she sat.

"Yes, I know. But you're friend's in very grave danger."

Maggie looked shocked. "She is?"

"How did you two connect online?" he asked.

"Through a guy she used to date." She let out a theatrical sigh. "She met him on a dating site and moved here thinking they'd get married."

Athen stared at her for a beat.

"He works for the Saudi consulate." Maggie brushed an imaginary stray hair back from her forehead. Her hairdo was what Grady would have described as a Nancy Grace helmet-do.

"And did they get married?"

"No." Maggie shook her head. "It never . . . it . . . didn't work out that way."

"What happened?"

"He wasn't who he said he was."

"And this is the man you reported her disappearance to?"

She looked wide-eyed for a moment but recovered fast. "How did you know that?" She kept looking down at her phone. "I have to make a call," she whispered.

"Not yet. Explain why you called this ex of hers. And not the police."

Maggie winced. "I didn't think it was that serious. You know. Tash being missing. What's he doing over there?" She turned to watch Paulie.

"Eyes on me, please." Athen kept his voice stern as over the top of her head, Paulie indicated the location of another camera on a different wall unit. "Tell me about the ex."

She seemed to grow more nervous. "He still loves her. He

no longer works at the consulate. But yes, I called him. He's well connected. I thought he'd launch a discreet inquiry. I hardly expected Beverly Hills cops at my door." She suddenly swiveled around again. "What are you doing?"

"Nothing," Paulie lied. But he shot Athen a meaningful glance and held up three fingers. *Three cameras.* He kept moving around the room then held up four fingers. *Four cameras?* Why would anyone need that many cameras in one room?

Athen touched Maggie's arm. It made her jump. "And what is this man's name?"

"Jamie Fahdi." Her face twitched. "I really have to make a call. Please."

"But why did you call him, of all people?"

"I didn't know who else to call." Her tone was desperate more than defensive.

"How about the police?"

She glanced away from Athen, fixing her gaze on some point in the middle distance. "I panicked."

"You *panicked*?" She was the second person to say this to him today. The first being Cameron Deck. "So, you report her missing to some guy who used to work at the consulate."

"He's an agent for Mossad," she said.

"Mossad?" This thing was getting freakier by the second.

"That's what he says, but I Googled it and there aren't supposed to be any Mossad agents here. Not in real life, anyway."

"You're saying he's a Mossad agent. An Israeli covert spy. And he worked for the Saudi consulate? Are you kidding me?"

"I'm just telling you what he told us." She was starting to get upset now. "That's what gave us the idea."

"What idea?"

She looked at him. "I'm in trouble, aren't I." It was a statement. Not a question. "Look. He must have connections. Somebody contacted you, right?"

"The mayor." Athen blurted the words then wished he hadn't.

"That makes sense." Maggie seemed more relaxed now. "Scotty's poker buddies with Jamie."

Athen knew then that the Saudi consulate had never been involved. The mayor's gambling pal had called him, and *Scotty* tried to make it look official. And important.

"Where is Natasha King really from?" Athen asked, his voice low and controlled.

"She's an Arab princess," Maggie said, a strange, high squeak to her voice.

"No, she's not. They've never heard of her. What the *hell* is going on?"

"I can't. Oh, my God. This thing's out of control." She covered her mouth with her hands. Her whole body seemed to shake. She dropped her hands again. "Do I need a lawyer?"

"Maggie. Just tell me. Please. What happened to Natasha? Is that even her real name?" Athen put a steadying hand on her arm again.

She couldn't speak. Tears were falling down her cheeks. She shook her head. Man, she was dissolving right before his very eyes.

"Natasha is her name," she whispered.

"Okay. And where is she from?"

Maggie's gaze flew upward, then down again. Sobs wracked her body.

"Are you afraid of this Jamie guy?"

"No, not him." She shook, and when Athen slipped an arm around her he was surprised how bone-thin she was.

"Then who are you afraid of?" he asked, keeping his tone gentle as Paulie leaned in and handed her a wad of tissues.

"Her landlord," she said. "I'm petrified of Cameron Deck."

Paulie and Athen stared at each other over the top of her head a moment. Paulie held up a laptop bag. A blinged-out

Hello Kitty laptop bag.

"You need to talk to me," Athen said. "Is this Natasha's laptop?"

Maggie nodded. "You can't let him know it's here. He'll kill me."

"*Kill* you?"

"He's been looking for it." Her eyes widened with fear. "Oh, my God. Please do not tell him."

"Why?" asked Paulie. "What's on here?" He handed her more tissues as she patted down her face. "It's okay. Take your time. Blow your nose."

"Is this the original laptop she claims was stolen a couple of weeks ago, or the replacement?"

Maggie blew her nose, turning a bleary-eyed stare at Athen. "Cameron told you about that? He was suspicious. He knew she'd caught him." She shook her head.

"Caught him doing what?" Paulie promoted.

"She didn't tell me. She told Isla something once about him and it got back to him. Tash hasn't trusted her — or him — ever since. Don't ask me what he was doing. I've gone over the laptop a few times. There isn't much on there. Screenplays she started working on and never got past a few pages. A few poems. I thought she was really creative, until I Googled the poems and they're all somebody else's." She patted at her eyes again. "But go ahead. Maybe there are secret files I can't access."

"Is there a passcode to get into it?" Athen asked.

She looked at him. "Ask nicely."

Is she for real? Before Athen could ask, Paulie did, and she responded. "Jenolan," she said, spelling it out for them. She seemed to be ready to say something more, but tears rose again, her makeup running in multicolor streams down her face. Athen wondered if she'd be able to pull it together for her audition after this.

"She said she had something on here related to him. I don't know what. I couldn't find it. I was thinking maybe Internet porn or something. Anyway, she only brought it here two days ago and asked me to hold it for her. I was surprised because she told me she'd had a robbery, too. No idea where she'd hidden it. She said she was going away for a couple of days. She said she needed to rehearse her scenes and get away from Cameron." She sat back against the sofa. "This joke went too damned far."

"What joke was that?" Paulie asked.

"She isn't even Saudi, is she?" Athen asked. "Come on. The truth."

Maggie looked at him. "No," she said finally.

"Is she Australian?"

Maggie seemed stunned. "How'd you figure that out?"

"There's one long-distance call on her phone bill. It's to Australia."

"Really? Wow. She's been so careful." Maggie chewed her lip. "I wonder if Cameron figured it out. He's obsessed with her you know, but then, he's not the only one." She sat up. "Please don't tell him. It's her only leverage with him."

"Why does she need leverage?" Athen asked just as Pauli asked:

"Why did you go get her cat?"

She swiveled her gaze to him as she wiped her eyes with the back of her hands.

"Because she asked me to."

"When?" Paulie and Athen asked in unison.

"She texted me last night. I was sleeping and just got it this morning. I was a bit surprised she'd left Violet at home. She'd never normally do that." She looked at Athen. "You said she's in danger?"

"Can I see the text?" Athen asked.

"Sure." Maggie stood, and out of the corner of his eye,

Athen detected a figure silhouetted in the flat screen TV mounted on the wall.

"Gun!" he screamed. "Get down, Paulie!" Athen pulled a shrieking Maggie to the floor and covered her body with his. Somebody shot. *Bam! Bam! Bam!*

Maggie huddled against Athen, whimpering into his neck.

CHAPTER SEVEN

Grady knew he had to calm down. As he sped north up the 5 Freeway, his thoughts kept spinning out of control. At least Despina had stopped crying and screaming at him. Passing the Harris Farms always upset them both. The stench and the sight of all the cattle lying around waiting to be slaughtered had sobered her up.

Until that moment, she'd kept asking him to pull over so she could buy some food. Then she wanted to pee. Then she wanted to puke. Then she wanted to eat again. Grady glimpsed her tearstained face through the rearview mirror as she peered out of the rear passenger window. She'd refused to sit beside him. Maybe she thought the cattle's misery reflected her own. Grady focused on breathing. Suddenly, all the hours he'd spent studying transcendental meditation seemed useless. He couldn't get his anger under control.

Focus on driving. Focus on relaxing a little. Shake your shoulders out.

Bella paced in the cargo hold then finally settled in a comfy dog bed he kept back there. Grady knew he couldn't stop because he didn't trust Despina not to run. He suspected Athen hadn't called Sia to let her know they were on their way. *He's working*, Grady kept reminding himself.

Past the stinky cattle ranch, Despina stirred. "Can't we stop for a burger? I didn't have any breakfast," she whined.

"And whose fault is that?" He slung the tote bag loaded with leftover muffins and sandwiches he'd prepared that morning over to the backseat. "Food and bottled water. We're not stopping." He should have made them both wear adult diapers. *What the hell am I thinking? Who am I?* He felt like his mind had been possessed. Like that crazy astronaut lady who put on adult diapers and drove across country to murder her love rival. *This kid is driving me nuts. Literally.*

"Why can't we stop for a burger?" Desi moaned, a sandwich in one hand, a muffin in the other.

"Not now," he snapped. "And if you don't speak for the next two hours, I'll stop at Pea Soup Andersen's and we'll grab a bite there. And before you mouth off to me young lady, let me remind you they have those things you love." He held her gaze in the rearview mirror. "Yeah." He paused for dramatic effect. "Onion straws. I'll even get you some to go."

She grinned at him through a mouthful of food. *Phew. It was as though the sun had just come out.* Sometimes she acted like a two-year-old. Sometimes she acted as though she were thirty. *Damn. I love this bratty kid in spite of it all.* He stepped on the gas until he hit eighty. He wanted this over with, now. He kept his gaze swiveling from one mirror to the next in the vehicle. He took a deep breath. *Be calm. And stay alive. You have hot, breaded onion straws to look forward to.*

He could already taste the barbecue sauce they came with, and he swallowed. *Dang. I think I'm drooling.*

"Are you okay?" Athen yelled over at Paulie as one of the cats' paws connected with his scalp in its haste to scramble to safety.

Paulie coughed and spluttered as he got to his feet. "Yeah. You?"

Athen didn't respond. The shooter was trying to flee the scene but had collided with an elderly man who struggled to hold onto the suspect.

"Help!" the old man yelled.

"Keep an eye on her. Call for back up!" Athen instructed

Paulie and ran from the apartment. He tore out of the front door, down the garden path, just as the suspect managed to throw off the elderly man. Athen caught the guy before he fell to the ground. Athen steadied him. As other residents came running, he shouted, "Take care of him!"

He followed the suspect who'd run up Spalding toward Gregory way. He hooked a right. The shooter was dressed head to toe in black, including a mask over the lower half of his face. Must have been left over from the coronavirus quarantine. He moved fast, turning to look over his shoulder as Athen picked up speed, gaining on him. Athen was so close he could see the sudden fear in the guy's eyes. He turned to shoot at Athen, and got off a shot, missing by several feet. He tried again, but the gun jammed.

Athen had his gun out from his shoulder holster, and stopped, aiming at the guy's leg. He fired off a shot and the guy went down screaming. He rolled back and forth, tossing his weapon into the street. It connected with the right front tire of an approaching black Mustang. The passenger door opened. A woman screamed, "Get in!" to the shooter and scrambled into the backseat to accommodate him.

But Athen was close and grabbed the shooter by the bad leg.

"Leggo!" the woman shouted but the driver sped away, the woman screaming from the backseat. Athen wrestled with the shooter who tried to headbutt him. Athen dragged him to the sidewalk. He flopped the shooter facedown, straddled his back, and cuffed his hands behind him.

"I hope you're a cop, sonny," an elderly woman said, sauntering over to Athen.

"He's a maniac!" the suspect squawked.

"Shut up!" Athen responded. "I'm a cop. Lieutenant Mavromatis, Beverly Hills PD. Lady, you got a paper bag?" He realized she was munching an apple with one hand and recording the action with her cellphone with the other. How . . . surreal.

"Why d'you need a bag?" she asked. "You hyperventi- latin'?"

He gaped at her a second. "To bag the evidence. Hurry. Please. Before somebody comes by and drives over the weapon."

She glanced at the gun still lying in the street. "Huh. Puny gun for a bad guy."

"It's a Glock!" the shooter screeched.

"Didn't I tell you to shut up?" Athen hollered at him.

"Sorry," the old lady said to the suspect. "Without my glasses, I don't see so great. That's why I record everything." She trained her cellphone onto him.

Athen blew out a sigh. "Lady. Hurry! Please!"

"Keep your pants on, sonny," she muttered and walked off.

"What's your name?" Athen asked the man still lying un- derneath him.

"I'm not saying a word. I want my lawyer." The guy twisted his face around, his words muffled from the mask.

Athen chuckled. "Yeah, don't we all." He yanked the mask down so he could breathe.

The old lady returned with a piece of newspaper. "I saw on *The First 48* that you could use newspaper." She laid it on the ground, toeing the weapon onto it. A car came from the other direction, but she didn't seem to notice when the driver slowed and took in the action. The vehicle picked up speed and took off again. Another car came right behind him.

Athen panicked. He couldn't risk the shooter's gun being run over. "Bring it over here! Quick!" he urged as sirens blared from somewhere.

The old lady gave him a look of rebuke and picked up the newspaper, laying it on the grass beside him. She juggled the apple core still in her hand and her cellphone, bouncing on her toes in what looked like new tennis shoes.

A squad car arrived, grinding to a halt right where the gun would have been.

The old lady swiveled a surprised glance at Athen. "Boy, you're good."

"He shot me," the shooter bleated as the officers approached them.

"You tried to shoot him first," the old lady chided. "I got the whole thing on my phone." She swiveled it around to them.

Athen hauled the guy to his feet and yanked the mask from his face. Good-looking guy, but Athen had never seen him before.

The old lady was staring up at him, entranced.

"You know him?" Athen asked.

"Yeah. I've seen him." She shook her head after a beat. "Oh, maybe not. Say, you on TikTok?"

The guy ground out, "No!"

"Yes, you are. I've seen you on it. I've got you recorded. Hold on a sec."

"He's bleeding," one of the officers said as she rifled through her phone.

"This is you!" The old lady turned her phone around again. Athen and the uniformed officers clustered around to watch. The shooter's leg, which had clearly seen better days was kicking along to a Donna Summer song with the rest of him.

"Jamie Fahdi?" Athen almost laughed. "The alleged Mossad agent?"

"I never said I was Mossad."

"Yes, you did." Athen handed him over to the officers. "Get him to Cedars but keep him under armed guard. I want to come and talk to him."

"I want my lawyer." Fahdi seethed.

"I know you do. We'll get him for you," Athen said. "Text me your numbers." He handed one of the officers, whose badge read, *Brady*, a business card. He moved over to the old lady as the officers got him into the squad car.

"Police brutality," Fahdi yelled.

Oh, brother. Athen exchanged glances with Brady. "I'll be in touch," he said. His phone rang. Paulie.

The officers drove away and Athen held up a finger to the old lady.

"You okay?" Paulie asked.

"Fine and dandy. On my way back to you. Can you get the crime scene unit out there?"

"On it," Paulie said.

They ended their call and Athen turned to the old lady. "I want to thank you, Mrs — ?"

"Meyer. Like the cleaning products. Widowed. In case you're interested."

Interested? Athen stared at her a moment. The thought that floated into his mind was *dementia*. Then, *don't blink.* "Um, ah. Thank you, Mrs. Meyer. Can you send me the footage you shot of the shooting? I need to see it." He handed her a business card.

"Do I have to?"

"Unless you want to interfere with an official investigation. He tried to shoot me."

"I know. But I'm not supposed to be out here." She turned. "There's camera crews coming. Oh, boy! That's CBS news!"

"Where are you supposed to be?" Athen asked her, wanting to escape before questions could be asked.

Two gigantic media trucks pulled up. Mrs. Meyer's eyes darted back and forth as though trying to compute the question. "I'll send it to you." She looked flustered as she pecked away at her phone's keyboard.

"You need help?" he asked her.

"Naw." She took a deep breath. "I kinda let myself out of my son's house. I'm supposed to be resting. I just got over pneumonia." She smiled then. "And before that, I had coronavirus. There. You should have it. He shot at you right near the corner of Gregory Way. I'm glad you didn't die. You're kinda cute. You're the one that found the dead woman in the blanket, right?"

One newswoman was out of the truck but didn't seem to know what she was looking for.

"I didn't find her, but that was my case, yeah," Athen said, anxious to run. "She was rolled up in a rug and left out with the trash."

A guy with a huge camera on his shoulder joined the reporter.

Mrs. Meyer grimaced as a man started calling, "Ma!" from across the road. "I gotta run. My number's in your phone. Use it. If you need me. Or—" she lowered her voice, "*Want* me."

Athen nodded, trying not to laugh at the notion that he might want her. "I may have questions. Thanks for this."

She'd already started running across the street, past the news crew. Athen picked up the newspaper and gun and sauntered back toward Maggie Harman's place. He had to keep it casual. He did not need an audience right now. With his free hand, he went through the footage Mrs. Meyer had texted.

Man, I look fat in this shirt. He moved toward the house where Fahdi had fired at him, but he couldn't see the spent shell casing anywhere. He'd have to send somebody else out to look for it. Back at Maggie's, he saw two squad cars out front. He sent one unit off to the house to search for the casing, after forwarding them the old lady's footage.

"Where's the crime scene unit?" he asked Paulie who greeted him outside.

"On their way."

The neighbors who'd gathered, drifted away as the uniformed officers stood guard outside the building. The news crews had started rolling up now. *Damn.*

"Keep 'em away," Athen muttered to the two officers. "Please."

Paulie seemed anxious. "I don't like leaving Maggie alone. She keeps trying to post on her Instagram. I just took custody of her cellphone."

"Good for you." Athen still held the newspaper with the gun.

Paulie went on. "I put the cats in the bedroom. There's glass everywhere."

"Did you find shell casings?" Athen asked.

"Yep. Spotted two but left them there. Every time I made a move away from Maggie, she got big ideas."

"The shooter was Jamie Fahdi. The guy she claims worked for the Saudi consulate—"

"And supposedly Mossad."

"Right. And if he's Mossad, then I'm Brad Pitt."

Paulie grinned. "Where is he now? The shooter, I mean, not Brad Pitt."

"On his way to Cedars. I shot him in the leg."

"Good for you." Paulie returned Athen's words to him.

In the living room, Athen laid the gun on top of Maggie's desk. He surveyed the damage. He replayed the scene in his mind, Maggie sitting on the sofa. The shooter had aimed for her head—three times—which was frightening. He hunted for spent casings.

Maggie was sitting in a chair by the wall now. "I saw the guy. Head to toe in black like a ninja. A Beverly Hills ninja!" Maggie seemed awfully excited for someone who'd apparently been targeted for death. "Nothing like this has happened in this town since Bugsy Siegel ate a bullet in his living room. Wait. I could have died!"

"Who's trying to kill you?" Athen asked.

"I don't know. But it's the most exciting thing that's ever happened to me in my life!"

Athen took her cellphone from Paulie. He wanted to check her text messages, but his cellphone rang. Within seconds, *Lucy* yelled in his ear.

"Shots were fired? What the hell? Are you hurt?"

"No, sir," Athen said. "The suspect's heading to Cedars."

"So I heard."

"I need you to background him for me, sir. His name is Jamie Fahdi." Athen gave her a quick rundown of what he knew. "He's close gambling buddies with the mayor. I hope you can get that lying son of a gun to tell you the truth. He lied to me when he said he'd been contacted by the Saudi consulate. We lost valuable time on this."

"I agree. I'll go see him right now. He's at Cedars, same as Jamie Fahdi. I'll have a little chat with both of them."

"Perfect." Athen felt his body loosen up just a little.

"Boss. You're gonna wanna see this." Paulie came over to him, shell casing swiveled on the capped end of a pen.

"What have you got?" Maggie asked, peering around his shoulder.

"Sit down!" Athen pointed to the living room chair again.

"I need the crime scene unit in here, sir," Athen said into the phone. "And another squad car. We've got company."

"News media?"

"Yeah." Athen focused on the casing.

"Nine-millimeter," Paulie whispered. "Luger R-P."

"Right," Athen agreed. Though the bullet casing was head-stamped Remington-Peters, there was an anomaly.

"What don't you see here?" Paulie pivoted the casing around so Athen could get a better look.

"Huh. Oh. No gun shot residue."

"Exactly. Starshape pattern inside. Not what you'd expect.

"These are homemade blanks."

Athen couldn't believe it.

"Blanks?" Lucy squawked in his ear. "What the hell's going on over there?"

"I don't know yet, sir. But Maggie Harman confessed that Natasha King isn't Saudi. She says Natasha is her real name. I think she may be Australian. Can you call that Australian phone number on her phone bill? We already know she's no princess. Maggie claims this was all a game that went too far. Maybe the blanks were supposed to scare her. Or us."

"Or, she thinks she's in the middle of her own reality show," Lucy muttered. "I just got through watching Natasha King's reel. Maggie Harman uploaded it last night to her management company webpage. Blackeye, dead or alive, Natasha King has to be the worst actress I've ever seen. Her demo reel is awful."

"Does she have an accent?" Athen asked. "I haven't had a chance to watch it yet."

"Poor attempt to sound American. Strange accent. She credits some vocal coach at the end of the reel. Before you could get to her, Maggie posted a YouTube video with the two cats, saying her friend and client, Natasha King, had disappeared. She's very obviously in her living room. She calls it her home office. The address is listed online if you Google her name. Can you believe her? Maybe somebody wants to shut her up."

"I know I do," Athen said. "And I've only just met her. Sir. I've got Sullivan Tang on the other line. She's at the crime scene."

"Take it. I'll call Australia," Lucy said. "CSU is on its way to you. I've got two more patrols coming over. We're gonna have to call in SID at this rate."

"Understood. This crime is bizarre and stretches our resources."

"Yep." Lucy went on. "I've called Natasha's beauty appointments. Been a hell of a chore getting them to believe I'm the police chief. Had to have people call me back to verify me. So far, it doesn't look like she showed up for any of her sessions. By the way, AB means anal bleaching. Detective Brand explained that one to me." A beat. "Don't ask me how he knew that."

Athen grinned, despite the circumstances. He clicked over to Sullivan and asked her to wait as new uniformed officers arrived on scene. Athen went out to deal with them as Paulie bagged the spent casings.

"Two of you stay here. Have the other officers go check with neighbors. Also check with the people across the road. Did anyone see the suspect come or go? Hopefully, somebody has security cameras." He glanced back at Maggie through the shattered living room windows. "And don't let her move out of that chair." He noticed her eyeing her landline phone sitting on her desk. "No phone calls," he yelled.

"Sullivan?" Athen said into his phone.

"Yes, boss. I mean Athen."

"Hold on." Lucy was back on the other line. He clicked over again. "Yes, sir?"

"It's five-thirty in the morning in Australia. I woke some woman up. She had no idea who Natasha King is." She ground out a sigh. "Said she's had a few calls from the US. It's a new cellphone number. She lives in Sydney and she's had it for a month. I'll call you with any updates. I'm sending the crime scene unit over to you now."

"Okay," Athen said. "Paulie found Natasha King's laptop. I'm sending it over to you with a uniformed officer. Somebody in IT needs to go over it. Maggie Harman says there is something on it that's related to Cameron Deck. She couldn't find it and obviously, I haven't had a chance to look at it."

"That's a good lead. One of the guys I sent your way is

Terry Stein. He's just completed a year-long course in cyber security at NICCS in Georgia. He's on loan to us from Homeland Security. Let's make use of his talents. Give him the laptop and have him come back to the office."

"Perfect. Thank you, sir." Athen ended their call, clicked back over to Sullivan, then asked Paulie to give the laptop to Terry Stein to take back to HQ.

"He's the man," Paulie said. "If anybody can crack it, he can." He paused. "Athen, I Googled Natasha's password. Jenolan. It's an Australian town in the Blue Mountains in New South Wales, a couple of hours away from Sydney. I'm thinking maybe Natasha comes from there."

"Great find. Maybe you can follow that up. I need to talk to Sullivan." He turned back to the phone as Paulie went off to find Terry. "Is Cameron Deck still there?" he asked her.

"Yeah. He's been getting a lot of phone calls. He told me about the shooting. He seemed really freaked out."

"Who told him?"

"I have no idea. But the uniformed patrol told me it happened on Spalding Drive. Guess everybody's heard about it now. News travels fast. Cameron overheard that conversation, and I thought he was going to have a coronary."

"Find out who told him about it." Athen was starting to put the pieces of the puzzle together and wasn't liking what he saw.

"I tried asking him and he was evasive. I'll try again," Sullivan said. "Mike's crew wrapped up here and they're heading over to you. Expect a call from him."

"Thanks. We're here waiting on them. Busy freakin' morning, huh?"

"You can say that again. And they told me there's no crime in Beverly Hills," Sullivan said. "So glad they were wrong."

"I've learned that our assumed victim is not a Saudi princess. Her friend Maggie Harman says it was some kind of joke, but it hasn't tickled *my* funny bone. Whoever she is, Natasha King's still missing, and it doesn't look good. What's cookin' over there? Apart from Cameron Deck's nerves?"

"Uniformed patrol went door to door. Nobody has cameras. Very trusting souls here in Beverly Hills. One house kitty-corner to this building has a vehicle out front that's been sitting there for a while. Owner says it's not his. There's a dashboard camera in it. We've left a note on the windshield for the owner to contact us. Maybe the camera caught something. If it's a functional camera."

"That's interesting." Athen was intrigued by this nugget of information. "Can you ask Cameron Deck if Natasha King drives? He told me that when she moved in, she arrived in a limo. I'm wondering how long she's been keeping up the charade of being a princess. Maybe she bought a car. Maybe this car you mentioned belongs to her, and she left it there. If she didn't leave of her own free will."

"I'll do that, Athen. It's definitely a local resident, or one of their guests. There's a valid area parking permit hanging from the rearview mirror. Want me to check the DMV records?"

Athen was surprised she could do that so fast. The Department of Motor Vehicles — Athen privately thought of it as the Department of Nightmares — was notoriously difficult to deal with unless it was an active murder case, which he didn't have. Yet. It was as hard to get driver info as it was to get cellphone records in California.

"Go for it," Athen told her. "Any news on Cameron Deck's facial recognition search?"

"Nothing yet. I'll let you know. And I'll get onto DMV now. I have an exceptionally good contact there."

"Excellent," Athen said. "Do me a favor. Contact the captain. Find out if we have an ALPR set up in the vicinity. There's been talk of doing it, but I have no idea if it's happened yet."

"That's a good idea. I'll find out," Sullivan said. "It would be great to know if there's a record of any vehicles coming and going."

"Exactly. We need to focus on the past two days. Natasha was last seen, according to Cameron Deck, leaving two days ago with her laundry. She also had visitors last night and this morning. I'd like to know if there's a record of their vehicles. Please keep me posted."

They ended their call and Athen thought for a moment. An ALPR, or Automatic License Plate Reader had become the hot new law enforcement gadget most investigators didn't discuss. It worked like a GPS but tracked all vehicles that entered a neighborhood. Once a particular license plate was tracked, its information could be entered into the ALPR system and its movements could be followed. The tracking device could be placed on telegraph poles and was undetectable, but it was an invaluable tool. It sure beat the heck out of the old-fashioned method of using cellphone tower pings to track a suspect's whereabouts. That relied on getting access to phone records, which took time. The ALPR system was precise, quick, and foolproof.

He tried to check Maggie's text messages, but her phone was locked. His phone rang, and Mike started speaking before Athen could even finish saying, "Mavromatis."

"This is the craziest crime scene I ever worked," Mike said. "And I've been doing this job twenty-three years."

"Tell me."

"There are fifty separate spots of blood where the attack took place. Looks like a knife. Maybe two. One big. One small. There's blood everywhere, Athen. Just invisible to the naked eye. Somebody tried hard to clean up. Must have taken forever." He paused. "There's even blood in the electrical wall sockets. Unbelievable."

"It sounds like a damned blood bath, but the place looked

immaculate until I stepped into the dressing room."

"That's where the bulk of the attack took place. I'm going to do a computer-generated mockup for you to give you an idea of where it started, but it looks like it started on the bed."

"On the bed?" That was a surprise.

"There's traces of semen, and two different blood types. The whole thing is weird."

"Yeah. I need you guys here though. We've had a shooting."

"So I've heard. We're on our way. They're calling in the Special Investigations Division from LAPD to help us."

"Lucy mentioned that. Thanks for the update." As they ended their call, Athen moved back to the living room. Maggie was chatting animatedly with two officers standing by her side. He glimpsed Paulie outside talking to other uniformed officers. As soon as Athen entered the room, Paulie sensed his presence and returned to the apartment.

"Maggie. Your phone shut off while I was talking to the precinct captain. I need your passcode. I want to check your text messages," Athen said.

"Do I have to give it to you?" She swept her gaze from the uniformed officers, to Athen, then focused on Paulie. Maybe she thought Paulie was a soft touch and he'd side with her.

"Either that or I can book you for interfering with an investigation," Paulie told her.

"I'm not interfering! Somebody tried to kill me!"

Neither Paulie nor Athen said a word. Athen wondered if she'd known about the blanks.

"Six-four-three-nine," Maggie grumbled. "I can explain the text messages."

Athen pressed the numbers then said to Sullivan as he waited for the phone to start up, "I need you to go interview a potential witness." He moved out of the living room again as Paulie went outside to deal with an irate neighbor.

"Her name is Isla Sanchez," Athen said. "She used to be best friends with our missing woman. She went to Natasha's apartment this morning and may or may not have vital information. According to Cameron, she and Natasha had a bad falling out. She had a robbery. Cameron claims Isla might have been involved. I have her number. No address. Please contact her and talk to her. In person only. Oh, and Sullivan?"

"Yes, boss? I mean, Athen?"

"Take Lorne Brand with you. I have no idea what's going on, but I have a feeling all of this is some wannabe Hollywood fakery that went wrong. Dead wrong."

He wasn't off the mark. As soon as he ended that call, he got a text from one of the uniformed officers looking for the shell casing from Jamie Fahdi's missed shot.

Bullet discharged from 9mm weapon. Looks like he drilled a hole to turn it into a blank but it isn't. It was a live round. Lucky he didn't hit you.

CHAPTER EIGHT

Despina had been asleep for two hours, so Grady bypassed the freeway he would have taken to cut over to the 101 freeway that ran parallel to the coast to the town of Buellton.

He pressed on. *No pea soup for her. Or me. Man. She ate all the snacks. Even the sliced apples I brought for Bella.* He longed to listen to the radio. To music. News. Anything. But he worried that the slightest noise would waken her. He sang in his head, but his mental repertoire was lousy. He kept wanting to sing love songs. He wanted to think about romance and the Celine Dion song, *I Drove All Night*. It was the song that always came to mind whenever he thought about Athen. In fact, it had been Grady's ringtone he used for Athen until they moved to Beverly Hills.

Both he and Athen thought it was better to make it something more generic, more cop-like, so he'd programmed the theme song from *Hawaii Five-O* instead. Though he wanted to think Celine, what his crazy mind kept playing over and over was, *Say Something*. Its haunting refrain of *I'm giving up on you* almost drove him crazy. But he wouldn't give up on Athen. Never. He took a deep breath and caught Bella's gaze in the rearview mirror. His dog was the most fantastic being ever, and so undemanding, but he knew her well enough to understand she needed to pee.

When you gotta go, you gotta go. He approached the town of Los Banos and spotted signs for two gas stations, a McDonalds and Starbucks. Los Banos was ninety minutes from Santa Cruz and involved cutting across the 152 Freeway to reach it.

He needed to pee. Then he wanted a coffee. Talk about conflicted. And he wanted a burger. In that order. Damn. Could he trust Despina not to run off or do something stupid? Could he risk taking a leak? He turned off the freeway overpass and pulled into the small complex that housed the quartet of businesses.

He pulled up to a gas pump. His was the only vehicle here. Good. Quietly, he got out, let Bella out from the cargo hold and she dashed off to some scrubby greenery to his right. She took a long pee and Grady filled his gas tank even though he didn't really need to. He had three-quarters, thanks to Athen who regularly checked and drove his SUV to the gas station to fill it. He got a lump in his throat knowing that thanks, too, to Athen, he had three bottles of water in the cargo hold, a well-stocked first-aid kit, a spare cellphone battery, and probably a note of love tucked in there.

How can I love a man so much and be so damned mad at him? He topped off the gas and sighed. So far, Despina was still sleeping. He tried to shake off the high anxiety he felt. *I should call him. Wait. I wonder if he called Sia yet to let her know we're coming? I don't want to have a confrontation with her about bringing her wayward kid home.* He replaced the gas nozzle, pressed the button for no receipt since he'd heard that the print from gas receipts could be toxic on wet hands, and called for Bella.

She came running. He filled a water dish for her at the back of the SUV and thought about tossing her a ball for a minute, but his phone rang. Speak of the devil, it was Sia. He took the call. She was screaming.

"Where's my baby?"

"Calm down. She's right here." Grady glanced down at Bella who lapped frantically at the cool, clean bottled water.

"I want to speak to her."

"Calm down, Sia. We're in Los Banos. On our way to you." Suddenly, he realized she was sobbing.

"So she survived the shooting? My baby's okay?"

Grady's body went cold. "What shooting?"

"It's all over the Internet. Some guy shot Athen. Are you really in Los Banos?"

"Somebody shot Athen?" Grady swayed. He was aware of Bella nuzzling his thigh. He reached out a trembling hand to pat her head. How had he not known this? *Oh man. I had the radio turned off.* He blinked. Hard. *My God. Athen. My Athen.* "Is he okay?"

Sia was crying so hard her husband took over the call. "The shooter missed," Jordan said. "Sorry if Sia scared you. We've watched the damned thing three times now. Some guy dressed like a ninja warrior shot at Athen. Sia freaked out. Sorry. It's all over the news. Some old lady and her son sold the footage to CBS news. You don't know about it?"

"What's going on?" Despina opened the rear passenger door and must have seen the anguish in Grady's face. She barreled into his arms and hugged him.

Within seconds, Grady had her on the phone with her parents, and Bella was back in the cargo hold. Grady practiced deep breaths until Despina ended her call, apparently thrilled to be going home now. Together, they watched the footage of Athen's terror in Beverly Hills.

Despina's eyes flickered. "Somebody tried to kill our man."

"Yeah," Grady said, blinking back tears.

"We need to call him," Despina said, her eyes huge, dark, pools of fear.

Grady called but got Athen's voicemail. They left him a joint message, Grady begging him to call.

"Let's get out of here," Desi said, leaning back against the front passenger seat. She held Grady's hand as he tore out of the gas station. "And G, drive like you mean it."

Athen went through Maggie's text messages. Fury rose in him as he realized she'd lied to him. "You need to come clean with me. Now. Natasha King didn't text you asking you to pick up her cat. Cameron Deck did. He wrote, *Get the damned cat outta here*. Why did you lie to me?"

"I panicked."

This was the second time she'd said this to him today. Deck had had also used this excuse when he'd lied to Athen about allowing Maggie into Natasha's unit. Athen's phone kept ringing. He handed it to Paulie and kept his focus on Maggie. "You need to tell me what's going on."

"Cameron said the cat wouldn't go inside Natasha's apartment. Then he said he didn't *want* the cat in there. I dunno. It was weird."

"Okay. So, when was the last time you actually heard from Natasha?"

"Two days ago. I wasn't lying about hearing from her."

"There are no messages from her for two days here."

"I spoke to her two days ago. She called and wanted to know what was going on with Cameron. She came here with the old laptop that was supposedly stolen then asked me to go get the new laptop and hide it."

"So, you have both laptops?"

She shook her head. "The new one wasn't there when I went this morning. I tried to go yesterday because I was surprised when I heard from Felice that Violet was outside running around. Violet doesn't go outside. Felice tried to catch her but told me the cat was acting very strange and skittish. I went over, but Cameron wouldn't let me onto the property. He acted weird. Real . . . distracted."

Athen had a feeling he'd been too busy cleaning up the crime scene to let her inside. It also explained why the cat had been left outdoors. "You said you could explain the text messages. I assume you mean the ones where you're telling Jamie

Fahdi not to come today." He held up the phone. "The ones that say, *Cops are coming. Let me know you got this.*"

She winced. "I told you it went too far."

"That doesn't explain things."

"Athen," Paulie said, "Grady needs to speak to you. He's blowing up your phone. He knows about the shooting. And, ah, one of the neighbors outside says he's the actor and scene partner Cameron Deck told us about."

Maggie twisted in her seat to check who was outside. "Oh, no. I forgot about Bryce." She sagged against the chair.

Paulie whispered to Athen, "Bryce Felton says he has information for us."

Athen nodded but kept his focus on Maggie. "Did you ask Cameron about the cat when you went there yesterday?" Athen asked her.

"No."

"Did you see the cat when you went there?"

"No." Her shoulders shook as tears filled her eyes. "I would have brought her home. I knew it was unusual to say the least. I was honestly surprised that Tash left her there. I tried looking for Violet, but Cameron yelled at me. He turned the hose on me!"

Athen wished more than ever that there was security footage to verify all of this.

"And Natasha gave you no indication what was going on?"

"None. Look. She had issues with Cameron." She paused. "She had issues with Isla too. Said she was going to go there and return the red dress Isla lent her but insists was stolen. She said she had other errands to run."

"Did Isla really lend her the dress?" Athen asked.

Maggie winced. "According to Isla, no. The whole thing. Oh. Losing a friendship over a dress." She flapped a hand.

Oddly, it was the same gesture Deck had used. "Tasha is convinced Isla broke into her place a couple of weeks ago to steal it back—"

"So, she did steal it." Deck had mentioned the break-in and had suggested Isla Sanchez may have been behind it.

"Forgot to return it." Maggie frowned at Athen. "The whole thing got way ridiculous. Anyway, she said she had these errands, like I said. Cameron was driving her."

"Why was he driving her?"

Maggie held his gaze. "She can't drive. I guess she never needed to before she moved here. It helps the façade of being a princess. She hires Uber drivers and sometimes Cameron takes her around." She pulled a face. "He's like a whipped puppy with her one moment, and a rabid dog the next. One day he wants to drive her everywhere. The next, he screams at her saying she's using him. So, after I got his text I went and got Violet today. I was relieved when she came straight to me. As for Tash, she hasn't returned my calls or texts."

Athen knew this was true about the texts. He'd noticed dozens of them on Maggie's phone. She's made every effort to contact Natasha King. He wasn't sure however, if it were true that Natasha couldn't drive. He wondered if she was an illegal immigrant. If so, she wouldn't be allowed to obtain a driver's license without a social security card in California. And she couldn't get that if she were here illegally. He wanted to hold off asking Maggie about Natasha's legal status because the woman was sobbing now.

"Maggie, is Natasha here illegally?"

"No. She has a valid visa. She won the green card lottery, believe it or not." She dabbed at her tears with the now-crumbling tissues Paulie had given her.

"Then why hasn't she learned to drive? Wouldn't it make her life easier?"

Maggie's gaze fell on her trembling hands. "It was a deci-sion we made when we decided she should pretend to be a Saudi princess." She glanced up at him. "Do you think this um, charade got her in trouble?" She let out a jagged sob. "Something bad's happened to her, hasn't it?"

Athen kept his voice low. "Yeah. I think it has. We'll do our best to find her. I promise you that. Now please explain this elaborate hoax. Why did you girls do it? And how many peo-ple know?"

"Just me and her. Oh, and her husband, Gary Goldman."

"She's married?" This was shocking news.

"Yes, but he's out of the loop. Gary's in New York working on an off-off Broadway musical. With the money she's been giving him, he's been able to salvage a condemned ninety-nine seat theater on Cornelia Street. He's putting together a one-man show. They've been planning a swanky opening night." She blew out a breath. "Oh man, he's gonna freak." She lapsed into silence.

"Is he in love with her?" Athen asked.

"He's gay. But he adores her. When she first came to LA, over a year ago now, the three of us went to lunch one day at Spago. Gary was smitten with her. Every man who comes near her is. She's not only beautiful, but lovely. Such a great personality. He had just booked an episode of *Criminal Minds*, and he wanted to treat us. He splurged. It was so exciting. We all had dreams. His was Broadway, hers was Hollywood. Me, I want it all." She gave Athen a tremulous smile. "It seems like such a long time ago now." Her face took on a blank expres-sion.

Athen waited a beat. "Please, go on."

"Suddenly, the waiter thought she looked like royalty. It was so crazy. On the spur of the moment, she said she was. Gary and I said we were her personal assistants. The chef, and all these people came out to meet her. Even the owner, Wolf-gang Puck. He happened to be there that day. They all believed her! We got a good laugh out of it. And a free meal. She was staying here with me trying to figure out how to be here permanently.

"Then she found out her mom had had a stroke and was in the hospital back in Australia and went home. She had really struggled here and suddenly, her mom died, and she got an inheritance you know."

"No. I didn't know."

She blushed. "Well, she got all this money, then she found out she'd won the green card lottery. She's one of those people. Fantastic things happen to her. Well, I mean, apart from losing her mom. And now this." She spread her hands. "The green card was like this miracle. She sold off everything and moved here. At first, she just wanted to make it here as an actress, but the green card lottery isn't everything it's cracked up to be. It doesn't guarantee employment. You still have to jump through hoops to stay here. She hired a big shot immigration attorney and had to prove she could live here on the money she had, which she could. But things got difficult. She really had to do something. She wasn't getting work and she stressed about it. The classes, all her hard work, well, it's her life. Then came a couple more lunches at Spago on her dime, and we got the idea to create this princess persona fulltime. Gary was desperate for money, and he's always wanted to go to Australia. She said she'd give him ten grand if he'd marry her. Seemed like a win-win for both of them."

"Is that when she broke it off with Jamie Fahdi?"

She skewered Athen with a sharp glance. "Exactly. I'll admit, she wanted to marry him because things were kinda hot between them, until she realized he wasn't rich, and, or, connected. He wasn't even a spy. Well, she wanted to think so. Who doesn't love a James Bond fantasy?" She let out a laugh but Athen didn't. "Anyway, she didn't tell him, or any of the other men around her, that she and Gary got hitched. She really felt she settled, but she was desperate, like I said. When she started telling people she was Saudi royalty, we decided together that we'd act like she was letting them in on a big secret. She couldn't leave a paper trail—"

"Is that why she gave Cameron Deck a year's rent up front in cash?"

She looked stunned. "He told you that?"

Outside, there was a commotion. Paulie was talking to a group of people. Athen figured he could handle it."

"Yes. I was looking for a rental lease, passport, driver's license, anything that could verify her identity."

Maggie turned around and looked, heaving another sigh. "Three months of planning," she said. "Oh. The permits. We'll lose all our money." Her hands went to her face again.

Athen wanted her to focus. "What about Natasha's ID?"

"Oh. Um. She kept all of that hidden in my car trunk inside a first aid kit. She came and took it out a couple of days ago. She kept it there because she knew Cameron sneaked inside her apartment when she wasn't home. He's a real snoop, that one."

"Is there any chance Deck caught onto the princess ruse?"

"No. He's so invested in the idea that he has royalty on the premises. He slips it into every conversation he has. Even with the gardeners. *"You have to keep the noise-blower down. The princess is sleeping."* You would have heard the screams coming from his building if he'd figured out she was a commoner.

"No. The only one that knew the deep dark truth was Gary. Even though he's gay, I don't think he's ever had a real relationship with anyone. I'd say he's asexual more than anything but getting married was another part of the game for him and Tash. And for me. They got married and he applied for a fiancée visa, to solidify her green card process. Her immigration attorney didn't think they needed it, but he said to look at it as extra insurance. It was just starting to pay off. Gary even said he'd turn it all into a musical one day. And then things went haywire a couple of days ago."

"And you're sure Deck has no idea."

"No. No way. Up until now, you're the only one who guessed. Even when she got tangled up with Jamie Fahdi and we realized he was a gambling addict with his own fantasy life, he never twigged. He acts obsessed with her, just like Cameron to be honest, but I think with Jamie, he just wanted a rich wife."

"And she rejected him," Athen said.

"Yes. And he was angry." She lapsed into silence again.

Was he angry enough with Natasha to kill her? Athen wondered about that. So far, he knew of two men who had issues with her. Three, possibly, if he included the husband. "Where can I find Gary Goldman?"

Maggie shook her head. "He's not involved, I swear. He's a playwright and he's back east working on his dream of an off-off Broadway musical. He's so happy to have her money. She gives him a monthly stipend. He's come to rely on it. The fiancée visa came through in October. And that's when we stepped up our plans and she rented the apartment in Felice's building."

Now the pieces were falling into place. "Okay. Now explain why Jamie Fahdi was here firing blanks at you."

She didn't seem surprised to know they were blanks.

"I—"

"Athen. Grady's going crazy," Paulie came into the room muttering. He pressed the phone into his hands. "Please, talk to him."

"Got it." Athen handed Maggie his business card. "I want Gary Goldman's contact info. Text it to me, and *do not* tell him

I'll be calling him."

She nodded, looking petrified. He was grinding his teeth as he took the call and stepped into the hallway.

"Oh, my God!" Grady yelled. "Do you know how long I've waited to talk to you? That asshole shot at you! He could have killed you."

"But he didn't. And I'm fine." Athen felt the mother of a migraine building up behind his right eye. "Where are you?"

"At Sia's house."

"You're in Santa Cruz already? You must have driven like a bat outta hell."

"Several of them. I knew when I signed up that being with a cop meant that this could happen. You said there was little to no crime in Beverly Hills!"

"That's what they told me." Athen ground out a sigh.

"There aren't enough Tums in the world," Grady said, sounding more freaked out than Athen had ever heard him.

"Hon. I'm okay. Please. Calm down."

"I don't want a life without you in it," Grady said.

Athen had no privacy and no time to talk, but he appreciated his lover's words. "I feel the same way. You know that, right?"

"I'm gonna have to buy stocks in every antacid on the market!"

Athen bit back a laugh. "I gotta go. Is Desi okay?"

"Yeah. She needs to hear your voice. She's okay about being up here with her mom."

"That's good news. Oh, heck. I forgot to call Sia."

"You were too busy taking down a Beverly Hills Ninja." Grady's sense of humor seemed to be coming back. He put Desi on the phone. She sounded worried. Just like the Desi Athen used to know and love.

"Don't scare me like that anymore," she told him.

"I'll try not to."

"I love you."

"Love you too, hon. You take care of each other."

"We will," she said. "People say you're a hero taking down the jerk with the gun. All my TikTok friends are jealous that you're my uncle."

Athen grinned. "Yes, I am. Talk later, sweetie." He ended the call. "Paulie, I'm sorry."

Paulie put a hand on his shoulder. "No worries. This is the freakiest case though, right? Wait'll you hear this one." He inclined his head toward the front door.

They headed outside and Paulie said, "This is Bryce Felton."

Felton was exactly how Cameron had described him. *Handsome as shit.* He wore a scowl that only made him seem even hotter. He was so damned sexy he made Brad Pitt seem like regurgitated dog food. He even made Grady look like . . . *No. I am not going there.*

"Sorry to keep you waiting." Athen tried not to stare at Felton. If there was such a thing as star quality, this guy had it.

Felton seemed to relax immediately and Athen's gaydar went on red alert. This guy was as attracted to Athen as Athen was to him. But he also suspected the guy was probably as closeted as Athen's collection of winter coats.

"I'm sorry to get straight to the point, but Detective Hansen said you have information about the shooting."

"I was supposed to be the shooter." Felton's face went a dangerous shade of red. His anger wasn't so attractive now.

"Excuse me?" Athen gaped at him.

"I was supposed to be the shooter."

Athen and Paulie exchanged looks.

"All this." Felton waved his arms around. "It's all a live set. We're all actors, some better than others. Today was the day we were supposed to shoot our sizzler."

Athen stared at him. "A sizzler is like a promotional sample for a TV series, right?"

"Yeah." Felton snapped his fingers and pointed the index fingers at Athen. "You know the biz."

"Not really. So, go ahead, explain."

Felton huffed out a breath. "We all put in money. Tash put in like thirty K."

"She put in thirty thousand dollars?" Paulie asked.

"Well, sure. She's a Saudi princess. She's good for it. But that freak, Cameron Deck, he didn't turn in his portion. She covered it. He was supposed to pay her back. He didn't. Felice Farmer covered it, but Tash seemed cool with it. They're buds. If you ask me, if Tash is missing, look at Isla Sanchez or — " he pointed over Athen's head to Maggie's unit.

"You think Isla and, or Maggie, have something to do with her disappearance?"

"Well." He scrubbed at his chin with two grimy, nail-bitten fingers. He was looking less appealing by the second. "I don't think Deck was involved. He didn't stand to gain anything by Tash not being in the sizzler. I mean, he's using his contacts to get it to people at Paramount and of course, Steven Spielberg's office."

Athen stared at him. "You think Natasha King was abducted by what, actress rivals?"

"Yes." Felton's expression was earnest. "Hollywood's a tough town. Anyway, the media think that's what's happened."

Paulie was on his cellphone in seconds. Athen's heart sank. So much for keeping things contained. He would have bet all of this had been one big, phony, cooked-up mess had it not been the crime scene in Natasha King's apartment.

"How well do you know Natasha?" Athen asked.

"Not well. We kissed once. She freaked out. Don't ask me why. We like each other." He twisted his lips into a grimace. "I suspect because she knows Maggie and I fooled around some and she didn't want to hurt her feelings."

"Do you think Natasha is dead or alive?" Paulie asked. He showed Athen the social media reports that had popped up on TMZ and Deadline.

"Dead? Are you kidding? She's alive. Probably at the Peninsula, having a great laugh at our expense. She knows how to milk some PR that one."

Neither Paulie nor Athen responded for a moment.

"But you just said Maggie or Isla has to be behind it," Athen reminded him.

"These girls fight like wild cats over everything. Ask Isla about the red dress sometime. I think Maggie probably put her up to going into hiding to give the sizzler some street cred."

Athen took a deep breath. So, he knew about the red dress, too. He quickly texted Sullivan. *Ask Isla Sanchez about a red dress.* He glanced at Felton again. "What's your TV show called?"

"Terror in Beverly Hills."

Oh, man. How apt. Athen thought it was eerily prophetic and after this, maybe it would sell its socks off. "And why did Jamie Fahdi get to play the ninja and not you?"

"He put in more money than me." He let out a harsh laugh. "He won twelve thousand dollars in a poker game with the mayor. Brought it all here in ones and fives. Lording it over everyone else. But I got the memo that you were on your way here and he didn't. And he got shot. Now he's a martyr and my career's still in a holding pattern."

"A martyr?" Athen stared at him. "He shot at me. He shot at a police officer."

"Blanks. He was using blanks."

"That bullet wasn't a blank. It was a live round. Maybe that hasn't hit social media yet."

"No. That's impossible." Felton shook his head. "I made those blanks myself."

"Well, you missed one. But thanks for admitting your culpability. Is the gun yours?"

Felton looked nervous. "Yes."

"Is it registered?"

He shrugged. "I was told if we were shooting blanks for a TV series it was okay to use it. Oh, hell. Am I in trouble?"

"Of course, you are. But I have bigger fish to fry right now. We'll be in touch." Athen gestured to Paulie. He'd scrolled through the lurid headlines on Paulie's phone. *Saudi Princess Vanishes. What happened to the Saudi Princess?* And his personal favorite, *Missing Princess's Scandalous Rendezvous.*

What rendezvous? he wondered, but the headline was misleading. Somebody had posted a photo of her they'd found online. It was the same photo of Natasha and Jean-Claude Van Damme Athen had seen earlier in the day. Athen had no idea who'd leaked the information about her disappearance, but it was out there now. So much for keeping things contained.

"You look how I feel," Paulie said. "Maybe this isn't as bad as we think. Maybe this will get us more leads."

"There's always that."

Paulie was still holding Athen's phone, and a strange beeping sound came from it.

"What's that?" Athen asked.

Paulie turned a troubled gaze on him. "With everything that's been going on I forgot to tell you that I remotely set your motion sensors and camera activation to send you alerts when somebody enters your house."

"You can do that? Wow, that's cool. I didn't realize it was turned off." *Oh man. Maybe Despina did it. To cover her tracks. I'm gonna have to check days and days of recordings.*

"Well. Maybe you won't think it's so cool when I tell you that Taylor James just let himself inside your house."

CHAPTER NINE

A then's body went cold. He let Paulie take the wheel of his car, which he almost never did, but he didn't trust his own driving. His thoughts raced as they sped to his house. Paulie activated the blue lights on the dashboard, but not the siren. This gave them clear access to run red lights, without making a sound.

"ETA one minute," Paulie said.

"Perfect." Athen called Cricket and got his voicemail. *Damn. I don't have his partner's number.* He left a message for Cricket. "Tyler James is in my house. Can you get back to me?" As if this day could not get more chaotic. He received a text from Sullivan.

Luxury car dealership on Doheny has an ALPR. Owner in Aspen. Will download info and email you ASAP. No official ALPR for the city, but this is great news!

Athen texted back, *Yes!* and switched over to the activity going on inside his house. "Sullivan found an ALPR," Athen told Paulie.

"Yep. She texted me too."

"Oh, right. I asked her to keep us both in the loop."

"She's got some awesome contacts, doesn't she?" Paulie asked.

"Impressive." Athen watched James standing in his hallway. Athen's front door was ajar behind him. He was on his cellphone. *Man, he's wearing gloves. What the hell is he up to?* Tyler appeared to get somebody's voicemail. He said a few words, ending the call quickly. He made another call.

"Holy shit. He's calling me," Athen muttered. "Should I take it?"

"Oh, my God. I don't think so," Paulie said. "Let it go to voicemail. Unless you want to mess with his head a little."

"I like that idea." Athen took the call as Paulie swerved around an ancient old lady driving an equally ancient Daimler. "Lieutenant Mavromatis." He realized too late he'd just made it impossible to view the footage as he talked to Tyler.

"Athen? Oh, hey. It's Tyler."

"Hey." It took some effort to sound casual, but Athen did it. He fiddled with some key functions on his phone and to his shock, the live camera feed popped up on his phone.

Tyler was poking his nose around the hallway, opening the drawer to the hall table. He turned the handle to Athen and Grady's bedroom. Tyler smiled.

Creepy. "What's up?" Athen hated when people used this expression with him, but he was beyond aggravated with Tyler. Athen waited for a response, but suddenly his and Paulie's cellphones went crazy with text message pings.

Paulie glanced at Athen.

"Take it," Athen said.

"What's going on?" Tyler asked, opening Athen's bedroom door. Athen went rigid as he watched Tyler walk inside. Athen and Grady hadn't put cameras in their room. He caught Paulie shaking his head. He pulled over and showed Athen the text from Sullivan.

Vehicle opposite Deck's property is a rental car. Was reported stolen yesterday. Dashboard cam is active. Not sure who the car was rented to. Rental agency being stubborn.

"What's all that noise?" Tyler asked, coming out of Athen's room.

What the hell are you up to? "I'm working, Tyler. What's going on?"

Tyler stared at Athen's bedroom door for a second, then closed it. "I just thought it was time to catch up."

"Catch up? I'm working on a missing person's case, Tyler. I'm about to go home. I'll call you from there."

Tyler froze, his face a mask of panic. "Shit!" he mouthed.

Athen watched him run. He made it through his front door as Tyler disappeared out the back door, closing it behind him. He blew past the windows facing the back garden. Athen thought about chasing him, but for what? Tyler would have a million excuses and Athen didn't want to mess up Cricket's surveillance. *I want justice for Allie Madden.* His phone rang. Grady. He took the call.

"Despina got hold of her phone. She texted Tyler and told him she and I were out of town."

"Oh, great. That explains why he was just in here, Grady. He was in our bedroom."

"Aw, man. This is just getting creepier and creepier. Hold on a sec." Grady seemed to be moving around. "I took her phone away from her. Sia's talking about putting her in a reform school. It's some horse ranch out in Montana, but it's really a lockdown facility that provides intensive therapy and the staff works on self-esteem and other issues."

"Maybe it's not a bad idea." Athen's phone kept ringing. Calls and texts were piling up. Paulie was beside him in the hallway. He let Cricket into the house. Paulie pointed to the bedroom and Athen nodded, watching them head in there. Athen's headache grew worse. He walked to the kitchen and popped a K-cup into the brewer. Just in time he realized it was decaf, tossed the pod aside and inserted a fully leaded one.

Grady went on. "I just Googled the place they want to send Desi. It has a bad reputation for mistreating GLBTQ youth."

"Shit." Athen rubbed at his head. Desi had come out to him and Grady, but not her parents.

"Tell Sia to hold off on making any decisions for now. You and I will drive up there when this case is over, and we'll help Desi tell her parents what's going on. We both know we can't take care of her. She's just getting worse. And please, keep that phone away from her."

"I will. Just wanted you to know. And something else—"

"Yeah. Like I said, Tyler James was just in our house. Maybe you should check your video. I'm in there now."

"No. I was going to tell you that Desi tells me Tyler has been texting her for two weeks. He found her on Facebook, and she admits she gave him her key a few days ago. He's never told her why he wants to come in here so badly."

"I'm thinking it's time to move." Athen looked up to where the drop camera had been mounted discreetly among a row of vintage baking molds Grady had hung above the shelves.

"You're on top of things then." Grady blew him a kiss. "Love you. Talk later."

"Love you back."

Athen checked the time on the oven clock. Three p.m. Man, this had been a long day with no end in sight. The sandwich he'd eaten earlier seemed like hours ago, and it was. He pulled out the coffee from the brewer and dumped in milk and two sugars. Grady would moan about the sugar, but he wasn't here and Athen needed the energy. He gave a finger wave to the camera as Paulie entered the kitchen.

"You want a coffee?" Athen asked.

"Yeah. Thanks." Paulie rifled through the drawer filled with exotic flavored pods. He picked up Athen's discarded decaf pod and slipped it into the brewer.

"I can't tell what James was doing in your bedroom. We didn't find anything at first glance," Cricket said, coming in, fixated on the coffee maker.

"Help yourself." Athen waited a beat. "I need to get a camera in the bedroom. Either that or change the locks. Maybe he doesn't know that I know he was in here." He looked at Cricket. "What do you want me to do?"

Cricket opened the fridge door and removed a plate Grady

had left with two sandwiches on it. "He's obsessed with this joint. My partner Murph saw James coming here. He walked up your garden path, rang the bell then took off when nobody answered. Then he came back a half hour later. Murph has footage of him walking around, looking in the windows. Made a lot of calls on his cellphone. Murph saw him go around the side gate. He called me, but James must have detoured to his other house two doors down via the backyard."

"So, you *have* been watching him?" Paulie asked.

Cricket slid a glance in Paulie's direction.

"You can trust Paulie. He doesn't know anything other than the fact James's been letting himself in here. We think my niece gave him a set of keys."

"That was nice of her." Cricket blew out a frustrated sigh as he put the plate on the counter and took a half sandwich. Athen and Paulie snatched up halves themselves before Cricket could demolish them all.

"James came back here just as we were switching out vehicles," Cricket said. "He's obsessed with your house, like I said. And your bedroom for some reason." He picked out a hazelnut flavored coffee pod. Athen hated flavored coffee. Cricket was welcome to it.

Athen's cellphone rang. A text from Sullivan. *I'm outside your front door.* He went to let her in. "How did you know I was here?" *Man, this chick has some skills!*

"Paulie told me via text. Since I'm here, can I come in?"

"Of course. I was beginning to think you were psychic."

"I am," she said, straight-faced. She started reciting her lengthy list of updates. Things were okay until he realized Detective Lorne Brand wasn't with her.

"Where's Brand?"

"At Cedars with the captain. We're keeping a watch on Jamie Fahdi. He's tried to escape from the hospital. Twice. Turns out he has two warrants out on him. FTA's."

"Failure to appear? On what charges?"

"Robbery. Turns out he's part of a ritzy crowd that likes to rob rich people. He's also got a bench warrant that might take precedence in Nevada. Clark County's dukin' it out with LAPD's sheriff's department on who gets first crack at him."

"What's he wanted for in Nevada?" Athen asked as they approached the kitchen.

"Same thing. He and a few other people targeted high-stakes winners from poker games for their winnings. Followed some to their hotel rooms and roughed 'em up. Amazing those pit bosses haven't arranged for his disappearance in the desert by now. Either way, the captain will arrange transfer of custody to the winning bidder as soon as the hospital releases him."

"Wow. Who knew so much skullduggery was going on in Beverly Hills?"

"Right? I did text you, but I know you've been busy."

"Soup!" Cricket called out.

"Cricket!" Sullivan rushed past the kitchen island and barreled into his arms.

"Soup?" Athen and Paulie asked in unison.

"Girl. You are a sight for sore eyes." Cricket kissed the top of her head and pushed her back, letting his gaze traverse her trim body. "I always was warm for your form," he said.

Sullivan just laughed. "You are such a Neanderthal. You and your decrepit old jokes."

"I take it you two know each other," Athen said, unable to keep the smile from his face.

"We worked together up in San Francisco on a cross country drug case," Cricket said.

Athen bit into his sandwich, sliding the remaining half to Sullivan, who mouthed, "Thanks" before extricating herself from Cricket's grip. Man, it felt good to eat.

"Her old man was the best," Cricket said between bites.

Sullivan, who'd been smiling, suddenly looked shattered. Athen knew her story but never talked to her about it. Grady had. They'd developed a bond Athen encouraged, but even Grady had been careful to sidestep Sullivan's devastating recent past. Nobody said anything for a moment. Sullivan and her husband, Alvin Tang, had been a crack team of investigators with the Drug Enforcement Agency. Alvin had been shot two years ago in an undercover meth lab sting that had gone wrong.

After quitting the DEA, Sullivan had, by all accounts, been teaching at a couple of colleges until a chance meeting with Lucy. She recruited Sullivan to the Beverly Hills Police force. That was as much as Athen knew. When Lucy told him she'd hired Sullivan, he'd suspected that the prospect of a more peaceful existence had appealed to her. That, and Beverly Hills' fabled palm trees. Both aspects of the job had been alluring to Athen.

"So how did you get the name Soup?" Athen asked, wishing he had another sandwich.

She grinned then. "Tang, my last name, is also soup in China. Alvin and Cricket used to eat soup together all the time. So, he gave us both the nickname Soup." She narrowed her gaze at Cricket. "I'd hoped in time Cricket would get some new jokes and I'd be able to upgrade my nickname."

"To what?" Athen asked.

Sullivan's grin grew wider. "I'm thinking maybe gorgeous. Or sexy."

"I like Soup," Paulie said, making everybody laugh.

All their phones rang. They checked.

"Lucy wants updates," Athen said. "Since we're all here, let's take this to the table shall we. Refills anyone?" He texted Lucy to let her know the team was in his house and they would join her in a Zoom conference call.

"I'll give you some privacy," Cricket said. "I'm gonna go

check out the backyard. I'd like to know how he's getting to his house from the backyard. I also wanna check the bedroom again. Just to be sure our favorite movie star didn't leave behind any nasty surprises."

"I appreciate it, thanks," Athen said, waiting for his turn at the Keurig.

Cricket let himself outside and Soup, because she would forever be Soup now to him, said, "You gonna tell us what's going on?"

"As soon as we're done talking to Lucy." With a heavy heart and a fresh cup of coffee, he took himself over to the kitchen table. He set up his laptop and entered the code for the Zoom session. Lucy was back in her office, sipping her customary green tea, judging by the tea bag floating over the edge of her cup.

"Hit me," she said. Paulie and Soup had signed in on their phones. It was weird sitting next to them and seeing them on his screen. He always felt like he was *The Brady Bunch* on these types of calls with everybody's faces in boxes on the screen. Seconds later, Lorne Brand signed in.

"I'm at Cedars in the waiting room," he said, a Bluetooth in his ear. "Waiting for that idiot Jamie Fahdi. The hospital approved his discharge and as soon as I get the word, I'll have to sign off. I'm escorting him to LA Sheriffs. Nevada won the coin toss. They'll send him over there."

"Good," Lucy said. "That gets him out of our hair and off the streets. One less thug to worry about. Athen, please bring us up to speed."

"So far, we know that Natasha King is Australian, not Saudi, and she arrived in LA approximately a year ago, not November, as her landlord Cameron Deck believes. In October, she began laying down the elaborate princess ruse. She won the green card lottery according to her friend and manager, Maggie Harman. Maggie tells me that Natasha was having trouble living and working here, even with a green card. She not only won the lottery but got a substantial inheritance when her mother died back in Australia. Apparently, she panicked and married a friend of hers, a playwright named Gary Goldman.

"Never heard of him," Lorne said.

"I don't think he's famous. Far from it," Athen said. "I also don't think he's involved in Natasha's disappearance, because his Facebook page reveals an incessant need to update. He's been in New York City working on getting an old theater up and running. I haven't contacted him yet because I, ah, had an urgent personal matter to attend to, but as soon as we're done talking, I'm going to call a buddy, who's a Manhattan detective for the fifth precinct. The theater's right on the south-east edge of the city. He could walk over and have a chat with him. It's the kind of conversation that should happen in person. It would be easy for him to check if Goldman's been there the last few days. And who knows, maybe the guy has pertinent information."

"I like that," Lucy said, as the others nodded. "Better than calling him. Was this a love match?"

"No. Not romantic love." That got a smile out of Soup. "According to Maggie, he's gay, but they're great friends. I have a feeling in my bones he's not involved. He's been posting like nothing's out of the ordinary. He stands to lose a lot financially if anything happens to Natasha." He waited a beat. "He relies on the monthly stipend she gives him."

"Interesting." Lucy jotted a note.

Athen looked at Gary Goldman's Facebook page as they spoke. There were no mentions of his wife, but she appeared in two older photos with no captions. He right clicked both images to retain copies of them. Both were taken in September, right before she began the princess charade.

"He's been in New York the entire time last few days if his timeline is correct," Soup said, flicking through her phone. "It doesn't look like he's posted a single thing about her. Don't you think it's strange if they're married? I mean even it's a marriage of convenience."

"No," Athen said. "Maggie told me that Natasha wanted it kept secret. Being married would detract from her allure. And she had all these guys just hanging off her. I guess she liked to feed them with a long spoon."

"That's an interesting expression," Paulie said. "A dangerous game she was playing. Think somebody found out she was no princess and went bonkers?"

"I think so," Athen said. "I mean, all the guys we know of needed money. All of them relied on her financially one way or another."

"Then I'm glad we're getting NYPD involved," Lucy said. "Let's find out what the husband knows. Just quickly from my end, then we'll cross over to you, Lorne. I've checked her packed schedule of appointments and Natasha hasn't shown up to a single one. It took me a long time to get people to be forthcoming, partly because they were worried about infringing on her personal life, but they all believe she's a princess. The woman who does her anal bleaching—"

"Her what?" Lorne spluttered."

"It's a thing," Lucy said, blushing. "So I hear."

"Anyway," Lucy said, working hard to keep the smile from her lips, "She said Natasha's become increasingly imperious, demanding discounts and favors."

"Huh." Athen thought a moment. "I have no idea what kind of money she inherited, but Maggie said every dime has been going into her career. Maybe she's been running low, or afraid of running low. If she's been here for a year and made no income, no wonder she was starting to panic. The imperious thing was probably all an act. She's probably trying to cut deals so she can keep going."

"Sounds feasible," Lucy said. "We need to get hold of her bank records, but we don't even have ID let alone information like that."

"Bryce Felton said he was supposed to be the ninja shooter in the sizzler this morning, but he couldn't come up with his portion. Natasha covered Jamie and that was how he got to get a mangled leg." Paulie grinned.

Lucy shook her head. "Wish we knew her bank account details."

"Maggie Harman told me she kept everything in a first aid kit in Maggie's trunk," Athen said. "Natasha doesn't drive and relies on rides and Uber transportation."

"That gets expensive," Soup said.

"Right. Well, she told me that Deck snooped in Natasha's apartment all the time, so she kept nothing of evidentiary value in there. She kept it all in this box in Maggie's trunk but took it out right before her disappearance," Athen said. We could start contacting all the Beverly Hills banks. See if we get a hit. See if she's been using her credit cards."

"Good idea." Lorne fiddled with his bluetooth. "Chief, you get the search warrant, and I'll start as soon as I drop off Jamie Fahdi. Damn. They're ready to release him. Gotta go." He signed off the chat.

"Over to you Paulie," Lucy said.

"I talked to several residents. The apartment building Bryce Felton and Maggie Harman live in is a kind of set. They have every unit wired for filming. The big acting thing that was supposed to happen today turns out to be a super-secret sizzler being filmed at Maggie's place. They've got hidden cameras everywhere. Even in parked cars on the street. I talked to several neighbors while Athen was getting the nitty-gritty from Maggie on Natasha."

"That ties in with the rental car Sullivan reported kitty-corner to Natasha's house," Lucy said. "The vehicle was rented by Jamie Fahdi three days ago. His credit card was declined after an initial acceptance, however, and he somehow managed to disable the GPS. There is an active dashboard camera, but it doesn't belong to the rental agency and isn't part of the rental agreement.

"When I talked to Fahdi at the hospital, he claimed Natasha was supposed to pay for the rental as of two days ago. The agency says a woman was supposed to go there two days ago to cover a week's rental but never showed up. They're going to let us have the vehicle towed to SID so we can go over it. For all we know, it was used in the commission of the crime against Natasha King."

"And it will give us access to the dashboard cam," Soup said.

"Right," Lucy agreed. "According to Fahdi, it was supposed to be part of the TV show process."

"I have no idea how she thought she was going to get away with the princess act once she actually nailed a gig," Athen said. "I don't think she and Maggie thought that far ahead."

"I thought she seemed remarkably . . . naïve about the industry for somebody who's posing as a manager, and markets herself as a show producer and actress," Paulie pointed out.

"Agreed," Athen said. He blew out a sigh. "Soup, what's your update?"

"Athen, you know about Soup?" Lucy chuckled. "So glad you guys are all becoming so chummy."

Soup shook her head. "As long as y'all don't start asking me to make you soup, we'll get along fine. As you know, I talked to Isla Sanchez. According to her, she and Natasha were the best of friends until Natasha suddenly revealed to her one day that she was a princess. This caused a rift between them because she says Natasha went to her apartment about a week before and stole a red dress."

"We keep hearing about this red dress. Deck mentioned it. Felton mentioned it." Athen looked at Paulie, who nodded.

"It's a classic retro red evening dress. Tom Ford featured it in his two-thousand-twelve collection. Highly prized by the fashionistas, from what Isla told me," Soup said. "About a dozen were made for different runway shoes. She bought hers online for three thousand dollars. She told me it makes you feel like a woman when you wear it. She said, and I quote, *I felt lit from within when I wore it.* Anyway, I've sent you all photos of both women wearing it. I hate to say so, but Natasha looks amazing in it."

Everyone grabbed their phones. Athen stared at the images. It was a beautiful dress, for sure. He was surprised that it was a ruby red, off the shoulder floor-length sheath with a matching cape. Isla looked beautiful but . . . *Wow.* Natasha just glowed. She looked like a real princess in it. He stared at the photo and realized he'd seen it — or part of it — before.

"Holy crap!" he yelled. "I know what Tyler James is looking for!"

"What?" Paulie responded at once.

"What's he talking about?" Lucy asked.

"Don't know," Soup said.

Paulie said nothing.

Athen almost knocked over his laptop and coffee cup in his haste to rush to the kitchen pantry. Tyler had been a pain in the ass since day one about his private collection of décor in the house. He'd insisted on his paintings being left on the walls and keeping certain art pieces on display.

"Some of his things just give me the creeps," Grady had said more than once. Together, they had slowly removed things they disliked and stored them in a box in the pantry. Among the items were three photos, that made no sense for them to have in their possession.

Athen fumbled around, pushing aside sacks of rice, potatoes, chilis, and flour. And there it was. He dragged out the box, going through it until he found what he was looking for. Grady had wrapped each picture and weird tchotchke in acid-free tissue paper. One of the packages contained a framed photo of a certain phony princess. Beside her, Tyler James stood, laughing and smiling for the camera.

But that wasn't why Tyler James had hidden it. Discreetly hidden among the strange jewels glued in one corner of the frame, was, Athen realized now, a teeny, tiny camera.

CHAPTER TEN

A then returned to the table. He showed the others the photo frame. "Camera," he whispered. "I don't think it's wired for sound." Then he called Cricket. Nobody said anything until Cricket came back inside and examined the frame.

"Are there more?" he asked, his eyes black with fury.

"Yeah." Athen was surprised. "Two others. It's a set. Grady and I put them away several days ago."

"Get them for me." Cricket covered the camera with his thumb then turned the frame over and with a gentle tug, picked away at a corner covered in tape. "These are state of the art, but they're visual only. No sound."

Soup snapped her fingers. "I saw something like this in the latest *Bosch* series. The wife who had her husband bumped off had no idea he'd been watching her from a spycam in a picture frame."

"Where did Tyler keep these?" Paulie asked.

Athen grimaced. "In our bedroom."

"Ah. Then he must have realized he wasn't receiving images anymore. That's why he's been invading your house." Cricket nudged Athen. "Go on. Git. I wanna see the other frames."

Athen felt numb as he went to retrieve the other photo frames. He could hear Soup and the captain asking about the home invasion.

"What's going on?" Lucy asked a couple of times.

Athen pulled the two remaining photos. Both were pictures of Tyler. One from a movie set, in a WWII costume, the other was Tyler on a beach somewhere in sunglasses. Despina had wanted them in her bedroom until she discovered a passion for the Kpop band BTS and the singer Dua Lipa. There wasn't enough room on her desk, bookshelves or her dresser for all the photos she printed from her computer and framed. She'd agreed to give up the photos. Now Athen was angrier than he'd been before he realized Tyler had been spying on them all.

He returned to the table with the other frames. The jeweled embellishments on all there had been elaborate coverups for pinpoint cameras.

Cricket dismantled them all. "He realized they were missing. Exactly when did you put them away?"

Athen ran a hand over his face. Ever since the coronavirus outbreak he kept telling himself not to do it but kept doing it. "Like I said, several days ago. About four, five days. Less than a week"

"Around the time Despina gave Tyler your house keys," Paulie said. "Do you think he had anything to do with Natasha's disappearance?"

"Good question," Athen said. "Let's bring him in." He was so incensed at this point, he didn't know what to think beyond wanting to get the hell out of this house as soon as possible. And getting Tyler James off the streets.

"So what's going on?" Lucy asked.

Athen gestured to Cricket. "It's your story to tell."

"It's our case. You have as much right to it as I do."

"Go ahead," Athen said. He drew another chair from the wall over to the table. Cricket sat and gave everyone a brief rundown of the Allie Madden case.

"Five years ago, Athen and I were brought in as US Marshals to work on a missing person case. Allie Madden had been gone for several months from Virginia Beach. She was separated from her husband, Phil, but they couldn't seem to stay away from each other. They met up in a bar one night, the last time anyone saw her. There is video of them arguing." He sighed.

"The video shows that Phil slapped her, but he left long before she did. She was there for two hours after him. She was drinking and dancing with her friends. Athen and I, heck, dozens of law enforcement officers studied that footage. We even interviewed and re-interviewed people we identified from the bar. Everyone confirmed Allie was calm and happy when she and her friends all left together. But she wanted to walk home. Didn't want a ride. You gotta understand, from the surveillance footage we've seen, she seemed sober enough to walk, and Virginia Beach is a pretty safe place. In fact, it has the lowest crime in the country for a city of its size.

"But Allie never made it home. Her friends still blame themselves for letting her walk the six blocks to her house alone. We've got nothing beyond two street cameras, one out- side a bank, one near a parking lot, where she's seen walking. Then she's just gone."

Nobody said anything for a moment.

Athen looked at Cricket and took up the story again to give his former partner time to regroup.

"Cricket and I worked that case hard. We came in with fresh eyes and an open mind. We were surprised that Phil Madden had a mistress. Leta Gordon claimed Phil had killed Allie and that she witnessed it. She confessed this to both of us."

"You didn't believe her," Cricket said.

The words hung between them a moment.

Athen drew in a breath. "No. I did not." He'd never told anyone that his feelings about Leta Gordon's confession had caused a wedge between him and Cricket that had never mended. They'd worked together on a couple more cases, but Cricket then asked for a new partner. Athen didn't challenge him.

"Long story short," Athen said, "I got a call from a young man whose grandfather, a water tracker, offered to come to Stumpy Lake, the place where Leta Gordon claimed Allie had been murdered and dumped in the water. We didn't find the body. The old man said she wasn't in there."

"Why did Leta Gordon confess to a crime that never happened?" Soup asked.

"Phil Madden dumped her for somebody else. She wanted to get him into trouble."

"Oh, brother," Lucy said.

Athen nodded. "She never dreamed we'd work with a tracker, or that the feds would dredge the lake. But we did."

"I think Leta believed that she'd get Phil arrested, and away from the other woman, and that she herself would be given immunity in exchange for her help. Well, we were never able to charge Phil Madden and the case went colder than a polar ice cap."

Everyone listened with rapt attention as Athen said, "Until a few months ago. Right, Cricket?"

"Right. We found Allie Madden's body. I know Athen hasn't had time to review the material I've emailed him, and he only found out about all this today, but a couple of field workers literally tripped over her body left buried in a shallow grave in a field located about three miles from the bar. It was being soil tested and observed for grading for a big property development. We assume she was abducted at some point between the bar and her home. The man who took her, raped, and shot her in the head. Buried her. And we found DNA on her clothing. It's amazing that we were able to get it after this amount of time, but we got lucky, and science as you know, advances every day. As I explained to Athen this morning, the DNA is not recorded through federal databases, which means the suspect has never been in jail for a crime.

But through Genetic Genealogy, which I ran myself, we've got a good idea who the killer is." He paused. "We think it's Tyler James."

"Holy shit," Lucy said.

"I've been watching him trying to get hold of his DNA." Cricket spread his hands. "What do you think the chances are that another woman's gone missing, and he's not involved? A woman he apparently knows?" He pointed to the photo.

"We don't know yet," Athen said. "But we'll find out."

"Was he living in Virginia Beach five years ago?" Soup asked.

"Nope. Pennsylvania. I've sent all this to Athen, like I said. He pointed out it's a five or so hour drive to Virginia Beach. According to his acting resume, Tyler James was in a play in Philadelphia at the time. His family lived in the city. I believe it was a production of *American Buffalo,* and it was a theater on Walnut Street, the hub of the theater community. By the way, it was his mother who went on one of those genealogy sites looking for long-lost family. And that's how I got the DNA."

"That's fascinating," Soup said. "I know that play. I bet he was playing the young heroin addict. What do they call him?" She paused. "Bobby. Yes. Bobby. He's a great character and he seems to launch careers."

"That wouldn't surprise me," Athen said. "He's had a fast trajectory."

"How do you know him?" Lucy asked. "I never did find out."

Athen sighed. "I met him on a movie set in New York. I was protecting his co-star from a stalker. Tyler and I became friends. Actually, he and Grady became close."

"It figures," Cricket muttered.

Athen frowned at him. "What the hell is that supposed to mean?"

Cricket waved a hand. "Nothing. I'm just frustrated. I want this guy nailed."

"Get him to the station," Lucy said. "And offer him a drink. We'll get his DNA. Does he smoke?" When Cricket nodded, she went on. "I'll even offer him a damned cigarette. Even if it sets off our smoke alarms. We need his DNA. And of course, we'll ask him a few pertinent questions. Any idea where he is now?"

"He's in his other house. Two doors down," Cricket said. "My partner's out front watching him. If he'd left, Murph would have told me."

"I think we need to keep the information we have about Allie Madden a secret," Lucy said.

"Agreed," Cricket said. "I don't want anything to compromise that case. Maybe the two women are unrelated cases. But I don't think so."

"We can ask him about Natasha. We have physical proof he knows her. And I'd like to know why he's been spying on Athen and Grady. It's disgusting, not to mention illegal," Lucy said. Go grab him. And bring those photos with you. Oh, and Cricket, please send me your DNA profile on your suspect."

"Will do," Cricket said just as Athen responded:

"Yes, sir." He stood. "Come on, Paulie, let's go." He started packing up his laptop and realized he'd need to grab a few essentials. He had no idea if Tyler had cameras or microphones anywhere else in the house. From day one, the guy had been overly insistent on being in control of the household objects. Now he knew why.

"Think he's good for Natasha's disappearance?" Soup asked him as they prepared to leave.

"I don't know. Maybe I'm too cynical, but it seems too perfect. Hey, do me a favor?"

"Anything."

"Call Grady and tell him I'm gonna find a hotel for the night until I can get SID in here to sweep the place for anymore spycams or microphones."

"I can do it," Cricket said. "And I can stay here if you like. I can change the locks, too. I'll get Murph to pick up one once you have Tyler James in custody."

"Do it," Lucy said from Paulie and Soup's phones. She was still in on the Zoom call. "I don't like my staff being victimized. Athen, go get this little douche canoe. I'll get the warrant for his DNA. Cricket, I'll make sure we get an extra sample for you. Both cases are our priority."

"I appreciate that," he said. "Just so you all know. Nothing about my case leaves this room."

"You betcha," Athen said.

"We haven't talked to Felice Farmer yet," Paulie reminded him. "What if she has info on Tyler James?"

Athen blew out a sigh. He looked at Soup. "Do you want to take a swing at Felice? Isn't she at her cigar bar?"

"She'll only talk to you, remember?"

"Yeah. I must remember not to blink." When Soup laughed, he added, "Paulie and I can go to her cigar bar after we talk to Tyler. I wonder if she or any of Natasha's other friends knew that she'd met him?" He took a photo of the collection of frames and emailed them to Soup. "Why don't you go visit Cameron Deck, and Maggie Harman? See if they remember anything. Maybe Natasha talked about him."

"I can do that." Soup looked at her cellphone. "I'm still waiting on the facial recognition search for Cameron Deck. And I'm also waiting for the info to download from that ALPR tracking system. Maybe I can swing by the car dealership and sweet-talk them into speeding things up a little."

"Good idea," Athen said. "Call Lorne Brand and ask him to go with you now that his babysitting duties are over." He snapped his fingers. "Tyler's got a distinctive yellow Porsche.

Let's get the license plate and check it against the ALPR data. Let's find out if he went to Natasha's house in the last few days."

"Will do."

"Perfect." Athen hesitated. "Cameron Deck said two men came looking for Natasha early this morning. The ALPR must have picked up license plates. Let's see if we can get something." He gathered his belongings and tossed them into a messenger bag. "I'll call my cop friend in Manhattan and ask him to go talk to Natasha's husband. He can check with him about Tyler, too. Maybe Natasha mentioned meeting Tyler James. His name is Albert Ngo. Great guy. I'll give him everyone's contact details so he can keep us all in the loop."

"Do it. See you back at the station," Lucy said. "I'm getting the warrant now." She checked out of the Zoom call.

Athen called Albert, who took his call after a few rings. "Hey, stranger. How's it hangin'" Since Athen had him on loudspeaker, Paulie heard it. He'd been in the process of taking a sip of coffee. He almost choked on his laughter.

"Hey, crazy guy." Athen grinned. "Listen, I need help." He ran through the case info and asked Albert to contact Natasha's husband.

"No problem. Text me all the numbers for your team. I'll be in touch. It'll take me about an hour to get to him. I'm in the middle of monitoring a controlled drop-off on a drug bust for ICE."

"You sure you got time for this?"

"For you? Yes. For a missing woman? Absolutely. Hit me back." Albert ended the call. Athen took a few moments to text him Lucy, Soup and Paulie's numbers. An hour. They could wait. He wanted this done in person, not by phone. He went to the bedroom, tossed some shirts, socks, underpants and a pair of jeans into a duffle bag then realized he'd need toiletries. Old marshal habits had been ingrained within him.

He still kept a packed bag of overnight essentials in the bathroom cupboard and stuck it in with his clothes.

Athen strode out of the house with the messenger bag slung crosswise over his body, duffle in hand, and an increasingly bad mood packed into his soul.

Soup and Paulie ran to keep up with him. "He's coming out of the house," Paulie muttered. "Oh, man. He's starting to run."

"Shit." Athen and Paulie were on the move and reached the bright yellow Porsche before Tyler James could get inside. "Tyler," Athen said, slapping his hand on the driver's side door. "I'd like to ask you a few questions. Mind coming down to the station with us?"

"I gotta be someplace," he said. "I'm running late." When Athen didn't respond, he said, "Do I have to?" For the first time in the years Athen had known him, the veneer of charm slipped, and Tyler seemed to ooze hatred.

"Yeah. You do."

Tyler shook his head. "Can I drive myself?"

Athen almost laughed. "I'd rather you didn't."

"Can I ask what this is about?"

"Spying on me. Oh, and a missing woman."

Tyler's eyes widened. "What missing woman?"

"We'll discuss it at the station." Athen glanced in the car and noticed a pile of cigarette butts crushed in a dashboard cup holder. Not only was it disgusting and stinky, but all car rental companies prohibited drivers from smoking in their vehicles. They imposed heavy fines and cleaning fees on cars returned with any trace of cigarettes.

"Paulie, can you please escort Mr. James to my car please?"

"Sure thing."

"Wait. I gotta lock my car," Tyler bleated.

"I'll do it." Athen extracted the keys from Tyler's hand,

waiting until Soup and Paulie led Tyler away from the vehicle. He almost texted Cricket with *Cigarette butts in the yellow Porsche. Get them now.* He cursed the fact that it wouldn't be considered legal procedure since technically speaking, Tyler hadn't abandoned the butts. Or the vehicle. He beeped the Porsche locked and walked over to his own car.

Tyler seemed to be resisting getting into the backseat, but quickly complied once Athen arrived on the scene.

"Make sure you call Lorne," he warned Soup. She gave him a radiant smile and a wink and went off to her car once Tyler was secured in the backseat.

Tyler seemed nervous now. Athen had never seen him so freaked out. "What's all this about?"

"All in good time." Athen got behind the wheel, tossed Tyler's keys over to him, and fired up the engine, doing a quick U-turn. Tyler had his cellphone in hand.

Paulie whipped around. "I'm sorry. I can't let you make any calls right now. I'll need to take your phone."

"Seriously?" Tyler gaped at him.

"Yeah." Paulie took possession of the phone. "You need me to contact someone for you? Since you're running late?"

"No." Tyler slumped back against the seat and stared out the window.

Paulie went through Tyler's calls. He nudged Athen who pulled over for a moment. He was shocked to find Despina's phone number there. She'd texted him numerous times asking for puffers.

He turned around to Tyler. "What the hell is a puffer?"

Tyler mouthed *fuck* but didn't look at him. "They're vapes with marijuana in them."

"And you've been giving them to my thirteen-year-old niece?"

"One time. She's been bugging me ever since."

Athen didn't want the guy to insist on a lawyer so he let

the matter drop and sped off to the station. He tossed the phone to Paulie who seemed to understand Athen wanted him to look through the calls. Athen noticed Soup heading up toward Wilshire. He wasn't sure who she would target first. Deck or Harman, but he wanted to make sure she got hold of Lorne Brand before she did anything. He didn't want her alone around either Deck or Harman. Both of them gave him the creeps.

"Can you text Soup and make sure Brand goes with her?" he muttered to Paulie.

"Roger that."

Athen marveled at the dexterity with which Paulie handled his phone and Tyler's. Athen reached the Beverly Hills Police Department headquarters on North Rexford Drive and found a parking space outside the mayor's office. He didn't want to venture down to the subterranean parking lot. Not with a suspect in hand. He took a deep breath. The entire department once consisted of a single US Marshal, Augustus Niestrum, who in 1914, ran both the police and fire departments from his home in Beverly Hills.

Things weren't so much different now. Both departments were still in the same place, albeit a much bigger one, along with a shooting range, crime lab, City Hall, traffic and records division, the mayor's office, and the Beverly Hills Public Library. He suddenly remembered the post office receipt he'd found in Natasha's possessions.

He switched off the engine, rifled through his phone and sent a copy of the photo he'd taken to Soup. She and Lorne could chase that up. The post office had security cameras. Maybe she'd been caught on tape.

"Is this going to take long? I'm a busy guy you know," Tyler said, leaning forward.

"Shut up," Athen said just as Soup texted him back a thumbs-up emoji.

Tyler slouched back in his seat.

Athen glanced at the 92,000 square foot building. Lucy Lane had hired him as a special consultant, making use of Athen's Marshal status. Like the first city marshal, he worked out of his house, except when doing interviews or working in the field. Beverly Hills was its own entity and the enormous complex was fast becoming outdated. The police chief who'd left in some disgrace before Lucy was hired, had wanted to revamp the building. Despite expensive plans drawn up with a projected budget of seventy-one million dollars, it was looking like the entire department would have to relocate.

In the meantime, Lucy was working overtime to rehabilitate a department hampered by the former chief's reputation for racism and homophobia.

Lucy was nothing if not inclusive. Athen respected the hell out of her. He hoped her interim position would soon become a fulltime one. He had to do her proud. That was the best way to help her.

Within seconds, he and Paulie had Tyler out of the vehicle. Though he wasn't cuffed, he seemed to realize he had no choice but to let them each take an arm and muscle him into headquarters. Athen led him to an interview room.

"Take a seat against the far wall," Athen said to him. He pulled the door closed for a moment. "Find anything in his phone?" he asked Paulie as Lucy met them there.

"No calls to Natasha's number. There are some troubling conversations though."

"Troubling? How so?" Athen asked.

"Well, he seems to be texting guys about a crab shack and buying seafood. A lot of ah, fishy conversations. He was heading off just now to pick up a pound of crabs. Who does that? I suspect these are drug conversations. I think Tyler's dealing marijuana."

"Shit," Lucy said. "Here's your warrant." She slapped it

into Athen's hand. "Keep him busy. I'm gonna sweet talk the judge into getting a search warrant for his house."

"Go for it." Athen checked over the warrant for Tyler's DNA, and a swabbing test kit. Correction. Two. *One for me, and one for Cricket.*

"What's that?" The actor's eyebrows shot up, revealing his alarm as Athen and Paulie entered the interview room. He seemed to be pacing the floor.

"Please take a seat," Athen responded.

"Can I get you a cup of coffee, or a bottle of water?" Paulie asked him.

"No." Tyler sat in the chair against the wall, looking glum as Athen scanned the terms of the warrant. He was pleased that he'd been approved for Rapid DNA, a type of analysis previously only seen in science fiction shows. Thanks to Lucy's quick thinking and the proximity of the local courts, not to mention her pristine reputation, she'd been able to procure the spanky new test that would give them DNA results in two hours. Reality was finally catching up with TV.

He took a seat opposite Tyler, sitting beside Paulie. There was an electronic button on his side of the desk, which Athen pressed, announcing the time of 3:40 pm. It activated a recording system in another room, where he knew other officers would be watching the interview.

"Am I being recorded?" Tyler looked alarmed.

"Yes. Nothing to worry about. I'm talking to Tyler James regarding a missing person case. With me is Detective Paulie Hansen." Athen then focused his attention purely on Tyler.

"I don't like to Miranda people unless I have good cause. Are you willing to help with an investigation currently in progress?"

Tyler's gaze shifted from left to right. His Adam's apple bobbled and he looked petrified. He adopted a head tilt however, and a sly smile that didn't seem genuine. *Man, I had no idea he was such a bad actor!*

"What investigation?" he asked.

Athen said nothing for a moment. Though he and Paulie hadn't worked out their game plan, he knew Paulie would ride shotgun with him on this. Athen wanted to make Tyler feel uncomfortable. It worked.

"Look, if you're trying to tell me your niece is missing, I saw her this morning with Grady. They left your house. With the dog. So, if something's happened to her, I had nothing to do with it." He brushed his hands across the space in front of him.

"Why would I think you had anything to do with Despina?" Athen made himself sound surprised.

Tyler's shoulders sagged a little. "She texts me sometimes. Like I said before. She can get someone else to buy vapes for her whenever she wants. I'm just the idiot who said yes."

Athen agreed but didn't say so. He could add this crime of procuring drugs for a minor to Tyler's growing list of infractions, but he needed to keep his eye on the real prize. A possible homicide.

"Hmph. Well, this isn't about my niece, but since you brought it up, I'd like to know when she gave you the keys to my house so that you could come and go at will."

"That never happened."

"So, you weren't in my house in the middle of the night trying to get into my bedroom?"

He blinked. "I—no. Never. Is that what she told you?"

"We have surveillance footage. What about this afternoon? When you thought the coast was clear?"

"I never—I. Jesus. Surveillance? Why do you need that?"

"Why do *you* need it Tyler? The US Marshals alerted me to the three photo frames you wanted kept in our bedroom. There are mini cameras on them." He pulled out the sealed packages from his messenger bag and placed them on the table.

"I don't know what you're talking about. They're just photos."

"Who's this?" Paulie spoke for the first time, jabbing a forefinger at the photo of Tyler with Natasha King.

Tyler flicked an annoyed glance at the photo. "I don't know."

"You don't know?" Paulie scoffed. "And yet, you wanted to make sure this photo stayed in the bedroom. Why?"

Tyler huffed out a breath and put his arms across his chest. "I just like to know what's going on."

Athen's phone rang. He checked the screen. Lucy had texted, *Not enough probable cause to get the warrant to search his house. We can still hold him for a while based on the warrant we have. If his DNA matches the sample Cricket sent me, then we can hit the judge for the search warrant.*

Athen ran a hand over his face. "So, Tyler. You like to know what's going on."

"I'm a control freak. I'll admit it. I need to know what's going on in my home."

Geez, Louise. This guy's a wingnut. "Technically, it's my home. I pay you rent. You like spying on me and Grady? Is that what you mean?"

"Yeah. Sorta." Tyler shrugged but had the grace to look embarrassed. "People are always watching me. And so, I like to watch other people. I, ah, I'm a bit of a voyeur."

"You like to watch gay sex?"

Tyler's face turned beet red. "That's not what I meant."

"Oh, cut the crap, Tyler. Why have you been watching me?"

"I get . . . obsessed with things. I like you and Grady. I'm just no good with tenants." His was grinding his teeth. "And your dog is shedding everywhere."

Athen stared at him. "We keep that place spotless."

Tyler shrugged. "I don't like dogs."

That was news to Athen. Now he was afraid for Bella's

safety if they stayed at the house any longer. He took a calming breath. "And what is your relationship with Natasha?"

Tyler looked confused. "Natasha?"

Paulie jabbed at the photo. "Natasha. You've forgotten about her?"

"There is no relationship with Natasha. I don't know her. Somebody took that photo of us."

"Where and when?" Athen asked.

He stared at the photo then glanced up at Athen then Paulie. "Wait a second. You're saying she's the missing person?"

"Yeah. Been all over the news. Don't tell me you missed it." Athen couldn't keep the sarcasm from his tone.

"I don't know her. I'm telling you. And I know that's gonna sound weird because that photo was taken in her apartment."

Athen went still. *Holy crap. He's trying to tell me that if we find his DNA in her apartment that's why. Smart move, Tyler. Smart move.*

"When?" Paulie asked.

"Maybe two, three months ago. I know her friend, Isla. They're a weird pair."

"How so?" Athen asked.

"They hate each other," Tyler said.

Athen sensed Paulie growing rigid beside him. A glance in his direction showed that he'd kept his game face on.

Tyler seemed oblivious. He ran a hand through his hair. "I guess you could say they're frenemies. Isla took me there one night trying to talk me into investing in this reality show they wanted to produce." Recognition flashed across his features. "We rang Natasha's bell but got no response. There's a landlord. Cameron something. Deck. That's it. Cameron Deck. His dad used to be an old-time producer. I'd never heard of him, but Isla said he was famous. Said he had lineage." He rolled his eyes. "Anyway, Cameron came out front and let us in. He was involved in this show idea, too. Told us Natasha had been on a date and was coming home. He had a whole presentation package. I thought the concept was great to be honest."

"What was the general idea of it?" Athen asked.

"Beverly Hills starlets getting murdered. You know. Dying for fame."

Athen stared at him. *Wow. Everything he's telling me seems plausible.*

Tyler poked a finger at the photo frame. "I entertained the idea of investing until the fight happened."

Athen and Paulie exchanged looks. "What fight?" Paulie asked.

Tyler shifted in his seat and rubbed at his scalp again. "Let me explain. I met Isla . . . I wanna say a year, year and a half ago. She works or *was* working in that high-end cigar bar over on Brighton Way. You know, they play fantastic Cuban jazz from the golden age, give you the good cigars, and charge a fortune for bottle service. I was going there a lot. There's a group of these girls working there. All hot. All super sweet. There's a girl called Felice. I liked her the most. She's the least pretentious of all of them."

Athen knew this had to be Felice Farmer. Next on his interview list.

"Isla knew who I was and slipped me a few extra bottles of champagne here and there. One night she mentions her friend who's a princess and how they're doing this show. I went over there with her. Like I said, Cameron let us into his apartment. You ever been in there?"

Athen shook his head. "No. Why?"

"It looks like something from an old silent movie. I mean, it's amazing. I was pretty . . . impressed. Each item he has, came from some movie set or other. His great grandfather worked with Theda Bara. You know, the original vamp from the nineteen-twenties. Together, he and Isla wove this spell over me, man. Here is this apartment dedicated to the first vamp in history. And now we have a real Arab princess." He glanced from Athen to Paulie. "In case you don't know, Theda Bara was an anagram for Arab Death.

"The Hollywood moguls claimed she was a princess and drank blood, and all kinds of crazy stuff. Deck's telling me this story about this new princess. New to Hollywood. He makes me sit on the throne that Theda Bara used in *Cleopatra*. He really has some fantastic set pieces. And I know they're the real deal. He has big Hollywood coffee table books with some of those items photographed in them." He lapsed into silence.

"Go on," Athen said. "So, what was this fight about?"

"Oh. Well, Isla and Cameron gave me the presentation package. I can show it to you if you haven't seen it. I was sold on the show's premise. Especially since they were going to try and make it look real." He lifted his hands and dropped them. "They were waiting for Natasha to come home. Isla went to use the bathroom and Cameron heard Natasha at the front gate and went and greeted her. We went with her to her apartment. She acted excited to meet me. She's a gorgeous girl. Fun. Flirty." He paused, then sort of giggled. "Beautiful teeth. She wanted a photo. Cameron took one. He texted it to me. I'd never met a real princess before." He paused.

"What was your impression of her?" Athen asked.

"Gorgeous. Elegant yet naïve. A very alluring combination. The photo came out well, as you can see. Cameron encouraged me to post it to Instagram, which I did. Hey, that will back up what I'm telling you. It's still on there probably. I captioned it, *So, I met me a princess.* Got a lot of likes, like twenty thousand. That's why I printed it out and framed it."

"So, you're a bit of a star fucker," Athen said.

Tyler blinked. "I haven't thought about her much since then." He leaned forward. "She's a wackadoodle. So's Isla. I haven't been to the cigar bar since. Those girls freaked me out."

"What happened?" Paulie asked.

"Everything was great until Natasha found out Isla was in Cameron's apartment. She kept saying, "I have to get changed. I have to get changed." Next thing I knew, Isla was in there screaming about how Natasha was wearing her dress. She flew at her like a wild thing. We had a real cat fight on our hands. It was horrible. Cameron and I tried to break it up, but it was vicious. There was hair-pulling and slapping. Then came the punches. We got scratched and *bitten* if you can believe it. Those women can fight! Let me tell you it's not as much fun as watching a real-life cat fight as it is on daytime soap operas."

Athen said nothing for a moment. He had nothing to gain by continuing to probe Tyler further. Everything he'd said could—and would—be verified. He'd ask Deck himself, or better yet, if Soup was still there, she could ask him about the fight. And checking Tyler's Instagram account would be easy. Soup had talked to Isla, but as far as he knew, she hadn't mentioned the fight.

"And you haven't seen her since?" Paulie asked.

"Hell, no. I haven't been in touch with any of them. I had to get a tetanus shot!" He flicked a hand at the photo. "I never went back to the cigar bar. I felt used. Lied to."

And he doesn't like dogs. Athen wanted to bite the guy himself. "Lied to? How?"

"I don't know. Just a feeling I got. The whole thing was weird. Desperate somehow. Can't put my finger on it."

So, he doesn't know Natasha's not a princess. I don't think he's lying to me. "Excuse me a moment," Athen said, getting to his feet. He left the room and called Soup. She picked up instantly.

"Hey, boss."

"Did Isla Sanchez mention having a fight with Natasha?"

"No, she didn't."

"You were in the middle of telling us about your conversation with Isla when I made the connection with the photo in my pantry. According to Tyler, the two women had a vicious cat fight in Natasha's apartment. I want to know if Cameron can verify it. Tyler says they both tried to break it up," Athen said. "Another thing. Cameron says he last saw Natasha walking out of her apartment two days ago with the dress to have it cleaned for today. He said that was at two p.m."

"Yeah. And he's sticking to his story about the cleaners. I'll ask him about the fight. I tried to get a name for the cleaners earlier but all he told me was it was some kind of Chinese laundry."

"He told me the same thing. Anything you can find out would be great, thanks."

Soup responded, "Something's not adding up. Well, a lot of things aren't. Isla told me she got a text message from Natasha asking her to come get the dress yesterday, but when she got there, Cameron Deck wouldn't let her onto the property."

"She got the text yesterday? But nobody's seen or heard from Natasha for two days now. Can you ask her if she'll give us permission to access her phone? I'd like to check the data. The same thing happened to Maggie. She got a message. *Go get my cat.* Then Deck refuses her entry. I checked her phone. The text appears to have come from Natasha's phone. So, either she's alive and playing games. Or somebody has her phone and is texting her friends." Athen's frustration mounted. "And that damned red dress. What the hell happened to it? I'm not sure which is true. That she wanted Isla to go get it, or that she wanted to wear it today. And please let me know what Deck says about Tyler."

"Sure. We just got here. I went to see Maggie Harman, but she was busy getting her windows replaced. They're going ahead with the TV show."

145

"The show must go on," Athen murmured.

"I know, right?" Soup said. "I did ask Maggie if Natasha knows Tyler. I showed her a copy of the photo of them and she kind of snorted and said they'd met once, but Natasha wanted people to think that something was simmering between them. Maggie's words. Not mine. Maggie thinks Natasha was hoping he might ask her out, but he never did."

"Okay, thanks." That corroborated Tyler's statement. Athen returned to the interview room. Tyler and Paulie were sharing a joke about something. Tyler smiled at him. Huh. The guy seemed super relaxed for some reason.

"Hey, boss," Paulie said. "Mr. James consented to give us his DNA so we could exclude him from the apartment search. He understands we needed two swabs in case something happens to the first sample."

Nice one, Paulie! Athen smiled. "Excellent. Tyler, if you don't mind, we'll need fingerprints too. Just to eliminate them from the multitude we found in her apartment."

"Multitude? Wow. You know. I don't mind, but there's something weird. I thought it was strange that for a princess she had no household staff. Apartment was nice. Bit sterile. She fights like a street hooker though. I kinda liked her until she turned feral. Not very princessy. You never can tell, right?" He held up his hands and wiggled his fingers. "So how do we do this?"

"I'll take you to the charge desk. Relax, you're not being charged. That's just where we do things," Athen said. "After they print you, I'll make sure someone drives you home. And just so you know, Grady and I will be moving out by the weekend."

Tyler looked startled, then relieved. "Sorry to see you go," he said, not sounding it.

Sure you are. "Thanks for your time," Athen said, keeping it pleasant. He texted Lucy with his update and knew she would make sure Tyler was kept on the premises until they could exclude his DNA from Cricket's case. *Maybe he's not good for Natasha's disappearance, but I'm certain he's good for Allie Madden.*

Athen hoped never to see the guy again unless it was to watch him standing trial for the murder of Allie Madden.

CHAPTER ELEVEN

Athen and Paulie headed to Lucy's office. The rental car from Natasha's place had yet to be towed to the precinct's garage.

"We've been slammed," Lucy said, shifting a lock of hair from her forehead. "I will let you know as soon as it's here. We're all anxious for close examination. And I know you want to get hold of the dashboard camera."

"Thanks. I appreciate it. Has our computer guy, Terry Stein, found anything useful in his search on Natasha's laptop?" Athen asked her.

"No. He says it's a dead end. While we're waiting for the dashboard cam, are you going to the cigar bar to talk to Felice Farmer?"

"Yep. And If we find out which cleaners got hold of Natasha's laundry, I'll go talk to them. Maybe Felice knows where Natasha goes. After that, I'll come back here and chase up our contacts."

"Find me something," Lucy begged. "You've got no idea the looney tunes that have been calling here with crazy-assed leads on Natasha. We even got a psychic from that shop on Wilshire Boulevard telling me she was abducted by aliens."

Athen grinned. "That was *my* first guess."

Lucy laughed then. "Yeah, mine too," she joked.

"Have any of the callers revealed that they know Natasha's not a real princess?" Paulie asked.

"No. Which means Natasha and her friend Maggie did a damned good job of hiding her real identity." Lucy shot

Athen an anxious look. "Hopefully, we'll get something out of the husband. Or Felice Farmer."

"We all want that," Athen said.

She nodded. "Okay, cool. Let me know if you need backup on the spaceship that allegedly abducted her. They can be real tricky with all those lights and stuff. I'll let you know as soon as the dashboard cam's in house. Oh, and I'll call Soup and Lorne and update them. We gotta make sure Cameron Deck corroborates Tyler's story about the fight."

"Roger that." Athen was happy that Lucy's sense of humor was still going strong, but he felt as though he was going nowhere fast. As he headed outside, it felt like he was moving underwater through cement shoes. Nothing was falling into place. Yet.

"What do you think about Tyler?" Paulie asked as they reached the car.

"He's got balls of steel that one."

Paulie grinned. "Couldn't have put it better myself. He seemed quite happy to help. Which means he thinks we're all complete morons. Or, he had nothing to do with Natasha's disappearance at all. I just scrolled through his Instagram. And it's just like he says. That photo was taken just over three months ago. Right before you moved in."

Athen tried to relax. He'd noticed since moving to Beverly Hills that he was grinding his teeth a lot. His friendship with Tyler was over, and it bothered him that he hadn't sensed the guy's fastidiousness was borne of a need to control beyond anything Athen had experienced before. *He might not have killed Natasha. She's lucky. But what are the odds there are two psycho killers in her orbit?*

"I think he might have been attracted to Natasha. Thank God she got into that fight and he realized she wasn't going to be easy pickings," he said as he slid behind the wheel and buckled up.

"That is probably really accurate," Paulie said. "Something

about that guy really creeps me out though. I think he probably did kill the woman in Virgina Beach."

"I think so too." Athen couldn't wait for the DNA results. The sooner Cricket got the little weasel arrested and off the streets, the safer all women would be. As he made the turn onto Brighton Way, he tried not to think about the move he and Grady had ahead of them. Wherever he went would have to be dog-friendly, in a city that was becoming increasingly dog unfriendly.

He parked in a loading zone near the club and slotted his BHPD ID card onto the dashboard so he wouldn't get a ticket. That was another thing he wouldn't miss. The overzealous parking enforcement patrol at his home. He turned off the engine and checked Paulie's phone for Tyler's Instagram account.

There was the photo of him and Natasha. He got a few comments but over twenty-thousand likes. Wow. He scrolled up. Lots of photos of Tyler with hot young women.

"Fancies himself as a real ladies' man," Paulie said.

Athen nodded. "Sure does." He hadn't alerted Felice Farmer to their pending arrival. He wanted her slightly off guard. It was four-thirty by the time they reached the entrance, but there were already several well-dressed people waiting to enter. Things started early in Tinseltown. Despite the glamorous reputation, it was an industry business with start times of around three a.m. 11pm was a late closing in a city that was usually done by 10. He suspected the Cuban club here had a much later off-switch,

The doorman was dressed better than most people headed to the opera at Disney Concert Hall. He gave Athen a disparaging once-over. "I think you can go home and change," he said.

"Well, *I think* you can let me in, or I'll come up with a reason to arrest you," Athen said, flashing his badge.

The doorman opened the door, murmuring, "Ice, ice." He was wired for sound. Interesting. Athen suspected that the club was either providing drugs for a price, or there were illegally employed staff members inside. *Ice* covered a lot of sins in his experience. He entered, Paulie shouting in his ear, "He just alerted somebody to us being in here."

Athen nodded. Despite the obnoxious bouncer, he loved this place. It had been decked out like an old-fashioned speakeasy from the 1950s. His vibe for sure. Low-lying sofas, leather club chairs, dreamy wall sconces, candles flickering from inlaid crevices. It was a startling contrast with the mundane world outside. He visualized making out with Grady in a dark corner and couldn't wait to try it.

From somewhere the booming sound of Cuban artists Rene Alvarez y Los Astros performing "Yo soy Congo" filled the dark space. He knew this one-hit wonder very well. His father had loved music from the Golden Age of Cuban jazz and had played the record often. That was another thing Athen could do now; unearth his vast collection of records that he'd put into storage and bring them to the new place.

"Can I help you?" a young woman asked.

Athen narrowed his gaze. The room was filled with cigar smoke and it burned his eyes now. It had been so long since he'd been in an establishment that allowed smoking, he'd forgotten how unpleasant it could be.

"Felice?" he asked. She sure looked different with makeup, a bustier, and her hair teased into a dramatic beehive. She wore a black leather mini skirt and her dramatic, long legs were encased in gossamer black stockings. The whole effect was topped off with towering six-inch black high heels. "Wow, you look amazing."

She laughed. "Thanks." She crinkled her forehead and laid a hand on his chest. "Should I be offended?"

"Not at all. I know you're working. Is there some place we

can talk privately?"

"Yes. Follow me." She enveloped them both in a seductive smile as she led them toward the back of the club. She didn't totter or stumble, despite the spindly heels of her shoes. As Athen followed, he realized she had seams in her stockings. She was a vision of mid-century feminine beauty.

"If I wasn't married—" Paulie flicked his hand up and down as though his fingers were on fire, making Athen laugh.

As they walked, Athen took in the tables of men smoking and drinking. There were tables filled with couples snuggling over champagne. *Huh.* No food. What a smart idea this place was. No food meant a lot less trouble for the staff.

Felice led them to the back door, where people trooped up the stairs. Athen was surprised to see a payphone mounted on one wall, circa 1950s. "Does it work?" he asked her.

"Oh, yes. "And it only takes a dime. Just like the good ol' days."

The music still pumped out over the sound system but had now migrated to *Israel Cachao* López's mambo classic, Pamprana." Athen tried not to snap his fingers and swivel his hips to the music, even as he promised himself he was going to start playing all his records again.

"Is there any news on Natasha?" Felice asked as they stepped outside to a staircase leading to a small parking lot. She reached into the bosom of her bustier and extracted a cheroot, lighting it with a Zippo lighter. It looked vintage to Athen's critical eye.

"No," Athen said. "I don't have any news. And I don't mean to rush things, but I need to know why you wanted to speak to me privately. Do you have information that can help us locate Natasha?"

Felice drew on her cheroot and moved her weight from foot to foot. He knew three things in that moment. Her shoes were uncomfortable. She was very nervous. More than that, she was afraid. "I think she's dead," she said, blowing out a thin plume of smoke. Athen had never seen a woman smoke a cigar the way Felice did. It was thinner than the typical cigar, but she smoked it like a cigarette, dragging deeply on it. The effect of her whole ensemble was a bunch of smoke and mirrors. Just like the whole Natasha King case.

"What makes you say so?" Athen asked.

"I've never known anyone to play so many men at the same time. She had guys at the building constantly. A few she was sleeping with, or *wanted* to sleep with. Some who wanted to sleep with her. And, she had a stalker, you know."

"Really? No, I didn't know." Athen glanced at Paulie, who mirrored his surprise. "Who was stalking her?"

"I don't know. She wouldn't say. All I know is, she didn't want Cameron to know because she was worried he would throw her out." She puffed on the cheroot again, glancing around as though checking for skullduggery in the back of the Beverly Hills bar.

"Why would he throw her out? She paid for a year's rent in advance," Paulie said.

Felice made a *tsking* sound. "I don't know. She just begged me not to say anything. I saw lots of guys here, but she told me one guy was showing up at odd times of the day."

"Did she give you a name?" Athen recalled Deck telling him two men had turned up the night before. He still had no clue who they were.

"No. She didn't. Of course," she went on. "She didn't want to say anything to Cameron, because he was already pissed that so many guys were coming over. It's none of his business what we do. Way too intrusive if you want my honest opinion." She paused. "Then again, there was the fight. S'pose you heard about that?"

"We heard about it," Athen said. "Were you there?"

"No. But Cameron complained about it. He was mad because Tyler James was interested in being involved in the show, then went running for the hills."

Since she wasn't there, anything she told Athen was hearsay.

She went on. "Cameron was always there. Ready to pounce. He's scared off a couple of my boyfriends."

"Do you know anyone that Natasha actually dated?" Athen asked.

She shrugged, tamping out the cigar on the stair handrail beside her. She tucked the cheroot and the lighter back into her bustier. "Lots of them."

"Do you know if she was involved with Tyler James?" Athen asked.

"No. That was a bit of wishful thinking. Look, what I think you need to do is check out that guy from the consulate. Jamie Fahdi. He was over here all the time. Real obsessed with her."

"What about her husband?" Paulie asked.

She gave him a look of disgust. "The gay guy?" She rolled her eyes. "He's in it to win it. He needed money. She gave him the money. She just paid for some fancy dental work for him. She married him even though she already had a green card." She shoved up her breasts with her hands, so they almost poured over the top of her bustier. "I hope I'm wrong, but my money's on Jamie Fahdi. I have no idea what she saw in him, but I try and keep as far away as possible from him."

"What makes you think she's dead?" Athen asked.

Felice took a deep breath. "Because she never, *ever* would leave that cat." For the first time, apart from fear, her emotions seemed real. "I think something really bad happened to her."

The words lingered between them for a moment.

"And that's all you can tell me?" Athen asked.

"Yeah." Her eyes glistened with unshed tears. "I didn't have the money to invest in the TV show, so we've drifted apart a bit. I'm no longer on the inside."

"One more question. Do you know of a Chinese laundry where she takes her clothes?" Athen asked.

She frowned at him a moment. "That would be Wong's, over on Beverly Boulevard, but I don't think she's going to them anymore."

"Why not?" Athen asked.

"Because she had a bad falling out with them over a stupid dress."

"What falling out?"

"They ruined it." Felice shook her head. "Isla Sanchez has been pestering for her to return the dress, because it belongs to her, but Natasha was petrified to tell her it was destroyed."

"How did they ruin it?" Paulie asked.

"Whatever cleaning solution they used, they shrunk it. Natasha kept pretending the dress was okay. Kept promising to return it. She wasn't trying to keep it, but she was afraid of a lawsuit, because that's what Isla was threatening. As an immigrant to this country, she can't have a blemish on her record. She's been going crazy trying to find a replacement dress because the duplicate Wong's made for her was a disaster."

Pretended it was okay. Athen held back a long sigh. *Pretense seemed to be Natasha's stock in trade.* "She got a duplicate?"

"Wong's has a cleaning side to the business, but they're also a salon that specializes in duplicating couture gowns. They do it for all the Beverly Hills housewives. On the QT of course. People pay a lot to get those dresses made. Usually, you can't tell the duplicate from the original. It's a closely guarded secret but nobody would ever tell because the customers don't want to admit they're being cheap, and Wong's doesn't want to out their clients."

"Besides which, stealing somebody's designs is illegal," Paulie said.

"Um, yeah." Felice looked nervous. "They're like the Heidi

Fleiss of the fashion industry." She gave them a twisted, sad smile. "I actually felt bad for Tash. She spent a pretty penny having that duplicate made. You talked to Isla yet?" When neither Athen nor Paulie responded she said, "Tash showed me the duplicate and it's pretty bad. I could have done better, and I can't even sew a button on a shirt. She's been in a real quandary over it."

"Beverly Boulevard, you say?" Athen asked.

"Yeah. Let me tell you, that dress cost her almost as much as it would have to simply replace it, but she can't find the exact same dress." Something on her person beeped. "That's my phone. I gotta run." She dashed past them back inside the club. She turned at the door, the fearful look back in her gaze. "Don't get heavy with the people at Wong's. They're trained to deny everything. Just be nice and they'll be helpful." She banged the door on her way back inside.

For a moment, Athen and Paulie stood, saying nothing.

"Well, at least we understand the mystery of the red dress a little better," Paulie said.

"Yeah." Athen put a call through to Lucy and patched Soup into the conversation. He quickly told them about the conversation.

"Wow," Lucy said. "We've had a lot of complaints about many of our local businesses, but that isn't one that's familiar to me. You going there now?"

"Yes. Unless you have good news for me."

"None yet. I still have Tyler James here. He's busy playing the superstar getting selfies with everyone. We just got a group of school kids in for a tour. He's posing for photos with them now."

"Geez," Athen said.

"I know, right? Still waiting on DNA, still waiting for the dashboard cam, but the car is on its way here."

Soup spoke up. "Deck claimed not to know anything about

a fight between the two women, but then changed his story. Everything he said backs up what Tyler told you. I'll tell you something else he casually slipped into the conversation. He said Isla confided in him that she dated Tyler James. Once. Said he was a real weirdo and she wouldn't see him again."

"Smart girl," Athen said. "If she told him in confidence, that means she probably didn't tell Natasha. Paulie and I are heading to Wong's to find out about the red dress and the laundry Natasha was supposed to take there. You should talk to Isla Sanchez right now. We can hit the post office right after it."

"Okay," Soup said. "Talk soon."

Athen and Paulie made it to Wong's in four minutes. The salon was hard to miss with its leopard print façade bedecked with huge pink bows. Athen didn't think he would trust a dressmaker with such garish taste. *But what do I know?*

There was a closed sign on the door as they approached, but Athen spotted people moving around inside the salon. Paulie jumped out of the car and raced over, hammering on the door. Once Athen parked and made his way there, it was obvious two women were hiding behind the counter. They were visible through the window via the mirror that lined the back wall.

"This is the police!" he shouted. "We know you're in there. We can see you!"

The two figures dropped to the floor.

Athen cursed under his breath then caught sight of the store's phone number stenciled on the window. He called it. A woman answered.

"Wong's," she announced breathlessly.

"Don't hang up. This is Lieutenant Athen Mavromatis with the Beverly Hills Police. I don't want to talk about the phony clothing. I'm chasing up an active missing person's case. If you don't open the door right now, I'll get a search warrant and I'll make your life hell. I promise you that."

The two women peeped at him over the edge of the long store counter. He held his badge to the window, and they exchanged glances. One of the women got up and made her way slowly to the front door. As she did this, she ended her call from Athen.

"I cannot believe Felice Farmer called and warned them," Paulie muttered. "What's she playing at?"

"I don't know but I plan to mess with her hairdo," Athen responded.

The woman opened the door and stared at Athen in a haughty way. "What do you want?" she demanded.

Nice. "We're here about Natasha King—"

The woman's facial expression brightened. "You're here to pick up her laundry?"

"I'm the police," Athen said, his temper shredding. "I don't pick up people's laundry."

"Can I check your ID?" she asked.

He stepped inside, Paulie close behind him. Athen handed her his credential wallet and as she studied it, he took in the luxurious décor, briefly admiring the nod to old-fashioned sewing rooms. Antique modeling forms, large black and white photos featuring old-time movie stars in various stages of frilly undergarments, and walls stuffed with vintage sewing machines, spools of colorful threads, books, knitting needles . . . all of it gave an effect of having stepped back in time.

She handed the wallet back to him. "You're better looking on TV."

Gee, thanks. "And what's your name?" he asked.

"You may call me Mrs. Wong." She wore a tight black sheath dress with a gold and black scarf knotted at her throat. He recognized it as vintage Hermes. He knew the design was called *Ceintures et Liens* and that it retailed at around seven hundred bucks. His sister was a big fan of the line. He and Grady had bought her a similar scarf when she'd completed chemo. It had been a huge investment for them. As for Mrs. Wong, clearly, there was big money in producing knockoffs.

The woman's spindly black heels clicked against the polished floorboards as she led him to the back of the store. "Somebody was supposed to pick up her laundry yesterday. She has a three thousand and twenty-seven-dollar bill with us. I've tried calling her, but she doesn't answer. Unusual for her. She usually picks up straight away."

She reached the counter and stood behind it. Her shoulders dropped a little indicating she was a little more comfortable now. Maybe she thought the marble slab between them was a safe buffer zone.

Paulie strolled around the store as Athen continued talking to her. He was Athen's eyes and ears.

"How can I help you?" Mrs. Wong asked, flicking an annoyed glance at Paulie.

"Maybe you haven't heard but Natasha King is missing." Athen watched for her reaction.

She seemed skeptical. "What do you mean, missing?"

"Vanished. Last time anyone saw her was when she left her apartment to come here."

Mrs. Wong scoffed. "She didn't come here. She owes us money."

"How do you know she didn't come here? I didn't say *when* she was last seen."

Mrs. Wong's eyes hardened. Her hands fluttered to her elegant, glossy bob, her French manicure impeccable as she moved her fingers beneath her hairline. He hoped like hell she didn't have knuckle dusters or a flick knife under there. She was a scary lady. So much so, he almost took a step back.

"When did she last come here?"

"Two weeks ago. She claimed the dress we made for her

was—" Mrs. Wong stopped speaking. It was obvious she hadn't meant to say that.

"It's okay," he said. Out of the corner of his eye he caught Paulie trying to catch his attention. Athen shot him a swift glance. Paulie pointed to his eye then a spot above one of the shelves. *Ah. Cameras. Good.*

"We know about the dress," Athen said. "So, you made a reproduction of it and from all accounts the duplicate was terrible."

Her mouth dropped open. "That girl lied about my dress. And I have proof." She stared at Athen defiantly. "You want to see my proof?"

"Sure."

His response seemed to surprise her. "You're much nicer than the other man who came in to ask about it yesterday."

"What man?" Athen asked.

She closed her eyes a moment. "Do I need a lawyer?"

He gaped at her. "No. Why?"

"Because the man who came in about this dress threatened legal action."

"Who was he?" Athen asked.

Mrs. Wong looked distressed for the first time. "This could kill my business if he finds out I talked. But he was so mean! It was the mayor."

CHAPTER TWELVE

"The mayor of Beverly Hills came in about the dress? When?" Athen asked.

"Yesterday, like I said."

"What time?"

"Right before closing. He had another man with him. I've never seen him before." She gave Athen a terrifying smile that reminded him of cannibal tribe members who were proud of their pointed teeth. All the easier to tear into human flesh. "I have them both on tape."

Athen said, "I'm happy to hear it. Can you show me the tape?"

Paulie joined him at the counter as Mrs. Wong said, "It was the strangest thing." She thinned her lips. "He didn't want to pay for her cleaning either." She turned on her heel and opened a door behind her. It was narrow, and almost invisible until she pressed on it. It whisked open. Behind her as she stepped into another room, he spotted rows of workers pounding away on sewing machines. Many of them wore face masks. He wondered if this was a hangover from the recent coronavirus safety measures, or if they always wore them.

Mrs. Wong stepped back into the salon, closing the door behind her. She returned to the counter with a large folder. On closer inspection he realized it was a portable display device. Almost a cross between an iPad and a writer's journal. He'd never seen anything quite like it. "It's a one-of-a-kind fashion studio portfolio from Japan," she said. "A lifesaver for me."

She pressed some buttons and next thing, on the left side of the open portfolio, were thumbnails of images taken over various dates. "As you will see, she is hard to miss, this one. Last time she came in was two weeks ago."

He and Paulie saw images and footage of Natasha King coming into the store, then footage of her showing Mrs. Wong the dress.

In the footage, a man came out of the secret door and studied the garment. Athen was quite taken by his dazzling presence. He emanated the kind of contained beauty and grace that he'd seen in ballerinas. Both male and female. His long grey hair was held back into a ponytail by a yellow tape measure. His form-fitting black shirt was covered in pins of various shapes and sizes.

"Who is the man with you?" Paulie asked.

"This is Franko. He is a designer from Spain. He works with me. He handles the toughest cases. Stains, shrinking, tears. There was damage to the original dress that we didn't do. She brought it in that way."

"This footage is amazingly clear," Athen murmured, trying to place his accent.

"Yes." Mrs. Wong nodded. "We are very detail-oriented, as I am about to explain."

The footage was timestamped from three weeks ago. "The stain appeared to be gasoline. She told us she'd done a car commercial for Ford. The dress couldn't be repaired completely. She'd allowed the stain to set too long. We checked with Ford by the way, thinking we could get their insurance to pay for the work since she fretted about the price. They said they never use models for their ads."

Another lie from Natasha. *When does this girl ever tell the truth?*

"I promised her we would try," Mrs. Wong said. "And we did."

Athen was speechless watching the vignettes unfolding.

All of them time and date stamped. Natasha was showing Mrs. Wong the dress.

"She kept saying she could see the stains and I'm telling you, none of us could. The stains you will see are very faint. In fact, hardly noticeable." Mrs. Wong's voice held a note of pride as she pointed at the dress.

"I don't see a stain." Paulie bent his head to study the footage. Athen couldn't see a stain either.

"That's amazing," Athen said.

Even though the interaction appeared to be very unpleasant, once again, Athen was struck by Natasha's natural beauty. He was staggered by the short, *very* short pale pink dress she wore. She looked like an elegant fairy as she hugged Mrs. Wong and Franko then left the store.

The next video was from two weeks ago. Natasha was back. Mrs. Wong was holding the dress up for her. "She asked us to reproduce the dress for her. It was the only way she would feel good about paying us for our work. So, I had Franco make one for her. She is smiling and happy now."

She stabbed a finger at another clip. Natasha picked up the dress and seemed to be happy with it but ran off quickly, the dress floating behind her as she carried the hanger over her shoulder.

"You won't believe this next part," Mrs. Wong said. "She came in the very next day with a *completely* different dress. She tried to pass it off as the one I'd given her the day before. But it's not even the same fabric!"

"Why would she do that? To try and get a refund or something?" Paulie asked.

"Worse than that. She wanted yet another duplicate made. She just wanted a free dress. I think this girl is crazy. She really thinks I can't tell my own work? She found a similar dress somewhere and threw gas on it to try and get a free dress out of me." Mrs. Wong sounded bitter.

Athen swallowed hard as he watched Natasha's wide grin turn to fury as she slammed on the counter and threw a stapler across the room. She kept shouting at Mrs. Wong and at one point appeared to try and slap her, but Mrs. Wong pulled back. Natasha missed. She took off with the dress, running out the door.

"She did not pay for the dress. She had someone bring in her dirty laundry two days ago. That idiot landlord of hers. He said nothing about her being missing. We refused the laundry because she owes us money. I didn't contact the police." Mrs. Wong's hand shook a little as she let her fingers walk down the next set of images. "That landlord told us she'd complained about our work. He showed me the fake dress. He was trying to return it. For credit. Credit?" Mrs. Wong's voice rose. "She owed me three months' worth of laundry service, and I'm telling you; it was *not* the dress we cleaned. Or the one we duplicated. As I said before, you can tell it's a different shade of red, and much smaller. Again, I refused it."

Athen and Paulie focused on the footage of Cameron Deck with a pile of laundry. Mrs. Wong shoved it aside and waved at him, shooing him off as he tried to hand back the red dress.

"He left it all here. The laundry and the dress. I didn't chase after him, but I put it all in a laundry bag. Now I'm glad I kept it. I have a little leverage that way. I have no idea what kind of game they're playing, but I wish somebody would teach me the rules."

Athen was disturbed that Deck had never told him he'd brought Natasha's laundry here. He said he'd seen her leaving her residence with it to bring it here. *Oh, my god. He claimed he didn't know the name of it when he'd been here the day before!*

Mrs. Wong tapped at another set of images and there was the mayor, Scott Aubrey, and another man, walking into the salon the night before.

To Athen's astonishment, the other man was Lorne Brand,

Athen's least favorite detective. Paulie bristled beside him.

"What did he want?" Paulie asked.

"He wanted her laundry back. And he wanted the red dress. He also wanted me to forgive her debt to me." Mrs. Wong looked from Paulie to Athen with an indignant expression. "Why would I do that? Even for the mayor?"

She has balls. Athen suspected the two men who'd showed up to Natasha's apartment building the night before were the mayor and Lorne Brand. Deck said they'd stopped by looking for Natasha. It would be easy to check against car license plates if they ever got access to the ALPR. Cameron Deck should have recognized the mayor, but then again, maybe not. Scott was only the mayor of Beverly Hills, not the entire city of Los Angeles. Unless he was very civic-minded, he wouldn't be aware of him. He would also have had no reason to know Lorne, in all likelihood. Had Deck recognized Brand when he and Soup went there today?

Athen excused himself for a moment and took Paulie over to the shop doorway, relaying his feelings. "Can you call Soup and ask her if Deck recognized Lorne today? I wanna know what the hell he was playing at, being the mayor's muscle."

"I'm on it. That guy's a moron. Allowing the mayor to play him like that." Paulie stepped outside, his brow knotted in fury.

Athen went out too, and called Lucy, reporting everything to her.

"The mayor did that? Holy shit show. I knew he was a useless tool. I'm gonna get hold of Brand and get him back here. I want to know why he was acting the heavy and didn't tell me about it. By the way, the owner of the car lot with the ALPR is demanding a warrant for the data. These people watch way too much TV. They get all their ideas from reruns of *Criminal Minds*. I just got it and I'll send over two detectives with it. We should get the data within the hour. Still waiting on the DNA results.

"Tyler James was getting antsy, then somebody suggested putting him in the conference room with one of his movies uploaded to the big screen in there. I stole a bag of microwave popcorn from the detectives' room. They're sore as hell. I had to promise them free tacos tomorrow. They drive a hard bargain."

Athen laughed. "And Tyler's fallen for the distraction?"

"Are you kidding me? He's mesmerized. Never met anyone who loves himself so much and I've met some really big celebrities. I stuck him in there with our media relations rep. She's smitten and he's lapping it up." She blew out a breath. "And in other good news, the rental car is being towed from Natasha's residence now. I am beyond furious with Scott. Can you get Mrs. Wong to give you the footage?"

"I'll try. Hopefully, she won't make me get a warrant. I wanna get the rest of the laundry, too. She says she threw it all into one bag. The fake dress could be the whole key to this. Or maybe it isn't. I have no idea where the real one is though."

"If you need that warrant, hit me back."

"Will do." Athen returned to Mrs. Wong.

Her steely gaze penetrated his. "So, she's really missing, the little princess?"

Athen leaned against the counter. He knew then that Mrs. Wong didn't believe that Natasha was royalty. "You don't think she's a princess?"

She rolled her eyes. "I deal with actual royalty, lieutenant. They make private appointments. They don't behave like street fighters. They don't dress inappropriately, and they always pay their bills. They don't bounce checks. I had to stop taking hers. No. Real members of those kinds of families are afraid of repercussions that reflect badly on their families. And another thing. She doesn't speak a word of Farsi. That was a big giveaway. Now. What do you need from me?"

Athen was beginning to like Mrs. Wong. A lot. "I'm wondering why the mayor chose to involve himself with this matter."

She looked at him. "You really don't know?"

"Don't tell me they're having an affair."

Mrs. Wong smiled. "Ha! He wishes. No. She's the dealer for their private poker games at his house every Wednesday night. He has a crazy mad crush on her. She can do no wrong." Her lips pulled into a thin, disapproving line.

Athen became aware of Paulie at his side. "Natasha's a poker dealer?"

"She's a professional poker player but she got into debt with the mayor after a bad losing streak. Apparently, she won a tournament in Vegas about a year ago. I believe close to a million. She's squandered a lot of it. She thinks she's slick, but I know the truth. She and Maggie Harman floated a rumor she got an inheritance. I don't believe it. Anyway, even if she did, she started losing badly, and owed money to two Vegas casinos.

"She even owed money to the Pechanga tribe down in their casino in Temecula. She can't show her face at any of these places until she's cleared the debts. She's stopped going to any of the casinos, even the local ones that offer her free stakes to play, so she's not entirely stupid. A couple of months ago she started dealing for Scott, and her friend Maggie pours the drinks and serves them canapes."

Geez, Louise. Nobody had told him any of this. "And you know all this because . . ."

She heaved a sigh. "My husband owns the cigar bar where they all work. Or, used to work. Natasha and Maggie wanted different things. Natasha is a fantastic card dealer. Men love her." Mrs. Wong's eyes glittered like diamonds. "In fact, I believe she almost worked off her entire debt to the casinos in Vegas doing their high-end weekend events. Maggie could tell you more about that because she travels there as her hand-maiden or some such rubbish."

Oh, my God. She hates her. Natasha must have asked Scott to intervene with Mrs. Wong. But if she asked him to intervene two days ago, that was after Cameron came in with her stuff.

I need to talk to Scott. If I can stand it. And if he and Lorne had gone to Natasha's after coming here last night, then he didn't know then that she's missing. When did he find out? "Thanks," he said, giving Mrs. Wong a smile.

"I have to apologize to you," she said, touching his hand. "I lied earlier."

"About what?"

"You're much better looking in real life than on TV."

Athen threw back his head and laughed.

One minute later, Athen and Paulie were back in Athen's vehicle, Natasha's laundry bag stowed in his trunk. Mrs. Wong's footage and photo collection were on their way electronically to him and Lucy.

She had also promised to file an official complaint with the police department on Scott and Lorne. One way or another, the money owed Mrs. Wong would be paid, if Athen had anything to do with it.

"Soup told me Lorne didn't go into Natasha's building. He went with her then went over to the rental car to try and find out why it hadn't been picked up yet," Paulie said. "She told me he seemed nervous and she realizes now he didn't want Deck to see him. He told her he's played poker with the mayor a time or two and the mayor called him a couple of days ago saying that Natasha was upset and wanted to get her laundry back. He asked Scott to go and get it for her because he didn't think Mrs. Wong would say no to him."

That made sense. So it was Cameron who solicited the mayor's help. Not Natasha herself.

Athen had intended to go to the post office but asked Soup

to go for him. He called her and explained that he wanted to speak to Isla Sanchez himself since he had one version of the dress and she would know if it was fake or if it was her original. Or the very clever duplicate.

"Great," she said. "I'll be in touch."

"I'll see you back at the station," Athen responded. He drove to Isla Sanchez's house as Paulie accessed her social media.

"She loves TikTok," he told Athen. "And boy, can she dance. She calls herself IslaDreams. Nice play in isle of dreams. She just posted on Instagram about Natasha. Interesting post. She wrote: *My friend is missing. Sometimes friends fight. Sometimes they say things they don't mean in the heat of the moment. True friendship is never serene. Hope you're safe, lovely Natasha.*"

"Huh," Athen muttered. "That last statement is probably true." He headed to Isla's location in what was known as the Golden Triangle. Bordered by Santa Monica Boulevard on one side, Crescent Drive on the other and bottoming out on Wilshire Boulevard, its rents were known to be even more ludicrous than other areas of The Flats, as they were known in Beverly Hills. He called Isla from outside her apartment building on Camden Drive. These girls must have been making huge tips at the cigar bar to afford the rents on these luxury places.

She was running out of the front of the building as his call connected with her phone. She looked up at him, mouthed "Shit!" and looked like she might run, but she walked over to him.

"I recognized you from the shooting video." She had a gym bag over her shoulder and was dressed head to toe in the ugliest lime green unitard with matching shoes and headband. She was so beautiful though she could have worn a sack and looked attractive.

"I'm here about the dress," Athen said.

"The dress?"

"The red one?"

"Oh." She swung the gym back to her other shoulder. "It arrived today. She mailed it to me."

Athen and Paulie exchanged swift glances. "Mind if we look at it?" Athen asked.

"I really don't have time."

"Make the time," Paulie said. "Unless you'd like to come down to the station and help us with our enquiries."

"Maggie said you were a pain in the ass. Hold on." She walked over to the front door of her building. Paulie raced to join her.

Athen loitered out front for a few moments. He checked his messages. Seventeen unreturned calls. None of them urgent work matters. He sent a quick text to Grady.

We need to move. Finding a hotel room for tonight. Love you.

Grady texted back. *Find one that's dog friendly. Bella and I are heading home. We love you.*

Athen texted back a bunch of emojis he hoped conveyed the joy and excitement he felt about that information.

Seconds later, Paulie and Isla were back. Paulie clutched the packaging the dress came in. He checked the tracking label against the one that was on the receipt Athen had photographed. One and the same. *That saves me a trip to the post office.*

"You can take it," Isla said. "I don't want it."

"But you fought with her. You threatened to sue her," Athen said.

"It's bad luck that dress. I can't ever wear it again knowing the stress it caused her. The stain isn't bad. I gave her hell because I knew she was lying about it. Mrs. Wong does excellent work and I knew the dress Natasha gave me a couple of weeks ago was a fake. She wanted this dress so badly I . . ." She shook her head. "I never wanted things to go this far. And now, I really do have to go." She marched off down the street, slinging her gym bag over the other shoulder again.

"High drama," Paulie said. "Where to now, boss?"

"Back to the station. We need to start a war room." He tucked the dress and its torn packaging into the trunk. Things were coming together, but there were still so many things they didn't know. He stood at the trunk, lid up, for so long Paulie came to stand beside him.

"What are you thinking?"

"Just when I think we've got things lined up, all our ducks in a row, we get another cannonball out of the sky. I can't figure out if Natasha was targeted by casino gangsters, a disgruntled guy. She's got so many guys dancing on strings around her. The dress. Man. That was I think, a huge waste of time."

Paulie said nothing for a moment. "Maybe. Maybe not. I don't think Isla killed her but why didn't Cameron Deck tell us he was the one who took the laundry to the cleaners?"

"I don't know. I want to view that footage again," Athen said. "Maybe Natasha was in a car out front. Something. We need to talk to Deck again."

"Yeah, we do. Security cameras maybe?"

Athen nodded. "There's a bank across the road from Wong's."

Paulie smiled. "And banks have security footage."

Athen got a call. It was Lucy. *911. Get back here.* That was all. He and Paulie got back into the car and headed to the station.

"We still haven't heard what the husband has to say, have we?" Paulie asked as Athen tried reaching Lucy. The call went to her voicemail.

"Nope. Can you call the detective in New York?" Athen asked. "I sent you his number earlier."

Paulie got busy. Seconds later he said, "Voicemail. Leaving him a message now. I wonder what the hell's going on at the station?"

Twelve seconds later they were pulling into the compound parking lot. Neither Paulie or Athen spoke as they took in the array of US Marshals, a SWAT unit and abundance of uniformed police officers swarming the street-level lot.

A couple of officers tried to shoo Athen away until he flashed his badge. Athen spied Cricket now wearing an FBI flack jacket, coming out of the building. Athen parked and turned off the ignition. He and Paulie stood, watching as Cricket and a team of other marshals escorted a heavily shackled Tyler James out of the building. Tyler looked stunned.

Athen's phone rang. It was Lucy. "Just saw you pull in from my office window. Tyler James tested positive for the DNA on Allie Madden's clothing and the skin underneath her fingernails. Unfortunately, he doesn't match any of the DNA found at our scene—so far. SID is going to go over the crime scene again. We haven't found trace evidence pointing to a different suspect. Or any suspect for that matter."

"I thought there were two different blood types," Athen said. He desperately wanted to get a closer look at Tyler who was being loaded into the SWAT vehicle.

"Yes, there are," Lucy said. "But we don't know whose. We need probable cause to get the landlord's DNA. It wouldn't hurt if we could check his body for injuries. Again, we only think he's the one who's been doing a bang-up job cleaning out that place."

"He had a two-day head-start on us," Athen said. "Where are they taking Tyler?"

The crowd gathered in the central courtyard started moving back as the SWAT vehicle shot out of the driveway.

"Men's Central Jail," Lucy said, sounding as bitter and demoralized as Athen felt.

"Fingerprints, that's all we've got on Cameron Deck, and there's no reason those wouldn't be in there. He apparently repainted Natasha's place right before she moved in six

172

months ago. He emailed us receipts for the paint and rollers. That's why the fingerprints were up so high on the walls. He says the second set of prints probably belong to some handyman he picked up outside Home Depot to help him do the job. He has no idea who the guy is. Paid him in cash."

"So, we got nothing."

"Yet." Lucy paused. "Cricket's case is federal. He has jurisdiction. I couldn't fightd extradition. They're escorting Tyler back to Virginia Beach after he cools his heels at Men's Central tonight."

"That's gonna freak him out. Are we still gonna do a raid on the house two doors down from mine?"

"Tomorrow. No rush now that he's off the streets. It pisses me off that Cricket wouldn't let us keep him here overnight, but I get it. He doesn't want us interviewing him again. He's focused on the Allie Madden case."

"As he should be," Athen said. "Even if it means we still have a missing girl and no obvious suspect."

"Right. And if we do end up finding anything linking Tyler to her disappearance and or, homicide, it would be years, if ever, that we'd get him back here to stand trial. This day just blows, don't it?" Lucy asked.

CHAPTER THIRTEEN

With the arrest over and the SWAT vehicle gone, Athen and Paulie made their way into the station. It was high tech and gorgeous, but as Lucy often reminded them, obsolete. They passed the bank of 911 operators and got a wave from a few of them. He and Paulie waved back.

Lucy came to greet them. "I've got you an office with plenty of wall space, some computers, a fax machine, desks, phones. What else do you need right now?"

They stepped inside. The place was huge. And perfect. "I'd like you and Soup to join us when you can." Athen began assembling his laptop on the first desk he spotted.

Lucy nodded. "She's on her way. Text her and let her know you're in here. I need to contact the judge who signed off on Cricket's warrant. I'm hoping because I played nice about Tyler being whisked away, he might grant me permission to get a DNA swab out of Cameron Deck."

"Excellent," Athen said. His phone rang. "Hold on, chief, it's Albert Ngo, the New York detective who's helping us out with Gary Goldman."

"Oh, right. Natasha's husband." She perched on the edge of his desk as Paulie pulled up a chair in front of it.

Athen took the call. "Hey, Albert. I hope you don't mind, but I've got you on loudspeaker with my precinct captain, Lucy Lane, and my partner, Paulie Hansen." He noticed Paulie perking up at his words. Partner. It felt right.

"No problem. I'm just grabbing an espresso. So, if you're hear background noise, that's why. Hang on. I gotta add sugar." Athen grinned as Albert banged something on the other line. "Anyway, I had to wait for Goldman to show up and boy is he a weirdo."

"In what way?" Athen asked.

"He looks homeless. He's trying to open this theater, which I guess you already know. Doesn't look half bad, but still needs a shitload of work. I think he drinks or drugs, can't tell which. He was shaky and sweaty. I asked about Natasha and he was ready to run."

"Run? Why?" Lucy asked.

"Apparently, he'd already heard she was missing. Said he didn't want to get blamed because they had a big fight a few days ago."

"Why would he get blamed if he's in New York and she's here?" Athen asked.

"He says they had a real blow out and she asked for a divorce. She hasn't been sending him money. He thinks, and these are his words, not mine, she has a fancy man she wants to be with. Said she needed a divorce and she'd think about a settlement."

"That makes no sense," Athen said. "She needs to stay married for two years for the green card process."

"He says she's an emotional girl and says things when she's angry. He fully expected her to call him and apologize but she hasn't sent him money she promised and he's in a bind here."

"When did they have this conversation?" Athen asked.

"Seven o'clock in the morning Eastern Daylight Time, which would be four o'clock Pacific. Two days ago."

They would add this to Natasha's timeline. Lucy moved over to the board to add it as Albert said, "Goldman's been counting on it. She was supposed to Venmo him the money that day. Never did. He's been trying to get hold of her ever since. No luck. Says it's not like her at all."

Athen, Lucy, and Paulie looked at each other.

"Anything else?" Paulie asked.

"No, not really. Except Goldman's supposed to be opening his theater for rehearsals in two weeks. Guess he's screwed. Unless you can locate his wife and get her to send him his money."

"Okay, thanks," Athen said. "Did he give any indication who might want to harm her?"

"Ha! He says she feuds with everybody. Again, his words. Not mine. Oh, I gotta book. Pal. You owe me." He ended the call.

For a moment, Athen pondered the conversation. "We're back at square one," he said. "Guess it's time to repack the snowball."

"Yeah," Lucy said. "As Arnold Schwarzenegger once said, I'll be back." She hoisted herself off his desk.

Athen and Paulie got busy. She turned back to them. "So, this partnership thing. You both like the idea?"

"Yeah," Athen and Paulie said in unison.

Grady texted Athen. I can get us into the Beverly Hills Hotel for a couple of nights. We can't go home. People are all over it.

Seconds later, Athen texted back. *Holy crap! I had no idea until just now. Tyler killed a woman and his fans are acting like we're the bad guys for arresting him!*

Grady texted, *Are you okay with a bungalow by the pool? They're making an exception for Bella because you're a local hero.*

Athen called him then. "That's some posh digs, babe. Should we be spending that kind of money?"

"They've offered us a discounted rate." Grady longed to sleep in luxury without a petulant teen banging around their house. Even Bella, the most good-natured dog he'd ever met seemed tense around Despina. Grady had a lot to tell Athen about how hard it was, despite her horrible behavior to leave Desi with her parents. He'd promised her he and Athen would travel there right after his case was over and be there when she came out to her parents.

"I don't see what the big deal is," he'd told her. "Your mom never had a problem with your uncle being gay. Your father has a lesbian sister — "

"That's different," she'd said. "I'm her daughter. And the whole time she was going through chemo she kept saying what was keeping her alive was that she wanted to be there for my wedding and for her to hold her first grandchild."

Ouch. Grady was surprised this weighed so heavily on Despina's soul. She was always so disdainful of parental caring. He chose his words carefully. "Your mom knows she can do those things no matter if you marry a man, or a woman."

"Easy for you to say," she'd snapped. Grady tried not to fret about her.

"They offered us a discount?" Athen sounded surprised. His question brought Grady back to the present. "Why?"

"It's all thanks to Sullivan Tang."

"We call her Soup now."

Grady heard the smile in Athen's voice. "I'm sure there's a story to it but I still need to know. You like the hotel idea?"

"Sure, babe. You're my fancy man. You deserve the best." He dropped his voice. "Thank you for loving me. Sometimes I don't think I deserve you."

"Sometimes I agree with you." Grady grinned. He bit his lip. "Athen, can you believe Tyler killed someone?"

"Yeah." Athen sounded exhausted. "I can. Where are you?"

"Just blowing through Bakersfield. Did you know the city's motto is The Sound of Something Better?"

Athen laughed then. "For real? What's the sound, any idea?"

"I think it may be cow farts." Grady laughed too. "I almost stopped in Gilroy to buy fresh garlic."

"Ha! Glad you didn't. I'm planning on kissing you a lot tonight."

"I'll keep that in mind," Grady said, ending their call.

Athen and Paulie had put in a long day and by seven p.m., they'd established a working war room with photos of the main players and info they had, establishing a timeline for Natasha's last known forty-eight hours. So far, they knew she'd talked to her husband at four a.m. Cameron deck said she was a late riser which didn't really jibe with that early morning call. Her next sighting was two in the afternoon. What happened after that?

All missing person cases started backwards, but they had nothing else to go on. Yet.

Paulie went off to scrounge up a coffee maker and Athen perused the photos tacked to the wall.

Although they had Tyler's photo among the many, there was nothing really linking him to the crime. Apart from the issue of the red dress, Natasha's problem seemed to be men.

Who is her fancy man? He couldn't help thinking of the Rolling Stones song *Fancy Man Blues. Which one of her men hated her enough to kill her?*

"Look at this." Soup held up a printed page. The ALPR data was fascinating. Athen spotted his own car's details and many others.

"I had no idea so many cars passed through a simple intersection each day," Soup said, as she, Athen and Paulie went through the long computer printout listing all the license plates that had passed or come near Natasha's residence over the last two days.

Lucy walked in with bags of potato chips.

"I think I love you," Athen said, making her laugh.

She settled in with the others, going through the ALPR report.

It showed that a vehicle Athen knew to be a Beverly Hills undercover vehicle had made its way to Natasha's residence the night before. They now knew it was the one Lorne Brand, driven for the mayor, on their way back from Wong's.

According to Lorne, the mayor had been unable to reach Natasha and thought they'd drop by her apartment to see if they could catch her.

Meanwhile, Scott told Lucy he had no idea Natasha was missing until Jamie Fahdi called him that morning.

Lorne had been removed from the case since he was involved. He was now outside Athen's house with armed officers trying to clear the throng of movie fans and media that had assembled outside what they believed to be Tyler James' residence.

Unfortunately, the rental car's dashboard camera had malfunctioned. There was no footage. But it had an active alarm and the car's dashboard security system showed that it had been turned off at 2:07 pm two days before, when Cameron Deck said Natasha had left her apartment with her laundry. The navigation settings showed that the car had not gone far. Only to Wong's, then back again. The alarm had been reset at 2:27 pm and hadn't been moved since.

Deck didn't deny driving her once Athen spoke to him again by phone. "She was in the car waiting for me as I dropped off her laundry. She loves having an errand boy."

He sounded bitter. "Hey, can you people send some cops here? Please? I got looky-loos glued to the front gate. Everybody wants a piece of the princess. My tenants are afraid to come home."

"In a minute," Athen said. "Why didn't you tell me you were with Natasha that day?"

"I was too embarrassed to admit that I drive her around

town. Hey, wait. I just saw a report on Radar Online. They're saying she's not a real princess. Is that true?"

"Probably," Athen said. "I'll send you over to our traffic division right now."

By seven-ten, one of the tabloid TV shows revealed that Natasha was no princess and that she had a severe gambling problem. Her story soon slipped from the headlines, replaced by the news of Tyler James' arrest.

"That didn't take long," Lucy said after a news bulletin. "If Natasha was blonde, blue-eyed, and American, she'd still be big news. But she's foreign and has dark hair. They don't give a damn."

"Well, Tyler James is big news," Athen said. "Besides, it works for us really. There's been so much reporting all day and we still don't have any significant leads."

"All hell just broke loose," Paulie said as they watched endless news reports of the actor being wanted on cold case charges.

"You could stay in the house tonight since he's locked up," Paulie said. "Once we get rid of the media and the fans, you'd be safe there. Cricket couldn't find any other hidden cameras. Tomorrow, you and Grady can start house hunting."

"Yeah, we could," Athen said. He'd briefly entertained the idea until he learned from Lucy that news media, fans, and tour buses had invaded Arnaz Drive and people were camped out in Athen's bushes. It would take hours to get them to move. Beverly Hills officers had been swamped with a parade of passersby. Lucy said they'd get it under control with fresh reinforcements from the West Hollywood police department, but Athen didn't want to spend another night in Tyler's house.

What a crazy day. He shifted in his seat. He knew he'd have to start his investigation all over again. Comb the threads, follow up even the slightest details. He made notes. They discussed what they knew. They were still waiting for Natasha's cellphone records and Athen wanted to go over all the footage from Wong's again. Something niggled at him, but he didn't know what. He also wanted to check the bank's security tapes but they'd closed at five. He'd have to contact them again in the morning.

By nine thirty, most of the officers at the precinct had gone home and he wanted Lucy and Paulie to return to their families.

"I'll stay with you," Soup said. "I've got nobody waiting for me."

But Athen wanted her to get a good night's rest. He wanted to head to the hotel to be with Grady and Bella. The clues to his case, the answer, lay in the pile of information he had. Yet, he was no closer to solving the mystery.

"Let's call it a day," he said, bleary-eyed. "Start fresh in the morning." He knew that as exhausted as he was, he'd go over each minute of the investigation so far and wouldn't stop replaying it in his mind.

They all walked outside and Athen, laptop in his grip, wished he was already up on Sunset Boulevard lying in a swanky bed with his hot man with tropical flowers and a pool outside his door.

"How early do you wanna start?" Paulie asked.

"Eight o'clock," Athen said. "Oh, your car is still outside Natasha's. I'll drop you there."

"Great. Man, I'm hungry."

"Me, too," Soup echoed.

"My husband ordered Thai tonight." Lucy gave them all a thumbs up.

Athen bid them goodnight. He wanted a shower, sex, and supper. Not necessarily in that order.

Bella knew something was up. She stared out of the window as Grady steered the SUV around the circular driveway of the Beverly Hills Hotel. He and Athen loved what they called The Pink Palace and had come here a few times for late night frosty beers and their incomparable hot dogs before Despina came into their home. They'd often fantasized about renting a room or bungalow for the night.

Now as the valet opened the door, he couldn't believe it was actually happening. "I'll take your car, sir. The concierge is right here." A uniformed man appeared. He ushered Grady and Bella down the flower-lined path to the bungalows

"Will you be wanting to order room service?" he'd asked over his shoulder. He'd not only taken custody of Bella's leash, but wielded Grady's overnight bag, Bella's bag of toys and dishes, and the groceries Grady had bought at Bristol Farms before stopping here.

"Yes," Grady said, hurrying to catch up. *Did Athen grab some clothes from the house? If not, I'll dash back early in the morning and pick up some stuff before he goes back to work.*

The concierge led him to a quiet, beautiful, secluded cabana. "Mrs. Tang said you required our most secluded, most romantic bungalow with a private patio." The concierge beamed at him. "This is it."

Grady's breath caught in his throat. "It's perfect." He glanced at the name tag. Tony Thomas. "Oh, you're Sullivan's brother!"

"I am." Tony smiled. "Oh, do you hear that sound?" Tony tilted, a sweet smile on his face.

"What kind of bird is that?" Grady asked as Bella's head swiveled in all directions. She fancied herself a bird dog, a squirrel dog, and a cat dog. As in, she wanted to play with everyone and everything she ever met. The trilling bird song was the sweetest Grady ever heard.

"It's a mockingbird." Tony handed him Bella's leash. "We

182

used to get them all the time in Beverly Hills. They returned during the coronavirus lockdown. The unmated bachelor of the species sings all night."

"It's a lovely sound," Grady said.

"Some say they became disoriented and bewildered when people vanished into their homes." Tony looked misty-eyed for a moment. "I think they took the time and space to find their way home again." He unlocked the bungalow door for Grady and stepped inside with Grady's possessions.

"Oh, this is wonderful."

They exchanged smiles. Grady took in the welcome basket that contained fruit, chocolates, and bully sticks for Bella. The dog had no manners. She inched her nose past the wrapped goodies around the sticks and licked at them.

Grady laughed and pulled one out for her. She flopped at his feet and got busy. He unclipped her leash and left her to it.

The cabana was an enchanting, breathtaking space with a bed that Grady could have slept in for days straight.

"If you would like to order now, I can dial room service for you," Tony said, putting everything down and handing him the key.

"I might open the wine bottle I see there and sit on the patio for a few moments," Grady said.

"Ah yes, the wine is the compliments of the hotel. There's champagne in an ice bucket on the wet bar and complimentary bottles of mineral water. Tony handed him a business card. "Should you need anything, please call me."

"I will." Grady handed him a twenty-dollar bill. "You've been amazing. Thank you." For long seconds after Tony left, Grady took it all in. He got busy stashing the store-bought goodies in the fridge and examining the stuffed welcome basket. The champagne in the ice bucket was Veuve Clicquot. Grady knew that Athen would want a glass of it. Then he'd want sex. Champagne made him very frisky. "Want a little walk, girl?" he asked Bella who looked up at him.

If she could talk, her response would have been, "Don't bother me. I'm chewing."

Grady laughed and texted to Athen to let him know he was at the hotel. *I'm in the last cabana. Wait till you see it.*

Athen texted back, *On my way.*

"Good," Grady said aloud and went off to order a bunch of room service menu items. He hopped in the shower after selecting a gel he'd been wanting to try forever. In spite of the stressful day, he was happy, and he was drying off just as there was a knock at the door. He threw on a robe. It was Athen, looking sexier than hell.

"Fuck. Look at you in that robe." Athen pulled Grady to him and they kissed hungrily. The room service guy arrived seconds later, robbing Grady of his chance for doorstep sex.

"What did you order?" Athen asked, scrawling his signature on the receipt.

"Open the lids," Grady suggested as the room service guy scurried away.

Athen did as he was told, looking ecstatic at the Pasta Alla Vodka they'd had at the hotel restaurant one time. He let out a moan. "Strozzapreti. My favorite pasta. Oh. And we have the McCarthy salad. I can smell the grilled chicken." His hand hovered over the last dish. "What's in this one?"

Grady just smiled as Athen whisked away the lid. "Oooooh . . . you ordered a hot dog. I think I just died and went to Heaven. It's all beautiful, babe. But I want you first." He put all the lids back on. "Come here." He pulled Grady to him. He suddenly laughed and looked down. "Bella!" He reached down and ruffled the dog's head. "Daddy loves you, sweetie, but he has important things to do." He led Grady to the bed. Bella stood at the foot of it, watching them. She was always bored when Grady and Athen fucked. Which was fine by both men. Grady tried to ignore his impatient erection jutting from the folds of his robe. He arched away as Athen grabbed at it.

"Hold on." Grady went and gave Bella another bully stick and put the welcome basket on the wet bar. She was a good dog, but she was a food hound who couldn't be trusted around anything near her eye level.

Athen watched him, a smile on his face. "My turn now," he said, pulling Grady to him again. He held Grady tight, letting his hands roam down his lover's ass. He cupped his cheeks, making Grady laugh. "Yeah, I have some ownership issues," Athen murmured against Grady's lips. He quickly stripped Grady's bathrobe off leaving his black boxer briefs on. He enjoyed prolonging the moment they were naked together. Loved taunting Grady using the briefs as a weapon to heighten his arousal. Athen squeezed Grady's butt again, sliding the fabric up and his hands under it. He squeezed again, letting his fingers trail between the cheeks and into the crease.

Grady let out a gasp and ground his cock against Athen's. Athen almost ripped off the briefs to throw Grady on the bed and let him have it, but he wanted to wait. He grasped the butt cheeks again, pulling the stretchy fabric up again, letting it wedge inside Grady's ass crack. He tugged again, up, and around, then with his other hand, reached between their crushing bodies to take hold of Grady's swollen cock.

"Yes!" Grady let out a moan. Athen gripped the head with a light touch careful not to let Grady come too soon.

They kissed each other with abandon, their tongues dancing over each other. Grady was the best kisser Athen had ever met. Athen kept pulling up on the underpants, letting them rub against Grady's crack. Only when Grady seemed to be needing urgent attention did Athen reach between his lover's cheeks and rub three fingers against his hole.

He dropped to his knees, hiking down the briefs again, testing, tasting Grady's length with lips and tongue. Grady just wanted to be in his mouth but Athen worked slowly on the head until it was nice and slick enjoying the sounds of his own mouth-to-cock resuscitation. Nothing beat the sound of that in his mind. Grady whimpered until Athen sucked in the head, dragging more of Grady into his hot mouth. *Mmm.* He sucked until every inch filled his mouth then released him again. He could have let Grady enjoy a swift, hard release but Athen was inclined to resist.

Athen got to his feet, took off his own clothes, stepping out of his shoes and socks and whipped off his underpants. He got back on his knees and began cock-sucking again. Yeah, it was maddening for both of them. Suddenly Grady grabbed his head.

"Fuck!" he ground out, flooding Athen's throat. Athen swallowed it all, leaned back on his haunches and grinned up at him.

"You're a very bad man," he said. He let Grady have a minute or two to recuperate. He pushed him on the bed and opened his legs, flicking his tongue this way and that. Grady was always sensitive after an orgasm. But it was too bad. He'd come too soon for Athen's liking. Athen pushed Grady's legs apart, knelt between them then up and buried his face in his man's musky scent. He rubbed his tongue along every touch of skin then took one ball then the other into his mouth. God, he wanted to fuck.

"Do it," Grady began to chant, but Athen wanted to take his time. Grady grabbed him, centering Athen's hot head right where it belonged.

Still Athen didn't give him what he wanted. He rubbed his cock along the crease then against Grady's balls. He grabbed both their cocks in his hand and knew he couldn't last much longer.

Grady was still begging so Athen began the delicious assault on his lover's hole. He pushed and pushed until he was sliding in. Grady clutched at Athen's ass cheeks, pulling him in harder, deeper, faster. Athen gave him everything he had, loving the erotic pleasure they gave each other. He came hard, seeing stars and fireworks in his mind. A rich sense of peace overcame him, but he kept fucking Grady making him come a second time.

They kept kissing each other until they needed to breathe. Athen came out of him and rolled to his side.

"Yummy," Grady whispered, making Athen laugh.

They swapped gentle kisses and licks. Athen wanted more. They both did. But he was tired. So tired. He yearned for rest and lay wrapped around Grady who fell asleep seconds later.

But Athen couldn't stop the thoughts that kept tumbling in his mind. Desperate for some solace, he kept reminding himself he needed rest until at two a.m. His phone rang. He checked the call, trying not to waken Grady. To his delight, he'd received an alert that Natasha's records had been delivered to his email address. He knew that his team members would also have the alert. He took a deep breath and texted them all saying, *I'm on it. Checking records now. Go back to sleep.* There was no reason for them all to be awake and working at this hour.

He slipped out of bed, detangling himself from Grady's warm body. In the process of repacking his mental snowball he felt compelled to work, work, work. He walked out to the small sitting room away from the sumptuous alcove where Grady lay sprawled on the bed. Athen longed to hop right back into bed with him. Bella licked his leg. This meant she wanted to pee. She always wanted to pee in unfamiliar surroundings. He unlatched the door to the bungalow and walked with her to the dark foliage lining the building. She squatted and peed among some beautiful birds of paradise.

She went on and on. The night was quiet and cool. "Come on, girl," he whispered and led her back inside again.

Bella trotted over to the kitchen area. She dropped her head into the large stainless-steel bowl that went everywhere with her. The sound of her lapping at water always filled his heart with pleasure. He had had no idea why. At that moment he loved her and Grady more than he ever thought possible. *Did I make the right decision not becoming a vet?*

He fired up his computer as she jumped up on the sofa beside him and curled into a comfortable furry donut position. Athen opened the email with the phone records and scanned them. Natasha had made two calls the last morning she'd been seen alive.

The first was to a 310 area code number. That was at 4.30 a.m. The same number called her back a few seconds later. That had to be Gary Goldman. He would check. It was the last outgoing call that held his interest, however. He couldn't help smiling.

I knew it. I knew there was something weird about this! The last call she made was at 7:03 a.m. It was to the Australian cellphone number he'd found on Natasha's bill. Lucy had called it the day before and spoke to a woman who claimed it was a new number.

Bullshit. She talked to somebody on that call for eight minutes. What time would it have been in Sydney, Australia? He checked. Midnight. Right now, it was seven p.m. Sydney time. Perfect. He called the number.

The cellphone rang as he paced the small room. After several rings, a woman answered.

"Hello?" Her voice came out in a shaky whisper.

"Please, don't hang up," he said. "Please. And this is very important. I'm Lieutenant Athen Mavromatis with the Beverly Hills Police department. And I have every reason to believe Natasha is in very grave danger."

The woman on the other end of the line let out a gasp. "I

knew it," she whispered. "I *knew* it. He's killed her, hasn't he?"

CHAPTER FOURTEEN

"Who? Athen asked. "Who do you think killed her?"
The woman sobbed loudly. Her heart was broken and Athen knew it. He had no idea how long she'd been worried about Natasha, or who she was, but he needed answers. And fast. He needed to know more about Natasha's Australian background, but if this hysterical woman couldn't calm down long enough to help him, he was screwed.

"Please," he implored. "You have to talk to me. What is your relationship with Natasha?" He sat on the sofa again, studying the phone records. Thankfully, the cellphone tower her phone had pinged was listed. It was in the heart of Beverly Hills' Bermuda Triangle. *Ugh. How apt.*

"I can't say anything," she said between sobs. "I promised. I—I shouldn't even have answered the phone, but I've been so worried." Her voice fell into muffled shrieks.

"You're the last person to have spoken to her, and that was two days ago." Athen studied Natasha's calls, shocked at the dozens and dozens she typically made each day. After the call to Australia, nothing.

"I shouldn't have picked up. She's the only one who calls this line. And then yesterday a woman called me."

"My precinct captain." Athen blew out a breath. At least the woman was talking now.

"That's what she said. Lucy Lane. I thought she was having a go. That's a cartoon character's name, isn't it?"

"She gets that all the time. Please. What is your relationship with Natasha?"

"I'm her mother."

Athen sagged into the sofa. "She's told people here her mother died."

"She did. I'm her birth mother. I've only been back in her life a couple of years. Her adoptive mother died and left her money, but it dried up when the executor of the estate found out Natasha was in the States. The will specified she had to be here. She comes and goes to make it look like she lives here."

"You know she's posing as a princess here."

A silence so long ensued that Athen was worried she'd ended the call.

"Yes. But she doesn't say she's Australian. I—I've been frantic ever since the call the other morning. It was horrible."

"What happened?"

"This is a nightmare," she said.

"Please. You've got to tell me."

"She set a trap for him. I knew it was dangerous. But she was determined, even though she was frightened."

"What trap?"

"She knew he was climbing into her bedroom window in the mornings when he thought she was at the gym."

Athen's blood ran cold. "Who?"

"I'm afraid. You've got no idea. He's a terrible human being."

Damn. "I understand. Why was he doing that?"

The woman started sobbing again. "Because he got a thrill out of coming in there and tormenting her cat. She found a YouTube video he'd uploaded online. The video vanished after somebody else told him she'd seen it. But she'd shot a video of it on her phone. She intended to press animal cruelty charges. But she's afraid of him. Very afraid."

Felice Farmer had said something similar to Soup. He needed to talk to her again.

The woman on the phone's words came out in a rush now.

"She forwarded it to me. He's a sick, sick man."

"Who?" Athen asked again. "Just tell me. Who?"

"Her landlord. Cameron Deck."

Athen's thoughts raced. He could hardly keep up with the woman's frenzied explanation.

"He came into her apartment while I was talking to her. Normally she's at the gym by seven."

"Deck told me she's a late riser."

"No. Not at all. She's a farm girl. Born and raised. Dear God. I think I heard the whole thing."

"What happened?"

"She'd left her computer camera on the day before I spoke to her. The footage from the YouTube video vanished after she called the Animal Abuse Task Force in Beverly Hills. They were no help. They sent someone to talk to *him*! Can you believe it? She put the video on a thumb drive. She was planning to move out. She said he's crazy and violent. I've seen the way he treated that cat. It was terrible. Oh my God. Where is the cat now?"

"Her friend Maggie has her."

"How did she get her? Did Natasha give Violet to her?"

Athen took a breath. "No. She was outside. Natasha had called her and asked her to pick up the cat. She had to go over twice, but she has her."

"What was she doing outside?" Before Athen could respond she said, "Oh. Thank God. Wait. If Maggie has her and the cat was left outside, which my daughter would never do, then I know my baby girl is gone." The woman started crying again. "I was talking to her on the phone when she told me this. Suddenly he was there. I heard her screaming. She dropped her phone, but I could hear it. All of it. I could hear him hitting her. And Natasha's blood-curdling screams. And then the line went dead. Please, mister. Please stop him. He's a psychopath."

"I'll stop him," Athen promised. "Any idea what she did with the thumb drive?"

"She sent me the clip. She planned to stash the actual thumb drive in a safety deposit box. My daughter loves animals and she would never, *ever* allow anyone to hurt that cat. She was devastated when she found that video."

Athen's thoughts flew to Soup. She said she'd recognized Deck but didn't know from where. Had she seen the video? Had the Beverly Hills Animal Abuse task force forwarded the material to her to pursue a case?

"Can you send the video to me please?' he asked Natasha's mother. "By the way, what is your name?"

"Valerie Harman."

"Harman? Are you related to Maggie?"

"She's my other daughter."

Athen couldn't believe the twists and turns this strange case had taken.

"I had two daughters. I was forced to adopt them out. There's two years between Maggie and Natasha. Natasha's younger. When we became reacquainted, I already knew Maggie. Natasha thought it was fate that she was here. She flew to LA and met her. They adored each other but they cooked up this princess thing, so they couldn't tell people they were sisters. I was afraid that would get her into trouble. I never dreamed the cat video would be her, um, undoing."

"Okay." Athen took a deep breath. "Can you forward the video clip to me?"

"I'm not very good at this stuff. Can you walk me through it?"

"Sure." He explained how to forward an email and how she could make sure the attachment was there. As he spoke to her, he harbored fantasies of driving around to Cameron Deck's apartment building and kicking him in the ass. The email arrived. He ended his call with Valerie Harman. He still had questions for her, but at least now he had solid information.

He clicked the link for the video and experienced the most uncomfortable fifty-seven seconds of his life as it unfolded. Damn. The clip had thousands of likes. In it, Deck could be seen removing a screen from Natasha's window, climbing in and advancing on the poor cat sleeping on the bed. The cat tried to run but Deck grabbed her and threw a blanket over her. It could have been viewed as sick humor the way he was pummeling the cat's writhing form through the blanket, but the cat got away from him and shot under the bed.

There was no volume but like many viewers who'd commented on the video it was clear this was not an isolated incident. Beck grinned to himself, climbed out of the window again and replaced the screen.

Athen needed a hot shower after watching that. He took one, thrilled when Grady climbed in behind him.

"You okay?" he asked.

"No. Yes." Tears pricked at Athen's eyes. He leaned back into Grady, allowing his lover's hand to migrate down to his slowly reviving cock. Grady stroked Athen's sheath from behind under the hot spray.

Athen wanted him. "Fuck me," he demanded. He wanted his good, good man to cleanse his soul, remind him the world was a beautiful place. He forced thoughts of the video and the conversation with Valerie from his mind. He'd allow himself a little more bliss to carry him through.

Then he had to avenge an angel.

He let Grady stroke him with a soapy hand. "Don't think about anything else right now, just this," Grady urged. Athen did as he was told. It was hard to think about bad things when the hottest man in the world was squatting before him giving him the blowjob from hell. Grady knew what he was doing. He sucked Athen hard then backed off, letting the hot water spray work some magic on him.

Grady took possession of him with his mouth again and sucked in his length then let him go. He did this several times then told Athen to close his eyes. Athen knew what he was going to do but it always worked. Grady moved his mouth away then came back again. He let a mouthful of hot water soak Athen's cock. It always made him feel like he was coming and made him explode in his lover's mouth.

Athen gripped the walls of the shower as he came, peace flooding his senses at last.

They lay entwined on the bed. It was almost three a.m. As much as he wanted to bounce some ideas off Paulie, he wanted to let him, and the rest of his team get more rest.

Grady brewed coffee in the machine the hotel provided and poured Athen a cup. After a quick kiss, he took Bella out for a walk. Athen hated Grady walking the streets alone in the dark but Grady relished it. Besides, he had a black belt in Brazilian Jiu-jitsu. He could, if he wanted, seriously hurt somebody with his skills.

I'm just lucky he loves me. Athen sipped his coffee and perused his case notes once more. He was shocked to find that Cameron Deck had a Facebook page and like many other stupid criminals posted way too much personal information on it. Most incriminating was a photo of him beside his new car. A 2020 Lexus IS. A quick check showed the base price of these vehicles was thirty-eight grand. *Wow. He's rich.* Athen found an image with the license plate. SEZ WHO.

Okay. Athen checked the ALPR. It was easy to check the stats for the vehicle with that license plate. According to the rental car's dashboard time stamp, Cameron had returned the vehicle at 2.27. Was Natasha really outside in the car waiting for him?

Or was she already dead by then?

He suspected the latter. Once he checked the bank's security footage, he'd have a better idea. Hopefully, he'd see Cameron Deck in his car, and whether or not he'd been alone in the rental car. He made a note to get onto the bank footage first thing. In the meantime, he'd go over the footage he had. Maybe with closer scrutiny, he'd see something he missed. Maybe he'd see the car parked out front through the window.

Athen wanted to review the footage from Wong's. He realized he hadn't seen all of the video with Cameron's appearance in it. "If Natasha was already dead, why did he take her clothes to the cleaners?" he asked aloud.

He knew the answer then.

To make it seem like she was still alive.

He cued up the clips and watched as Cameron came in with her clothes. He had separated the red dress from her laundry. What was the red dress about? Why bring in the phony?

Holy cow! He saw it in her house and really had no idea of the drama over the second reproduction. Had no idea he was bringing in a phony! He cleaned her place up and thought he was slick bringing in the dress she coveted. He thought he knew all about Natasha and her life. He knew about the fight, obviously. But he had no idea she'd had a cheap knock-off made and tried to pass it off as the original duplicate to Mrs. Wong.

Oh, boy. He thought he was so clever. Nobody would have thought it was weird that he was bringing in Natasha's laundry. Probably did it dozens of times. Buying time for himself was smart. Next thing you know, he'd be telling people she'd gone back to Saudi Arabia.

And that makes sense because everything we know here is how repressive the regime is there, especially with women. He could say she told him she had to go home. Wouldn't be his fault if she disappeared.

Huh. He wasn't banking on me and Paulie showing up. He must have freaked!

It happened so fast, he almost missed it. Athen backed up the footage by ten seconds. Yes. There it was. No mistaking it. Cameron had turned to leave the shop after Mrs. Wong refused to give him back the laundry. He didn't look too upset. But as he turned, it was very clear he patted his jacket pocket and he turned. Now he looked panicked. He came back to the counter.

He had an argument with Mrs. Wong who made him leave. *What did he want? What was missing?*

Athen wasn't much of a lip reader and wished with his whole heart he had volume on the clip, but he was certain Cameron Deck had left something in the bag of laundry and wanted it back. He walked away without it. He hovered at the door a moment then left.

What the hell could have been in it?

Holy cow! I have the laundry bag in my trunk! He raced out of the bungalow and realized he'd valet parked his car. The valet guy was dressed and alert, making Athen feel like a homeless person in his outfit of yesterday's shirt, jeans and no shoes, the way he gave him a swift, sneering once over. He went off to get Athen's vehicle and returned with it within seconds.

"Did you guys wash it?" Athen gaped at the vehicle.

The valet stepped outside. "Yes, sir."

"Holy cow. I might just become a permanent resident." He popped the trunk and handed the guy a twenty-dollar bill. "Any chance you can leave it someplace close? I'm a lieutenant with Beverly Hills police and I'll be heading over there in about an hour."

The guy palmed the twenty so fast it was like seeing it disappear into a slot machine. "I'll see what I can do, sir."

"Thanks." Athen retrieved the laundry bag, closed the trunk, and sprinted back to the bungalow.

"What's going on?" Grady asked, greeting him at the door.

"My lead suspect left something in this bag."

"What?" Grady held the door wider as Athen came inside,

then shut it again before Bella could leap outside.

Athen moved over to the table where he'd been working and opened the bag. *Oh, man. She has expensive taste in undergarments.* Each item might have been dirty but didn't look it. Natasha favored La Perla and the individual pieces showed exquisite workmanship. He suspected Mrs. Wong would love them.

"I recognize that laundry bag. Wong's. They do a beautiful job," Grady said. "And you get what you pay for. Usually they return everything tied in a beautiful blue bow. And they tuck in a bar of Amedei Porcelana. Every actress I know gets their laundry done by Wong's, and they give me, and the other crew guys the chocolate. You know it retails for around ninety bucks a bar, right?"

Athen frowned at him. "And you never shared this great chocolate with me?"

Grady flashed him a guilty look. "No. Never crossed my greedy mind."

Athen shook his head but said nothing as he carefully hunted through the clothes. Nothing but underwear, beautiful as it was. It almost broke Athen's heart when he caught a faint whiff of Shalimar.

He looked up to find Grady watching him. "Babe. Look at this stuff. What do you notice?"

Grady stared at him a moment. "You want my opinion on somebody's undergarments?"

"Please." Athen stood back as Grady examined the clothing. "Wow. Somebody has excellent taste. This black robe retails for around seven-hundred bucks."

"What else?"

"Well, they seem clean. I thought so when you first went through everything, which was why I was surprised that there was no bow. Or the chocolate."

"Right. They seem clean to me, too." Athen paused. *Why the hell did Deck take clean clothes to the cleaners? I'm certain he was trying to make people think Natasha was still alive. And what was he looking for?*

"Hey, is there something I missed?"

"No," Athen said. "What about the red dress?"

Grady pulled a face. "Not up to the quality of the bras and panties." He ran his fingers over the fabric. "Not sure what this stain is." He dropped his face to it. "Oily feel to it. Not noticeable at first. Maybe oil." His face brightened. "It's perfume. Shalimar." He shook his head. "My grandma wore it back in the day. Said it made her feel exotic."

Athen said nothing. Mrs. Wong had seen the dress and the stain and assumed it was gasoline, but it was perfume. He had a sudden image of Cameron Deck frantically clearing out Natasha's apartment and spilling the perfume. He thought sending her stuff to the cleaners would buy him time. *Sheesh.*

"I'm gonna iron your shirt," Grady said. "Glad you thought to bring some fresh clothes. I'm gonna start house hunting today before I get the movers to help me collect our stuff from Tyler's."

Athen glanced at him. "Wait until I finish this case, babe. Or at least, give me a couple of days until I can do it with you. I don't want you going back there alone."

"My hero," Grady teased, running a finger along Athen's jaw. Athen kissed it then picked up his phone. He called Paulie and reported the latest developments.

"Hot damn. That fucker. What do you think he left with the clothes?" Paulie asked.

"No idea. I'd like to ask him though."

"Have we checked the ALPR to see if he was driving any other vehicles around between the time we think she was killed and when he drove to Wong's or maybe even after it?"

"Yes," Athen said. "I checked his registration. He drives a Lexus, vanity plates on it as SEZ WHO. Original eh?"

"God. And?"

"He moved it right after he returned the rental car. The

alarm's dashboard time stamp aligns with the time he moved his car outside the building a few minutes later. He doesn't drive off until around midnight, returns at two a.m. Leaves the car outside the building and moves it again around nine o'clock the next morning. This was the day before we were called. Paulie. Get this. He never leaves Beverly Hills. Unless he's got her somewhere here, someplace close, I have no idea what he could have done with her."

"Can you imagine what her mother's been going through? Having to listen to all that screaming then not knowing what's going on?"

The words hung between them for a moment.

Athen's other line rang. "It's Valerie Harman. I'll take that and I'll come get you."

"See you in a few," Paulie said. "Want me to call the girls?"

"You call Soup. I should have called Lucy first but you're my partner after all." He smiled at the thought.

"Yes, I am." Athen could hear the smile in Paulie's voice. "We're like Inspector Morse and Sergeant Lewis."

"Who?" Athen asked, genuinely puzzled.

"You damned Neanderthal," Paulie teased. "See you in a few."

Athen took Valerie's call. "I'm flying over to the States," she said. "I talked to Maggie. She knows you know everything. She bought me a ticket. Well, an electronic one. I arrive tonight."

"Excellent. Will you be staying with her?"

She hesitated. "I'm not sure. She's afraid of her apartment being broken into. All her windows are boarded up. I told her to find a hotel and we can stay there with the cats until her windows are replaced. She said her insurance company was being difficult."

"Okay," Athen said. "You have my number. Please, let's stay in touch with each other." He ended the call and turned to Grady. "Who's Inspector Morse?"

"Oh, darling. Don't." Grady stared at him. "You're serious. Oh my God. You've never seen the series?"

"No. What's this inspector like?"

"Why?"

"Paulie says we're like Inspector Morse and Sergeant Lewis."

Grady laughed. "How apt. I never thought about it, but you are. I didn't mean to eavesdrop, but did I hear you say something about, you're partners?"

"Yes. What do you think about it?"

"I love it. Oh, babe. You two really are like Morse and Lewis." He moved to Athen and hugged him. Bella moved her solid body between them. She wanted some love, too.

Athen kissed him.

"You got time for breakfast?" Grady asked. "I ordered pancakes, eggs, toast, strawberries and a giant pot of coffee."

"Sounds good to me. Tell me about Morse."

Grady shrugged. There was a knock on the door, and he answered it. The room service guy rolled in a cart covered in silver domes. Bella drooled.

"I can smell bacon, too," Athen told her.

Grady signed the receipt and the room service guy smiled and left them to it.

Athen looked at Grady. "Morse?" He lifted a silver dome and removed a couple of slices of bacon. One for him. One for the dog.

"It was voted the best British crime series of all-time last year."

"Is that so?" Athen poured himself some coffee and dunked a slice of hot-buttered toast into it. "And is Morse sexy?"

"No, darling. He's a curmudgeon. He scowls and frightens people. He's moody. He's a pain in the ass. Just like you."

"I'm none of those things," Athen protested. He tried not to scowl. But sometimes it was hard.

"Right," Grady said, trying not to smile.

Athen met up with his team twenty minutes later. He wished he could have eaten more strawberries and toast, but he had a job to do. He tried not to think about having his hot, handsome naked man in the shower. *Focus, Blackeye. Focus.*

"Natasha's mother called me while I was talking to Paulie," he told the others. She's flying over here. She's blaming herself for not being here sooner. She told me Natasha begged her a few weeks ago to come out here. Valerie Harman said she understood all about the princess ruse but knew she couldn't handle close scrutiny if anyone asked her."

"It's not her fault," Lucy said, plugging in the coffee maker.

"In the meantime, now we know Natasha and Maggie are sisters, we can ask her to come in do a DNA swab," Athen said. "That way we can check it against the massive samples we have."

"Excellent." Lucy spooned coffee into the pot. "I've contacted the corporate headquarters for the bank's security footage. Now we start building our case against Cameron Deck."

Athen called Maggie Harman and was surprised to learn she was already on the premises. "I'm at the front desk," she said. Everything seemed to be happening at once. Lucy got a phone call from the bank and Soup volunteered to go look at the security footage.

When Athen mentioned the cat assault video to Soup, she said she'd never seen or heard of it. "Unless it's necessary for me to view the footage and it's germane to the case, I'd rather not look at it."

"Fair enough. Do you have any idea why his face was familiar to you?"

"I'm still waiting to hear. I'm sorry I can't remember, but

he is familiar to me."

Lucy had a press conference coming up regarding Tyler James' arrest and needed to prepare for it. "Let's just hope they don't throw eggs at me for arresting their favorite actor," she murmured. "Keep me updated."

She sent Maggie into the room and Athen was surprised to see her accompanied by Gary Goldman, Natasha's husband. Athen recognized him from his Facebook page.

"I took the redeye in last night. Any news?" Goldman asked, looking pale-faced and worried.

"None yet, I'm sorry to say, but there has been a development."

"I know," Maggie said. "My mom called me."

Athen introduced himself and Paulie to Goldman and offered him and Maggie coffee. They both accepted, and cups in hand, they all settled down. Though the vibe was amicable, there was tension in the air that had Athen restless and uneasy.

"I have a record of my DNA, which should help you check the DNA on the blood you found in Natasha's bedroom." Maggie pushed a manila envelope toward him. "I ordered the tests to make sure Valerie was telling me the truth. That she's my mother." Her mouth twisted in bitter fury. "She didn't tell me I had a sister until a year later. We have the same parents, so I know these results will help with mitochondrial DNA."

Athen stared at her a moment. "You know your science."

"I watch a lot of cop shows."

"They will help a lot, thank you," Athen said. "We had no other record of her DNA. Not even a toothbrush or a hairbrush. Nothing." He paused. "Somebody really cleaned the place out."

"It was Cameron Deck. All his tenants know it. They saw him piling things into his trunk late at night."

"Nobody told us." Athen's fury mounted but he put the

topic aside for the moment. "How did you know we have blood in her bedroom?"

"Everybody knows in the building. Felice Farmer told me. She also told me that she mentioned to you and to the lady detective that they're all afraid of him. He's obsessed with my sister. Even steams open her mail. She had to have it sent to the post office."

Damn. Athen was worried Cameron Deck would run and hide before they could arrest him. "I need to—" He turned to Paulie. "Can I see you outside for a moment?" To Maggie he said, "I'll be right back."

Outside the war room, Athen handed the envelope to Paulie. "Can you take these to Lucy and have that fast test run on these? And she needs to have Cameron picked up and held until we can get the results back."

"On it," he said, striding down the hallway.

Back inside the room, Athen refilled their cups, buying himself a few moments. He looked at Maggie. "You know about what he did to the cat."

"No. She never told me. My mother did last night."

This was a surprise to Athen. "You and Natasha are close. And she didn't tell you?"

Maggie grimaced. "I dated him for a bit. I think he was trying to make her jealous. I realized pretty quickly he was a jerk."

"You dated Cameron?" Athen couldn't believe it.

"Yeah. He can be charming. For about five minutes. Anyway, she didn't tell anyone, except apparently our mother. You don't understand. She doesn't tell people here anything because Cameron has a way of calling and bugging you and questioning you. He'll make up stuff."

"It's true," Gary said. "He'll call and say that Natasha told him she was spending the evening with me when she'd said no such thing. He wanted to know where she was every second of every day. When he found out I was married to her, I think it caused her more problems that any of us expected. He calls me, hangs up on me. He has a really bizarre sense of entitlement. But I can deal with him."

Maggie picked up her cup. "I knew something was going on at the apartment. I also knew she was afraid that if he knew she was telling people, he'd kill her."

Paulie returned, giving Athen a nod.

"She thought he'd *kill* her?" Athen asked. "Wow. Why didn't she call the police?"

"She always said, "I can handle him.""

Gary snorted. "God. That's so true."

"Did she tell you she was planning to move out of her apartment?" Athen asked as Paulie took his seat again.

"No. Well, yes. She said she was leaving. She didn't say where she was going because she knew he'd hound me for her location, which he did. She was trying to protect me. She took a series of Ubers around town. I can show you my call log."

"I already looked at it, remember? Speaking of cellphones, we're waiting for Maggie's records from her service provider. Now I know you're sisters, any chance you share an account?"

Maggie gave him a swift, sad smile. "No. We don't tell people we're sisters. The only one who knows is Gary."

"Like I said before, I married her to protect her from Cameron," Goldman said.

"How would that protect her?" Paulie asked.

"He's obsessed with her. He has this . . . irrational need to be all things to her. It's insane. I pegged him as a sociopath long before she met him, and I hated the idea of her moving into what we call the Persian Palace. I knew one look at her, and he'd fall so hard he wouldn't be able to see straight."

"And you knew him how?" Athen asked.

"He and I were extras on the *Judge Howard* show. We'd be on it together a lot."

"They use the same extras over and over?" Paulie asked.

"Oh, yeah. They shoot five episodes in one day. You go and you take five changes of outfits. They move you around a little bit. Not much. But if you watch those shows and study the courtroom watchers, it's the same people all the time."

"I had no idea." Athen shook his head. "And that's how you met him?"

"Yeah. And Maggie and I threw a New Year's Eve party last year, and I invited Cameron. He saw her and stayed glued to her. She and I got married when he wouldn't leave her alone, then when we started the fake reveal of her real identity as a princess thing, he offered her an apartment."

"If you thought he was such a creep, why let her move there?" Paulie asked.

"You have no idea how connected he is," Maggie said. "He's a co-owner of the cigar bar where all the girls have worked at some point. They've all met their agents, their boyfriends, you name it, there."

Gary shifted in his seat. "He knows I'm gay and knew that ours was a marriage of convenience. He never saw me as a threat, Far from it. He felt it meant she was off the shelf because of it and it gave him a clear run to her once Natasha and I got divorced. You know, once she got her green card."

"So, having her in his building meant that he'd have her under his control." Athen shook his head.

"He pretended to me that she just showed up one day around October, November and moved in, but he knew her long before she moved in." He marveled at the way all of these people told lies and kept secrets. Deadly secrets.

"She's the only resident allowed to have a pet." Goldman stared off into the distance. "I know about the video. Natasha told me about it. I was the one who finally found it. That was a few weeks ago. She told Valerie. She had to talk to someone."

"But how did you find out about the video in the first place?" Athen asked.

"My vet told me," Maggie said bluntly. "Violet has been distraught since I brought her home. I took her there thinking he could give her something to calm her."

"Between Cameron Deck's assaults and yesterday's shooting, it's no wonder," Athen said.

"Well, he told me a few weeks ago that he'd warned my sister. He told her five months ago that Cameron Deck went in there to pick up Violet after her spay surgery that he was showing people in the waiting room the video on his phone. They were disturbed that he thought it was funny. The vet told her about it, but she couldn't find the video he'd showed everybody. So, this thing's been going on for all that time."

Athen blew out a breath. "And, Gary, you eventually found the footage."

"I did. We've been looking for it. She had no idea his assaults were still going on. The video had a lot of views and she was horrified that he just came and went from her apartment like he owned it."

"Maggie, how did you find out Valerie was your mother?"

"If I tell you all of this, can you please keep it out of the media?"

Athen considered the thought for a moment. "I can't promise. It may come out if there's a trial. It may not. But I will do my best to stop it from coming out. Whatever it is."

"My mother belongs to a cult."

Athen hadn't been expecting that one. He exchanged glances with Paulie who seemed as surprised as he.

"She's a member of the Rajneesh movement," Maggie said, her voice shaking.

"A sannyasin? I thought that cult was over," Athen said.

"I was born into it. Long story short, my parents were devotees. In Australia, there are still deep pockets of it. There was a commune in Nimbin, an abandoned dairy town in northern New South Wales. When my mother was pregnant with me, they came here to the US. They lived at the ashram in Oregon. I don't remember any of it. I was three when my dad and mum had a fight and he ran off with me. He moved to Salt Lake City where he adopted me out to a family I thought of as my own until I was sixteen. Once they told me the truth, that I was a cult kid, it was devastating. I had memories, flashbacks if you will of everybody being dressed in orange. We could only eat orange-colored food. I remember we sang *We All Live in the Orange Submarine*. Sometimes when I'm sleeping, I hear that damned song in my dreams."

Her voice fell away, and she rocked back and forth a little. "I was mortified. It was a free-love cult and as much as I wanted to know my roots, I wasn't sure if I would ever know who my father was. My adopted parents helped me track down my birth mother. I was surprised her name was Harman. Same as me. Turns out my dad had adopted me to his second cousin. She knew where I was all along! I might as well have been on Mars though. Our lives were very different."

"Did you ever go see her?" Athen asked, curious to know.

"Oh, yeah. She still lives in the commune. Let me tell you I swear I have PTSD from visiting her. No hot water, patchy electricity. She's a lesbian now and lives in a dinky hippie shack that she owns, but she's not allowed to sell the land. That belongs to the community. That's what they call this commune. I have to say they all work hard. She grows cotton and makes clothes to sell. All the money goes back into the community.

"My parents are no longer together, and my mum says

she'll never remarry. She loves her girlfriend and these days the free love stuff's over for her. She took so many drugs she always seems out of it. When we finally reconnected, she told me about Natasha. Turns out my dad went back to the commune after he left her. He knocked her up a second time and the local authorities in Nimbin took Natasha from her after my mother gave birth to her. Tash had NAS."

"Neonatal abstinence syndrome?" Athen asked.

"You got it. She had drugs in her system and the state wouldn't return the baby to my mother unless she left the cult. She refused. She signed Tash away. My dad didn't want her. Or me. He moved to Tasmania years ago. He agreed to DNA testing but wants no contact with any of us." Maggie's eyes glazed with unshed tears. "He has a new family and a thriving organic vegetable farm. As for Valerie, I'll never be able to have a proper relationship with her. We don't think alike at all."

Athen chose his words carefully. "From what your mother tells me, she's quite close to Natasha."

"Ha! She's close to Tash's money."

Gary nodded. "Tash and I went to Disneyland once. It's still one of the best days I ever had in my life. We were like two little kids. Then her mother called, and Natasha was really excited and put her on loudspeaker. Valerie called asking for money. You should have seen the look on Natasha's face. Hurt beyond belief."

Athen had a feeling this was the pot calling the kettle black.

"Once she discovered Valerie, my sister got generous with her," Maggie said. "Lieutenant, my sister is a fucking angel. She's the sweetest person I've ever met. She cares about everyone. She kinda came unglued over the dress issue but that's because she's never had anything nice in her life. She had an irrational desire to keep that dress. She was adopted by religious, unfeeling, very strict parents. She was shocked when her adoptive mum left her money. Unfortunately, she's met a few predators since she got her inheritance."

Nobody said anything for a moment.

"I got the DNA testing done last year." Maggie took a swallow of coffee. "Our father didn't have any problems with it, as long as Tash and I signed quitclaims to all of his holdings."

"He did that?" Athen was astonished.

"Oh, yeah. Anyway, he's definitely our father and like I said, I hope you find my sister's DNA in that apartment. Are you going to arrest Cameron Deck?"

Athen's cellphone rang. It was Soup. *911.*

"I'm working on it," Athen said, rising. "Thank you for coming in. Do you mind waiting a moment?"

Gary and Maggie exchanged glances. "No," Gary said but neither looked comfortable.

Athen took Soup's call and gestured Paulie to accompany him.

Outside the room, Athen said, "Soup, hold on." He pulled over a uniformed officer. "Please stand guard outside this door. Do not let either of those people out of here for any reason." He thought for a moment. "On second d thoughts, move the woman into interview room one. Offer her refreshments. She's likely to decline. Tell her nothing. Please stand guard outside the room. Don't let her out, or anybody else in for any reason. I'll have somebody stand guard outside our war room."

The officer looked startled. "Yes, sir!"

Athen and Paulie headed to Lucy's office. "You gonna leave Goldman in the war room?" Paulie asked.

"Yeah. I have a feeling he's up to his neck in this. He strikes me as a weak man." He encountered another officer, repeating his instructions. "And take his phone away, please. Bring it to us. We'll be in the captain's office."

"Understood." The officer moved away quickly and Paulie

and Athen walked into Lucy's office. She stood, looking perfect and polished in full dress uniform. Her makeup was
muted, not a hair out of place. She'd do a great job with the
news conference. Throngs of media types were filtering into
the station's conference center, but she was well-equipped to
handle the endless questions that would come her way.

"Come to wish me good luck?" she asked Athen, a nervous
smile on her lips. She glanced at Paulie then back at Athen. "I
guess not. What's the update?"

"I think she's in on it," Athen said.

"What?" Lucy gaped at him.

"The sister. Maggie. I just know she's mixed up in this."

"You have proof?"

"I do," Soup said on the phone. For moment, Athen had
forgotten she'd been waiting. "Sir," she went on, "I just pulled
security footage from the bank. She was with Cameron Deck
when he went to Wong's. She also went to the bank's ATM
and withdrew two amounts of cash totaling eight hundred
dollars while he was in the salon. She tried a third withdrawal
two hours later. It was declined. The account she was trying
to withdraw from belongs to Natasha King. And get this, she
brought a letter she intended to use as proof that Natasha
wanted her to have power of attorney over her affairs."

"They told you all of this?" Lucy looked as astonished as
Athen felt.

"They sent me to their fraud department. They started an
investigation two days ago into suspicious withdrawals from
Natasha's account. They said they froze her assets after the
realized the power of attorney letter was falsified."

"How did they know it was falsified?" Paulie asked.

"It was signed and stamped by a notary public who died
two months ago in a skiing accident on Mammoth Mountain.
By the way, this happened mid-May and the resort's been
closed since the twenty-fourth because of it." She paused.

This gave Athen, Paulie, and Lucy a few seconds to absorb this news.

"The fraud investigator just told me that he received a fax from Gary Goldman about an hour ago, filing a right of survivorship form."

"Against Natasha's account?" Athen was horrified.

"Apparently. They say it's the same notary's signature and stamp but dated yesterday."

"But Natasha's still officially missing," Lucy said.

"He's desperate," Athen said. "Man, oh man. She's got some treacherous people in her orbit."

"So, two counts of fraud. Let's see what else we can get them on," Lucy said.

"The bank tells me both letters appear to be the work of one person. They're excellent forgeries, but the signature witness is the same on both. Margaret Jane Harman." Soup blew out a breath. "Natasha has over two hundred thousand dollars in her account. Her funds are transferred monthly from her bank in Australia. That amount, they tell me is almost three hundred K in Australia."

"And her sister and husband are already fighting to take control of it." Athen said.

"Oh my God!" Soup shouted.

"What?" Lucy, Athen, and Paulie responded.

"The branch manager says that Maggie Harman texted him saying she needs urgent funds today."

CHAPTER FIFTEEN

L ucy stared at Athen. "What tipped you off that Maggie was dirty?"

"She knew about the blood in the bedroom. She said everyone in the building knew but I don't know. It felt fishy to me. She was quick to come in here with DNA reports. Really wants Cameron Deck arrested."

"I thought it was weird, too," Paulie said. "If we find DNA matching her, she has a good excuse. It's her sister."

"But why would she kill her?" Lucy asked.

"Money. Maybe. Heat of the moment. I don't know yet." Athen held up his phone. "Soup, has she tried to access the account again since those two withdrawals?"

"Four times," Soup said. "Like I said, they put a freeze on the account because Natasha was smart enough to get Lifelock. Any sign of suspicious activity and they take immediate protective measures of an account. The branch manager told me they haven't been able to get hold of Natasha. She hasn't responded to their text messages asking to verify that she made the two withdrawals, or the following four attempts at a withdrawal. So they froze her funds."

"If Maggie's asking them for emergency funds, she must be desperate, too," Athen said.

"Can you get hold of that ATM and bank footage? Bring it in?" Athen asked.

"And copies of the forged letters," Lucy added.

"Sure. Hang on."

Lucy, Paulie, and Athen, waited as muffled voices exchanged conversation on Soup's end of the line.

"Holy cow," she said. "The branch manager just told me that at two o'clock yesterday afternoon, Maggie went in there and tried to cash a check for five hundred dollars. Not a huge amount, but she kicked up a big stink when they refused to honor it. They said the signatures didn't match and as we said, the funds are frozen. By the way they tell me there have been no other attempts to use the account, except for Maggie's efforts in the last forty-eight hours. Guess she thought even if the debit card was closed, she might be able to cash a check. They asked her to wait but she took off. They have it all on tape."

"Can you bring that in too, please?" Athen asked.

"Sure, boss."

"And do me a favor. Can you ask the branch manager if we can see a list of her transactions going back say thirty days, and the actual account balance? Please let me know if Lucy needs to make a formal request."

"Hold on." Soup relayed the information then came back to Athen. "They will give me a printout. They know you and Lucy sent me here. Boss. I think they're all upset. They like Natasha and they hate what's going on."

"So do we," Athen said, his voice low. See you when you get here." He ended the call, his thoughts spiraling.

"If she didn't kill her sister, she's part of it, like you said. A big part." Lucy looked dismayed.

"I know it sounds crazy, but she and the others were obsessed with this TV sizzler. They didn't want anything to get in the way of getting it made yesterday," Paulie said. "Bruce Felton told us they were short on funds when he couldn't pay his share so Jamie Fahdi stepped in. And because of it, he got to play the ninja assassin part. Natasha was supposed to pay for the car rental and didn't. I'm thinking things got out of hand in her apartment. Cameron killed her. Maggie helped him clean up then the mayor got involved trying to get help when Natasha disappeared."

"He screwed their plans up for sure," Athen said. "I have no idea how they thought they'd get away with it but think about it for a moment. What if Maggie resented her little sister, the princess? What if she thought she could get away with bumping her off? Keep the limelight for herself."

Lucy nodded. "And her money."

"Right." Athen was warming to his theory.

"Sir," a uniformed officer said from the door. "We have Cameron Deck here, but he says he wants a lawyer."

"I've got get to that press conference." Lucy looked at Athen, alarm in her eyes.

"I'll take care of it," Athen said. He turned to the officer. "Can you put him in interview room number four, pleased?"

The officer looked dubious. "That's the one that still smells of human piss after that homeless guy squatted in there the other day."

"Yeah, I know." Athen grinned at him. "I want him uncomfortable."

Lucy chuckled. "Remind me to stay on your good side." She tugged at her uniform and strode out of her office. "Time to cast my pearls before the swine." She gave them all a wink.

Athen's phone rang again. It was Grady. He almost let the call pass except he'd texted *911*. Twice. Athen called him. "Are you okay?"

"Yeah."

"You don't sound it."

"Hon. I'm sorry. I was getting ready to go meet an officer who's given me permission to go into our house and empty it of our possessions. The governor's office is giving me an hour to do it. The US Marshals found weed growing, a lot of it, in

Tyler's house two doors down. A massive illegal grow. Anyway, with you being a police lieutenant, they let me know they want to go over our house. I said they could of course, but I'm allowed an armed escort in there once they make sure we weren't involved in a grow or anything like that.

"I booked a moving van. I'll put everything in storage. Shit, sweetie. I was running out of the door when I found that thumb drive you were looking for earlier. It was on the ground outside our cabana. It must have fallen out when you brought the laundry bag in here. Know I shouldn't have, but I plugged it in." Grady sounded hysterical. "I can never unsee what I just saw. Oh my God. That poor, poor woman."

"What's on there?" Athen asked.

"I think I saw her being murdered. A man and a woman. At first I thought it was two women. The man has long hair. It might even be a wig. Strangest looking head of hair I've ever seen."

How weird. Athen didn't know any of the men on the suspect list that had long hair. "Can you send it to me?"

"Yeah. Sending it now. I'm going over to the house. I feel so nervous knowing people like this live in our world." He ended the call on a troubling note for Athen who hated leaving Grady to deal with the house issue on his own.

Athen and Paulie's laptops were in the war room.

"I'll go get yours," Paulie said and returned a minute later. "Maggie's complaining about us making her wait. Told her it wouldn't be long. Took everything in me not to punch her lights out."

"You're a good man, Paulie." Athen opened up the laptop and got online. Paulie looked over his shoulder at Lucy's desk as he downloaded the footage from Grady's email. *Holy cow.* It was in color and started with a scene where Cameron Deck climbed into the bedroom and attacked the cat with a blanket. There was no sound, but the assault was a different one from the one Athen had already seen. The cat got away from him and vanished under the bed. After a fruitless couple of minutes trying to get the cat out, a furious-looking Deck thumped the bed, stood, folded the blanket up and climbed out of the window again.

"This looks like it's been recorded from a computer on the desk," Paulie said. "Very clear footage."

Neither of them said anything as the second piece of footage began to play. Natasha was in her bedroom and appeared to be adjusting her computer's camera angle. She stepped back and waved into the camera. She was wearing a pink and black slip. Athen blinked. It was similar to the one he'd found in her laundry bag.

She stepped back and kept staring at the camera. She blew kisses and gave them a couple more times. She seemed to be having fun. From her right, and what Athen knew to be her doorway, something moved. Her playful expression vanished and her mouth dropped open.

"God, I wish we had sound," Athen said. And suddenly, they did.

"What are you doing here?" she asked.

Cameron Deck came into the room. "You're supposed to be at the gym."

"You're not supposed to be here. I told you about this. I'm calling the police."

He took a swing at her, a hard, vicious punch that landed in the middle of her face.

"Oh!" Paulie and Athen exclaimed in unison.

She went down hard, and Cameron kept hitting her. Her hand came up, clawing at his shoulder, which seemed to enrage him. He dragged her by the hair, but she fought him, kicking, and hitting at him. Then a woman appeared. It was Maggie.

Athen watched in horror as she came at Natasha with a

large knife. She must have brought it from the kitchen. She stabbed Natasha in the stomach. Natasha went down again, and Cameron ran from the room, returning with a hammer.

"Jesus," Paulie said. The brutal assault continued, with Cameron raining blows with the hammer. A third person appeared, picking Natasha up. Was it a man or woman?

Athen was appalled when this figure joined in the fray. He picked up Natasha by her arm and dragged her out of frame. Probably to the dressing room where her assault turned fatal.

"Oh, my God," he said.

"Who the hell is that?" Paulie asked. "Soup's right. It looks like a wig. It's like he's trying to imitate Natasha King. Holy shit! It's—

"Gary Goldman," he and Athen said in unison.

Athen sat back in the chair staring at the screen. "How did Goldman get here so fast then back to New York again? And then back here this morning? He's like a damned yoyo."

"According to his Facebook page, there's almost no downtime between his posts." Paulie jabbed at the computer. "The wonders of modern technology. We can get a warrant to access his Facebook page and check. That might take some time. We're gonna need to separate him and Maggie. We've got all three suspects. Let's take a swing at them."

"Why did they keep it?" Athen squinted as he made a copy of the footage to Lucy's computer. He pocketed the thumb drive and picked up his laptop. "Deck was the one who kept it. Maybe he thought he needed insurance if Maggie or Goldman tried to pin it all on him."

"There's that. And what if they planned to use it in their stupid sizzler?"

"Oh, man." Athen shook his head. "Use it to their advantage. What a group of sickos."

The place was a bit of a ghost town as he and Paulie walked to Maggie's interview room. Probably the press conference had everybody except for a few in attendance. The officer standing guard said, "She wouldn't hand over her phone. Neither would Cameron Deck."

"Thanks," Athen said. Inside, Maggie was spitting fire when they entered the interview room. "I can't stay here all day!" she yelled. "What's going on? I have a right to know."

"We'll be with you in a moment," Athen said. He asked the uniformed officer to stay on duty outside the door. Though he itched to question Gary Goldman, he targeted Cameron Deck first. He was busy on his cellphone when they entered.

"You took long enough," he griped.

"We're a little short-handed today." Athen sat across the desk from him. Paulie sat beside him.

"Can I take a look at that?" Paulie held his hand out for Deck's phone. Surprisingly, Deck handed it over. Athen looked at the series of texts before activating the interview recording. He'd learned a long time ago the art of interviewing suspects went better if he acted as though they were friends having a chat rather than starting aggressively.

Deck had been busy texting somebody saying, *Help, I need help*. He'd also texted Maggie. Athen recognized the number. *Don't say anything*.

"I'm going to record this conversation," Athen said. Paulie took the phone and rifled through the contents. Cameron Deck became unhinged.

"What are you doing? I told the officers that brought me in here that I want my attorney. I've got nothing to say."

"Fair enough." Athen took a breath. "We'll need to take your phone though, Cameron. By the way, we don't need your statement at this time anyway. We've got the murder on tape. We know everything."

Cameron Deck stared at him. "That's impossible."

"I can't say another word unless you're willing to talk to me. But just so you know, we have the thumb drive."

"Shit! That's fucking impossible!"

"So, you want to talk to me now."

No. I want my lawyer."

"Okay. Come on Paulie."

Paulie and Athen rose in unison. Out in the corridor, Athen locked the room again. Lucy was hovering.

"He lawyered up?" she asked.

"Yeah." Athen rarely swore but he did now. "He's such a shitbag."

Lucy nodded. "Okay. We'll get him his attorney. How bad is the footage?"

"Horrible. I made a copy and it's on your computer. How did the press conference go?"

She huffed out a breath. "I think I pulled it off, but I hate those things. I left the mayor there to show off his new arm sling and to bullshit them a little longer." She grinned. "The media will probably take off in a minute because I warned him not to say anything. He's talking about his plans for state politics now. I saw people's eyes glazing over the moment he opened his mouth."

In spite of the circumstances, Athen let out a hoot of laughter.

She smoothed her already impeccable hair back from her forehead. "Who's next?"

"Maggie. Go look at the footage. It's her, Deck, and her cherished and adored husband."

"With friends like that, who needs enemies?" Lucy grimaced. "Okay. I'll watch from the other side."

In Maggie's interview room, she seemed glum until they sat opposite her. Athen realized she was angry. Very angry. He'd had a hinky feeling about her from the get-go.

"We know everything," he said. "And we've got the thumb drive with your sister's murder on it."

She blinked. "That's not a real murder. It was for our sizzler."

"With her blood. All that blood? You're the one who gave us the DNA report."

She dropped her head. He heard her soft expletive. "Shit."

"Why? Why did you have to kill her?"

"I want my lawyer."

Athen and Paulie rose. They went to see Goldman next. He seemed nervous and had every right to be. Athen pressed the button that illuminated the Interview in Progress sign.

"Gary, we know everything."

He looked astonished.

"We just want your version of the events."

"My version?" His eyes widened in total terror. "What the hell did they say?"

Athen took a gamble. "They both blame you."

His mouth dropped open. He stared at them in disbelief. "That is not true! They called me."

"I've seen the video. Nobody called you."

Gary's eyes narrowed. "Maggie called. She sounded frantic. I was outside. She said they needed help."

Athen would review the footage. There was a moment when Maggie dropped to the floor. Maybe she'd called him then.

"She called me from Natasha's phone."

Ah. So that was the call made to his phone from Natasha. The last call she made. Except it wasn't Natasha. It was her murderous sister.

"I went in. I was wearing—"

"A wig. We know. Why?"

He squinted. "I cross-dress." He turned beet red. "Sometimes." He began a strange hand-wringing gesture Athen recognized as typical obsessive-compulsive behavior. "I had offered to play a woman on the sizzler. A victim. We all met at the building. Things were already going down in Natasha's apartment. They had already attacked her. They dragged her to her dressing room. I begged them to call 911. They convinced me we could get her money."

Athen and Paulie stared at him.

"They assured me. Look. She was too far gone. She couldn't have survived the blood loss. Or the stabbing. Believe me. I have nightmares about it now. They've shut me out of everything. She and Cameron." His shifty gaze flicked from Athen to Paulie. "She was sort of breathing when I left. They told me to go back to New York." He shrugged. "So I did."

"And you never once thought to call the police?"

"Briefly. But it was a mess. A fucking mess by then! I knew they wanted me gone. I left town. I had blood on my pants. I had to throw away the wig. I sat on that plane pretending none of it happened. And then that New York cop showed up and asked questions. I was so freaked out! I thought he knew." He kept up the handwringing. "Nuts to them if they say I was the one who did it."

"What did they do with her body?" Athen asked.

Goldman flinched. "They won't tell me."

"But she is dead."

Goldman stared at his hands as though surprised they were moving of their own accord. He kept his gaze down. "Yeah. She's gone. They said Cameron buried her."

"Where?" Athen asked.

"I don't know." He lifted his head and there were no tears. Not even an expression of real remorse. "I don't want to go to jail for this. I did not kill her."

"Yes, you did. And as far as I'm concerned, you're as culpable as the others."

"I had nothing to do with the bank stuff. They're the ones trying to get their hands on her money and I'm her husband!"

"You signed a form asking for emergency funds," Paulie said. "A right of survivorship form."

Goldman gaped at him. "I have no idea what that even is."

"So, you know nothing about that at all?"

"No. I'm telling you. They said we'd split the money three ways once they got their hands on it."

Athen was surprised the guy was being so forthcoming. He was glad his gamble had paid off.

"They've been very secretive. They won't tell me anything. Maggie contacted me a couple of times. Said they weren't getting anywhere. Then she said I needed to come here today." He moved his hands underneath his thighs, keeping them there. "I'm in trouble if they don't give me that money. Natasha stopped sending me cash, in violation of our agreement. I was getting ready to report her to Homeland Security for our fraudulent wedding. Then I found it if I did that, I was liable too." He folded his arms across his chest, his chin stuck out in a defiant way. "I am royally screwed now."

Athen had no idea what to say to this. He and Paulie got up. They left the office without a word. In the hallway, Lucy waited for them.

"We've got enough to press charges, but I'm not sure the D.A. will move forward with the case without a body. You got a lot out of him, though. You guys are amazing."

"We can leave him alone for a bit and I'm thinking Paulie might want to go in on his own and have a crack at him," Athen said.

"Could work. In the meantime, I'll contact the D.A.'s office and see if they'll work with us. Maybe with murder charges hanging over their heads either Cameron Deck or Maggie Harman will tell us where she is."

Athen doubted it but liked his own idea of sending Paulie in alone. In the meantime, he intended going over the case notes. He wanted to check the ALPR records too. A closer scrutiny of Cameron Deck's car license plate might give him some clues.

And his cellphone pings. As usual with a homicide investigation, sheer hard work and painstaking detail was the key to solving a crime.

"We can hold them all for at least twelve hours, even though they've lawyered up. "We can hit all three of our suspects with multiple charges," Lucy said. "Apart from charges of homicide, we've got tampering with evidence, removing a dead body without a medical examiner's permission and multiple felony weapons charges." She paused for breath. "I wonder what the hell they did with that hammer and knife."

"There's also being an accessory after the fact to a felony for Maggie," Athen said. "Not to mention multiple fraud charges for the bank caper."

"Right." Lucy snapped her fingers. "Let me get on it. You and Paulie need help?"

"Anyone you can spare," Athen said.

Within minutes, Soup, Lorne Brand, and another detective on loan from the Special Investigations Division came in to help comb the ALPR report, which Paulie had duplicated on the copy machine. They also went over the calls and texts on all three suspects' phones.

An hour later, they were no closer to figuring out where, how, or who, helped Cameron Deck dispose of Natasha King's body.

"There isn't much time between when we know that Cameron Deck drove away from his building to Wong's salon," Athen said. "He didn't move his own vehicle during that time—"

"Maybe he used an Uber," Lorne suggested.

"There's no record of an Uber booking on his cellphone app," Athen said. "And a body's a hard thing to lug around." He was obsessed with the issue because it was the most vital one to his case. A conviction pivoted around the location of the body.

The others studied the reports.

"I think he and Maggie had the body with them when they went to Wong's," Athen said. "Looking at the timeline of his drive back from the salon, it took him longer than it probably should. What if they dumped her body on the way back and Cameron *walked* back later on his own and buried it?"

"Fuck," Lorne said. "That's brilliant. Want me to test drive how long it should take getting from Wong's back to the Bermuda Triangle?"

"Great," Athen said. "Do it."

Lorne took off with the SID detective.

In the meantime, Athen and the others went back over their notes from the beginning. Within twenty minutes, they knew from Lorne that the drive had taken Cameron and Maggie nine minutes longer than it should have.

"And that's me counting three different ways they could have driven there," Lorne reported to Athen.

"What about Maggie's car?" Soup asked.

But when they checked Maggie's license against the ALPR, she had driven to Cameron's place and left again hours later. There was no indication she had gone anywhere else other than her place.

They could check street cameras, but Athen would have to gain access to those. He had his crew look into that.

Then the DNA results came back from Maggie and Natasha. The blood in the bedroom belonged to Natasha King. The second set of blood drops belonged to Cameron Deck.

He'd been injured in the process of harming Natasha. They would have to get a warrant and deal with his attorney to get permission to strip him for photographs.

"I'll organize that," Soup said.

In the meantime, Athen and Paulie went over a topographic map of Beverly Hills, trying to figure out where Cameron and Maggie could have stopped to hide a dead body somewhere near or inside the Bermuda Triangle.

CHAPTER SIXTEEN

"Mr. Grady?"

He smiled to himself. "Please, just call me Grady." No matter how many times he told his best friend, Fera Montgomery's housekeeper, Consuela, to call him Grady, she couldn't wrap her head around the idea. Fera was Mrs. Fera to her. Athen was Mr. Captain. Not Mr. Lieutenant. He was Mr. Captain. Despina was Miss Desi. Bella was Miss Bella. Sometimes Miss Puppy Girl. Grady adored Consuela. His whole family did. Once, when Despina was sick with flu, she'd come over with a gigantic pot of homemade chicken soup. She'd even lugged a special container for Bella.

"Thees one got no noodles," she'd told Grady. "For doggies, noodles ees no good."

Maybe that was true, but somebody forgot to tell Bella. She adored noodles. She adored anything edible, truth be told. And at this moment she was at Fera's house being waited on hand and food by Consuela.

"Is everything okay?" Grady asked. He'd made three appointments to check on local homes for rent and thought it would be easier without Bella, but he missed her. He worried now that the dog was fretting.

"Ees okay," Consuela not sounding like it at all.

He tried to keep his tone gentle. "Is Bella okay?"

"Bella ees good. Consuela ees not so good."

Grady stood outside the swanky apartment building on North Doheny Drive and waited. "What's wrong, Consuela? Are you sick?"

227

Before she could respond, the front buzzer sounded and the door to the snazziest apartment building in Beverly Hills opened. He'd driven by this place so many times and always wondered what the apartments were like. He was about to find out. He'd had a harrowing morning and he didn't need more drama.

"No, no," she said.

"Consuela, can I call you right back? Just give me two minutes. I promise."

She hesitated. "Or-kay, Mr. Grady."

Grady put on his best game face and greeted the dark-haired man who stepped out of the elevator, making his way toward him. Grady took a deep breath. He'd been thinking of houses but most of the ones in Beverly Hills were ridiculously overpriced. After what he and Athen had just been through with Tyler James, he liked the idea of a two-bedroom corner apartment up high with no cameras. No landlords lurking in the garden. No pot grow two doors down.

"Hi, I'm Grady," he said, extending his hand to the guy who was so handsome Grady couldn't see straight for a moment.

"Hey, there. I'm Angelo. So glad you could come on such short notice."

Grady nodded. "Thank you for letting me come right over." He followed Angelo to the elevator. Inside, he admired the opulent finishes, suspecting the floor and walls were real marble. The gold bits gleamed like somebody had just spent hours polishing them. *I have got to fuck Athen in this thing. I can't remember the last time we had elevator sex.*

On the tenth floor, Angelo led the way toward the end of the plush, carpeted hallway. Grady felt as though as he was in a five-star hotel. All was quiet and smelled new and inviting. Huge windows giving way to a view of the city. Grady relaxed as his potential landlord pointed out the many security aspects of the building.

"There are security cameras in the garage, the elevators—"
So much for elevator sex.

"And there are security features that come with the apartment should you choose to rent it."

All Grady could think was, *Palm trees. I see palm trees and more palm trees.*

Inside the unit, he took an appreciative gasp at the roomy surroundings. There were two balconies in the living room facing the street. The open-plan layout appealed to his need for space and for total comfort. Huge sofas grouped around a wood fireplace and above it, a gigantic, mounted flatscreen TV would tick all of Athen's boxes. Grady's lover didn't require much. He smiled at the image of Athen sprawled on the sofa with Bella, beer in hand, watching *Drag Race*. Grady felt happy for the first time in days. *Yes. I can see us living here. The big question is the kitchen.*

"I know you said the kitchen is important," Angelo said, his gentle voice intruding his thoughts. "We recently installed an Aga." He let that little detail sink in as Grady followed him in there, dazzled by the beige and white fixtures. He touched the beautiful quartz countertop, opening cupboard doors and finally, allowing himself to manhandle the most perfect stove in all the world.

The cast iron Aga was beige and had four huge gas rings and four ovens. *Four!* Grady visualized huge family dinners. *My sister will come. Athen's family will come.* Then his attention fell on a beautiful antique wooden mold resting beside the stove. *No. I can't believe it!*

"That's an orthodox—"

"It's a holy prosphora stamp." Grady's words came out in a ragged whisper.

"Wow. You know about those?" Angelo seemed as surprised as Grady was. "My husband is Greek orthodox."

"So is mine." Grady reached into his messenger bag and pulled out the tissue-wrapped antique he'd taken from the

Arnaz Drive kitchen. "Athen has had this since he was a little boy. It belonged to his paternal grandmother. He inherited it. His sister got his maternal grandmother's prosphora."

"Harvey got his from his mom. Wow. Small world, big connection."

Grady knew he was talking too much but he couldn't stop himself. "This was the first thing I took out of Tyler James' house." Tears swelled then. Grady wanted Athen to be happy and safe. To focus on his work. The prosphora might have just been a wooden seal pressed into unleavened dough before baking it for Greek Easter, but to Grady, it was blasphemy for this precious object to be anywhere near Tyler James.

"You poor thing." Angelo walked over and touched his arm. "You've had a rough couple of days. I'm not going to pretend I don't know who you are. You're all over the news. I know you had a horrible time with that actor, Tyler James and I saw you being escorted into your own home this morning to remove your possessions. I'm a big fan of your husband. The two of you were having cocktails at the Four Seasons one night and I loved how he handled that purse-snatching incident with the fake valet driver. The lady who almost got her purse swiped is my sister-in-law. She would have lost her passport, her wallet, some jewelry she shouldn't have been carrying around, her insulin, and anyway, we are so grateful."

"Thank you." Grady recalled that night but couldn't remember having met Angelo. He'd talked to another man, calming him as Athen dealt with arresting the thief. Grady had been mad at Athen that night and felt badly about it afterward. All he'd wanted was a night out with his man, but as usual, Athen found some crime to thwart. *Man, I've been getting grouchy a lot with him lately.* The memory of the night hit him then. "Wait, your Harvey has a moustache, doesn't he?"

"Yes. That's him! You remember! And you two are adorable. Please say you'll move in. We'll look after you here. You'll have total privacy and lots of peace and quiet."

Grady blinked back his anguish. "I'm sorry. This just threw me. Athen won't believe it when I tell him. These prosphora could be twins. They both have bronze backings."

"I think this is meant to be." Angelo seemed emotional himself. He pointed to the right. "This farmhouse table was a recent find. It came from a Greek orthodox priest's family. They're relocating to a new church in Athens."

Grady took in the solid wooden rectangular table and the big windows with more tree top views.

"All the windows are tinted and double-glazed. Virtually soundproof and heat-resistant," Angelo said.

"You're driving a hard bargain." Grady felt himself unwinding. It would be perfect here for when Desi had homework to do. He could keep his eye on her, chit-chat with her and cook to his heart's content.

If we ever let her come back to us. Suddenly, he missed her terribly. *My beautiful little lunatic.*

He focused on the moment. He'd always wanted an Aga. "I can't believe it," he whispered again. He knew this model retailed at around nine thousand dollars.

"Believe it." Angelo seemed nervous.

Emotion pierced at Grady's very soul. This would be a temporary move since Angelo and Harvey were only offering a six-month lease, but, in his bones, he knew it was the right one. Ever since the news had broken about Tyler's arrest and everything that went with it, life had become impossible. Grady's phone hadn't stopped ringing all morning. People he hadn't heard from for years were texting and calling, wanting "the goss."

He just wanted to gag.

The federal prosecutor had warned him not to discuss the

case. Everything Grady and Athen had kept at Tyler's house now loitered with intent in a rental pod outside Fera's house. Not for the first time he was grateful for Fera and Consuela who'd come to help him pack everything. Of course, the media had seized on every little piece of information they could. They'd blasted Athen and Grady's names all over the place, as though they were silently complicity in Tyler's crimes.

Grady couldn't help fretting that Tyler was now being linked to other unsolved homicides. *It had nothing to do with us. We didn't know.* He hoped the media weren't bugging Fera or Consuela. The rental truck they'd used had lost the TV crew trucks before stopping outside Fera's place to unload everything, but still . . . a homicidal movie star made for non-stop news.

Oh, man. I really need to call Consuela back.

He felt protective of his friends. Consuela had had a fierce gambling addiction, one that caused the death of her dear friend, Paulina Martinez, another Beverly Hills housekeeper. Poor Paulina had been murdered in a casino and her husband had rolled her body in a carpet and dumped it with a stranger's trash one morning. Thanks to Consuela, Athen had solved the case. Thanks to Athen, Consuela had been released from an onerous debt to the casino.

As far as Grady knew, she'd made good on her promise to stay away from gambling. *God, I hope she hasn't started up again.*

Grady wasn't answering anyone's calls. He avoided everyone, including Athen's sister, Sia. She kept sending hysterical texts about some of the things she'd seen and heard on the Internet.

Tyler James could have killed my daughter! She'd written more than once.

Grady understood her concern but once Athen knew Tyler was a homicide suspect, he'd made sure Despina was no longer anywhere near the man.

"Let me show you the bedrooms and bathrooms. There's a bonus room, too." Angelo took him through the rest of the place. More than anything, Grady loved the fact they were up high but had no close neighbors. The bathrooms were huge and lavish with claw-footed tubs, and there was a bonus room that looked like a movie theater.

"It's a panic room," Angelo told him. "This is one of the security features I mentioned. There are others, but we can discuss that later if you like."

Grady took one more walkthrough and knew this was the best find ever. He stood for a long moment in the living room, staring out of the sweeping balcony windows.

"It's gorgeous at night," Angelo said, confirming Grady's suspicions.

Nobody can see us up here. The watched will become the watchers. We'll watch sunsets and stars and . . . He already pictured many happy evenings here at home with Athen and Bella.

"I think my husband will love it," Grady said. He and Athen weren't married. Yet. *I'm going to ask him though. Because my life is total crap without him in it.*

Angelo beamed. "I'm so happy!"

"Oh, wait." Grady's momentary pleasure became eclipsed by worry. "Did I mention we have a dog?"

"Yes! We love animals. Harvey and I live two floors down and we have three dogs and two cats. The city maximum."

Grady smiled at him. Suddenly his conscience got the better of him. "I'm going to say yes. And please don't be offended but I have a call to make. What do you need from me to make this happen?"

Angelo looked ecstatic. "How soon do you want to move in?"

"How about day after tomorrow? We're staying at the Beverly Hills Hotel and we're booked for three nights. Last night was our first. My husband is in the middle of an investigation and I'd like him to not have to deal with moving for a couple of days." *My husband.* The more he said it, the better it sounded to Grady's own ears.

"How about you come over and pick up the papers later today and you can sign everything. I'll just print everything out." Angelo's face flushed a little. "I will need to do a credit check just because Harvey's a stickler for rules."

"No problem." Grady smiled at him. "Do you want my social security number now?"

"Sure."

Grady rattled it off and Angelo tapped the numbers into his phone. "How is say, three o'clock?"

"Perfect." Grady felt better already.

"Wonderful. I won't show the apartment to anyone else."

"Yes, please don't. I love it."

Angelo smiled at him. "Grady, please know, it's our privilege to have you here. This is a very cool building with some wonderful people in it. We have your back. Anything Harvey and I can do to help ease this transition, please don't hesitate to ask."

"Thank you. I mean it. And when I come back, I want to meet your fur babies."

Angelo grinned. "You got it."

Downstairs, Grady waited until he was out of the building before returning Consuela's call. He felt terrible when she didn't answer. But after several rings she finally picked up.

"Mr. Grady?"

"Consuela. Are you okay? What's going on?"

"Ees my husband. He work at the monster house."

"The monster house?"

"Yes. Ees the house the monster buy."

"Okay." He tried to follow all this and realized she was probably talking about the house the actor Boris Karloff had bought many, many years ago at the height of his *Frankenstein* fame.

"My husband ees scared."

"Why is he scared?"

Consuela started to cry. "He say there is a dead body in the rose garden. He never seen it there before. He say he afraid the police will think he killed her."

"Killed who?"

"He don't know. Ees a girl. A girl in a red dress."

Athen and a large proportion of the Beverly Hills Police Department were there when the body of Natasha King was painstakingly excavated from the rose garden of the so-called monster house. The day had taken on a terrible grey pallor that matched Athen's mood. Seeing a dead body was never easy, but with the recovery of the young woman's remains, he and Lucy were able to move forward with their case.

Almost worse than seeing Natasha's bruised and battered body was the moment Cameron Deck was forced to remove his shirt and submit to photos. There was a deep gash on one hip that still seeped blood and probably required stitches. On his right shoulder were claw marks left by a young woman who, though flawed, didn't deserve to die the way she did.

Athen and Lucy went to the airport to meet Valerie Harman. She still didn't know one daughter was dead, the other on remand for her murder. She cried and wept in both the detectives' arms.

"I just have one question," she said. "Do you think this is my fault? I'd led a different life, would they still be alive?"

Technically it was two questions, but Athen gave her the only response he had. "That's something you will never know. You did the best you could."

In the end, Athen knew that Valerie Harman was as flawed as any human being and nobody could have expected the strange and shocking death of a Hollywood hopeful. Terror in Beverly Hills indeed.

By the end of another long day, Athen was anxious to be home with his man. He drove to the Beverly Hills Hotel, stunned when the valet drivers greeted him with applause.

"I never liked that man," one of them told Athen. "It didn't surprise me he was the killer."

"Which one?" Athen asked. Tyler or Cameron?"

"Tyler," the valet said. "He assaulted a friend of mine once but the police didn't believe her."

"I want you to call this man, please. And tell him everything." Athen gave him Cricket's number.

In the little bungalow where his heart currently lived, he threw himself at Grady and Bella, covering both their faces with kisses.

"I love you," he said over and over.

Grady kept trying to tell him that he'd found them a wonderful new place to live, and Bella wanted belly rubs. There was time and space for everything. Athen wanted to fuck his man and he also wanted to call Paulie.

"That can wait." Grady pushed him back on the sofa.

"Is that so?" Athen asked as Grady straddled him.

"Yes. That's so." Grady's eyes shone as he rubbed his ass across Athen's lap, making Athen get hard.

Oh, man.

Grady rose and pulled Athen to his feet, unbuckling his pants and pushing down his briefs before removing his own clothing. He straddled Athen again, still half-dressed.

Athen's phone rang. He glanced at the screen. An 808 number. He recognized it as Kai, the blind Hawaiian tracker's number. Clearly, he was calling to talk about Allie Madden. He'd been right about her not being in the water. He'd been right about a lot of things. He'd told Athen things he'd never believed possible.

"That blind man told me I'd meet you," Athen said, looking up into Grady's eyes.

"Really?"

"He described you to a T. God, Grady. I can't do this life without you. I can take anything. Shootings. Murder. Riots. I can take it all if I have you."

"Good thing I'm not planning on going anywhere," Grady said. "Isn't there a song called *If You Leave Me, Can I Come Too?*"

Athen grinned. "I think there is."

"So marry me."

"Just tell me when," Athen said, lifting Grady from his body for a moment. "I need to be in you."

"Your wish is my command." Grady moved his body so he was on his knees hovering over Athen's pointed cock. They never used lube because they both loved how it felt to work their way into each other. It took several minutes but Athen was finally in, letting Grady control the speed and depth with which Athen took him.

He smiled when they came together, Grady's cock erupting between them. Athen slumped back against the sofa as Grady leaned into him. They kissed for long minutes.

"I gotta make a call," Athen said, his voice husky from their passion.

"Of course you do," Grady joked, rocking back on Athen's cock.

"You're making me hard again."

Grady nodded. "That's the plan, Sam."

"Hold on. I gotta call my other husband. The work husband." Paulie took his call. "Hey partner," Athen said. "I got a question for you. How do you feel about a promotion? You want to go for your sergeant's exam?

Grady ran his hands over Athen's chest. There was time and place for everything. And it was time for a partner. In life and in work.

Anything to chase away those Fancy Man Blues.

ABOUT THE AUTHOR

A.J. Llewellyn is the author of over 250 M/M romance novels. She was born in Australia, and lives in Los Angeles. An early obsession with Robinson Crusoe led to a lifelong love affair with islands, particularly Hawaii and Easter Island.

Being marooned once on Wedding Cake Island in Australia cured her of a passion for fishing, but led to a plotline for a novel. A.J.'s friends live in fear because even the smallest details of their lives usually wind up in her stories. A.J. has a desire to paint, draw, juggle, work for the FBI, walk a tightrope with an elephant, be a chess champion, a steeplejack, master chef, and a world-class surfer. She can't do any of these things so she writes about them instead.

A.J. started life as a journalist and boxing columnist, and still enjoys interrogating, er, interviewing people to find out what makes them tick.

How to find/friend me:

email: ajllewellyn@gmail.com
website: www.ajllewellyn.com
www.facebook.com/aj.llewellyn
www.twitter.com/ajllewellyn
Newsletter sign-up: ajllewellynnewsletter@gmail.com—each month I give away a free ebook!
I'm an app! Download my FREE A.J. Llewellyn App for Android here: http://tinyurl.com/lkbc4wm

www.ingramcontent.com/pod-product-compliance
Lightning Source LLC
Chambersburg PA
CBHW070600130626
46556CB00001B/225